BELOW

THE BROKEN SKY CHRONICLES

BELOW

BOOK 1

JASON CHABOT

TURNER

Turner Publishing Company
Nashville, Tennessee
New York, New York

www.turnerpublishing.com

Below: The Broken Sky Chronicles, Book 1

Cover design: Maddie Cothren
Book design: Glen Edelstein

Library of Congress Cataloging-in-Publication Data

Names: Chabot, Jason, author.
Title: Below / by Jason Chabot.
Description: Nashville, Tennessee : Turner Publishing Company, [2016] |
    Series: The broken sky chronicles ; book 1 | Summary: "On the barren
    plains of Below, a teenage boy named Hokk lives in isolation amid the
    remnants of Earth's modern age. On the floating islands in the skies of
    Above, Elia and her family are enslaved in endless drudgery until a
    natural disaster sends Elia plummeting to Below, where she meets Hokk and
    together they face airborne and terrestrial dangers and discover a
    powerful secret"-- Provided by publisher.
Identifiers: LCCN 2016001215 | ISBN 9781681626017 (pbk.)
Subjects: | CYAC: Science fiction. | Survival--Fiction.
Classification: LCC PZ7.1.C468 Be 2016 | DDC [Fic]--dc23
LC record available at https://lccn.loc.gov/2016001215

9781681626024

Printed in the United States of America
15 14 13 12 11 10 9 8 7 6 5 4 3 2 1

Dedicated to my remarkable parents,
Jo-Ann and André

And in loving memory of my grandmother
Mabel Munroe

Chapter 1

A BOLT OF LIGHTNING TORE across the sky like a white-hot, bloodless vein. The churning clouds ruptured with its sudden crack. Half a second later, a body broke through the heavy underbelly of the storm, appearing to hover for a moment.

Then it fell.

Hokk's neck pulsed with excitement. *Let this one be real, not another hallucination.*

As it dropped, the body picked up speed.

Hokk had been kneeling, digging in the soil for worms to eat, but now he stood tall above the rippling prairie grasses, the explosive thunderclap still ringing in his ears. The white wrapping of the bundled corpse had unraveled into a long, fluttering tail, creating a stark contrast against the menacing sky.

As Hokk expected, the body's free fall slowed midway between the clouds and the grasslands, trapped momentarily in a layer of the atmosphere that seemed to oppose gravity. Yet the earth's pull was unrelenting, and the body slipped past the invisible barrier, continuing to fall. Hokk was too far away to hear the thud, but he saw it bounce and come to rest, hidden in the grasses.

Another flash and roar of thunder.

Hokk was not well camouflaged. He had to be careful. A vast and apparently empty prairie stretched around him, but he couldn't be sure that others hadn't witnessed the body's descent.

He hastily tied back his hair, paying no attention to the leaves and sticks tangled in his ponytail. His pale skin resembled gauze, with faint, bluish blood vessels tracing crooked paths underneath the surface. Burn scars discolored his hands and arms in patches, as though puddles of hot wax had cooled on his flesh.

He blew a shrill whistle. Behind him, the blond, furry face of a fox appeared in the grasses. Nym's large ears stood alert, like sails filled by a strong breeze.

Overhead, the lightning and thunder were growing fierce, and the wind blew litter everywhere, the entire landscape covered with a flurry of ancient debris. With Nym at his heels, Hokk ran toward the striped gazelk he had stolen a few days earlier. He vaulted onto its high back, and as the gazelk tossed its head, Hokk grabbed the animal's massive, twisting horns.

Nym gave a sharp bark.

"Up!" Hokk commanded. Nym jumped, and Hokk swung him onto his lap. With a kick to its ribs, the gazelk leapt forward. The ground rushed past and Hokk's torn leather cloak billowed behind him. He surveyed the prairies, trying to locate the body among the drifting rubbish.

From his pocket, he pulled out his father's compass. The instrument's needle was still spinning, as it had been for days. Useless. How far had he drifted off course?

The threatening sky lit up again. Gray sheets of advancing rain streaked down in the distance. Hokk and the gazelk flew along as if racing the lightning above. Ahead, a sudden gust made a flickering piece of white fabric dance up into the air. Hokk's eyes remained fixed on the spot. He urged the beast on.

Only a short distance remained when a thunderbolt exploded dangerously close on the ground. The blast's concussion slammed into Hokk's chest and the gazelk stumbled in blind panic until Hokk pulled back on its horns, veering the beast toward their destination. Yet the lightning had scattered burning debris. Flames trembled to life with the wind's encouragement, forcing Hokk to carefully maneuver the gazelk around growing patches of fire.

Reaching the bound corpse, Hokk leapt off the animal before it stopped. Much of the white fabric had come undone, and the body was bent unnaturally. The material was starting to smolder from grasses burning nearby, so he smothered the flames with his cloak and dragged the body to a safer spot.

Hokk carefully scanned the horizon. *No one. Good.*

Nym sniffed the body, but backed away as Hokk began unwinding the scorched fabric. The cloth was high quality, lightweight and finely woven. A promising sign. Normally the bodies that fell were swaddled in rags.

Hokk unwrapped the face of a middle-aged man whose dark skin and thick, blond hair were similar to all the others who had dropped out of the clouds. The man's eyes were open, but Hokk forced himself to ignore the vacant stare. Instead, he pried open the mouth, tilting the head. In the glow from a burst of lightning overhead, Hokk saw a glint in the back. *Yes!* A gold tooth. Hokk struggled to loosen it, bracing his knee on the man's chest. Finally wiggling it free, he triumphantly held up the shiny molar. Curious, Nym stood on his back legs and Hokk let him sniff it. At last, something of true value, he thought.

The few hairs still growing on Hokk's arms suddenly stood straight as if electrified by the storm. He glanced uneasily at the dead man's face, overcome by a strange sense of being watched.

And then the eyes blinked.

Hokk shot to his feet, horrified. He pressed both hands

against his head, waiting for the man's eyelids to move again. He gently kicked the body.

He kicked harder.

No response.

Of course not. The man was dead. They were always dead. Hokk had been betrayed by his imagination once more. "I'm relapsing," he sighed miserably as he sank to the ground and reached out to pet Nym. He'd been so convinced he had moved past this problem. Now to see it rear up again—

No. He would control it. He wasn't going to turn out like his brother. He simply needed to end this wretched isolation.

Hokk stuffed the gold tooth in his pocket. The tiny treasure was worthless on the prairies, but he could trade it later, just like all the other things he had found fallen from the sky, when his exile from the City of Ago was finally over. However, that was still four years away. For now, the tooth was a reminder that someday he would return home to rebuild his life. Someday, his mind would eventually heal too.

The first drops of the approaching storm hit Hokk's face. Time to leave. Rewrapping the body was pointless, so he would simply abandon it. That's what Kalus had always taught. If this dead man's family could discard him, then Hokk had no further obligation.

He hurried to the gazelk and lifted Nym onto the animal's back. He was about to mount too when the fox went rigid, staring over Hokk's shoulder, his nose quivering. Even before turning, Hokk had already guessed who had arrived—another roaming outcast to claim the body and whatever bounty it might offer.

Hokk whirled around, ready to fight. Through the storm's rolling mist and the smoke from the fires, he made out the shape of an immense bison with a rider on top.

A Torkin!

For a moment, Hokk suspected another hallucination, but Nym's reaction confirmed the sight was real. His hands started to shake. This was a warrior from the mountain tribes, not an exile from Hokk's city. But whose territory was this? Hokk had been so careful not to trespass, though he was reckless to trust his instinct with directions and continue traveling when his compass was so unsettled. And if the clouds hadn't been so low, he would have seen the jagged Torkinian Mountain Range piercing through the prairies.

In an instant, Hokk was on the gazelk, twisting its horns and kicking its sides. Glancing behind, he saw the rider crouch into position, preparing his bison to charge. Hokk urged the gazelk toward the oncoming wall of rain, hitting it head-on.

He pulled his cloak around himself and covered Nym in his lap. The rain whipped at his face, crawling down his neck and under his clothing like icy fingers.

Yet they drove forward, into the storm and its fury.

Chapter 2

EVERY PAIR OF EARS WITHIN these walls had heard the same whispered advice: *Work as though you are already dead. Try to feel nothing.*

Just looking at the glazed faces on the women and other young girls, Elia suspected they were all masters of numbing themselves to the fatigue and boredom. Unfortunately, Elia was always too painfully aware. She felt each cruel ripple of her washboard, every drop of water splashed down the front of her plain gray dress, each loose pebble digging into her knees as she crouched by the tub. She hated it here. Buried in the bowels of the Mirrored Palace, the laundry room was chiseled out of solid rock. Torches on the walls offered only feeble light against the gloom. Moisture dripped from the ceiling, and the centuries-old air was fouled by Cook's ever-burning fires.

Elia wrung a shirt and tossed it onto a pile of clothes sitting in a growing puddle. She clawed wisps of hair from her sweaty forehead, then dunked another shirt into the wash, disturbing the water's surface before she could catch sight of her image staring back. She scrubbed the cuffs clean and her knuckles raw, gritting her teeth with determination.

It had been ages since she had last seen her reflection. She remembered nothing beautiful about her face. She had a strong profile inherited from her father and her skin was dark like her eyes, her hair blond as if bleached in the sun, though she was hardly ever in it. Elia felt like a neglected workhorse—sturdy in frame, but underweight and lacking any curves.

Faint vibrations from the stone floor accompanied the familiar grinding sound of Cook's cauldron rolling closer. The cauldron stopped in front of Elia, yet the trembling below did not. Puzzled, Elia stared at the ground, her hands still submerged, as Cook poured water into her tub. The water was especially scalding today, the searing pain instant. Elia snatched back her arms and bit her lip to prevent a curse flying out, forgetting all about the slowly dissipating sensations from the rock.

"That's all you get," grumbled Cook, adding a scoop of soap pellets. "Make it last."

Cook was ruler of the laundry room and she could not tolerate waste, especially not water. Water was too precious. Though she didn't prepare meals, she was a cook all the same, stirring her cauldrons to melt the gelatinous waterballs delivered daily from the dewfields.

Elia dared to wait only a few moments before slipping her hands back into the steaming brew. Over a decade ago, arriving as a scared five-year-old, Elia suffered for weeks until her tender skin toughened. Now she had arms of blistered leather.

While she wrung another shirt, Elia's jaw cracked as she stifled a yawn. She had been yawning all morning, exhausted after spending half the night searching for her grandmother. The old woman's mind was deteriorating, and she had started wandering away while the rest of the family slept. Even by the glow of the moon, with its many pieces scattered across the sky, it still took hours to find her in the forest. Omi had tried to flee, terrified to see Elia approaching in the shadows, but Elia caught her in a tight embrace and did not let go until her grandmother recognized her voice. Trembling, Omi clung to her as they headed home, jabbering nonsense about the palace stables and how the Empress Mother was expecting her. Years had passed since Omi last tended the royal stallions, yet for all of her memories that had evaporated, somehow these remained vivid. And now, lately, they had become all-consuming.

The last shirt done, Elia grabbed a pair of white trousers with fine embroidery along the waistline. She scowled. Gravy stains everywhere. It was hard to believe a nobleman could be such a sloppy eater.

"Bunch of drunken animals," huffed Mrs. Suds, kneeling at a tub beside Elia's. She held up a tablecloth covered with wine stains and footprints. "Those fools climb over everything!"

Years in the laundry had taken its toll on the old woman's frail body. Around the same age as Omi, Mrs. Suds now had a permanent bend in her back and she grew stiffer and more stooped each day.

The woman dunked the tablecloth into her wash. "They can always find a reason to celebrate," she said, picking up a scrub brush with twisted, arthritic fingers.

No one responded. Only Mrs. Suds was brave enough to talk when they should be working.

As Elia lowered the trousers into the water, she felt something in one of the pockets. She reached inside to touch it, then quickly yanked out her hand, pushing herself away from the tub.

"Looks like your heart's about to stop," said Mrs. Suds.

Elia shot her a glance and then scanned the area for Cook.

"What did you find?" Mrs. Suds's tired face was lit with curiosity.

"I don't think I want to know."

It couldn't possibly be what it felt like: a severed finger.

"She's found something," Mrs. Suds whispered to the other washers. "Come on girl, pull it out!"

Hesitating, Elia stirred the water before coaxing herself to reach again into the pocket. Fleshy and greasy, it almost slipped from her hand as she eased out not a severed finger but—

A bone.

A half-eaten bone, with meat and gristle on each end. Tied in the middle was a long, blue ribbon, the type worn by women of the Royal Court.

"It's just a bone," Elia muttered, holding it up for the others to see.

Mrs. Suds's mouth fell open. She reached out a trembling claw. "Let me see that!"

The old woman slowly turned the bone between her fingertips, then clutched it to her chest, her gaze drifting up to the ceiling as if her vision could penetrate the many stone floors above. Dread creased her face.

"Just throw it away," said Elia.

Mrs. Suds's attention refocused. "We mustn't. We were meant to find this."

"It's only a fool's joke."

"By no means is this a joke!" Mrs. Suds tucked the bone into her apron. "We're lucky. We could have missed it completely."

"It's actually not the first," whispered Naadie, a young girl with a patch over her eye.

Mrs. Suds whipped around. "It's not?"

"I saw several bones in my washtub two days ago."

"Two days ago!" Her raised voice made everyone shrink back, eyes darting for trouble, but Mrs. Suds didn't care. "You should have said something before. Were ribbons tied to them too?"

"Yes, each one. The same blue," replied Naadie.

"I found one myself yesterday," another woman quietly offered. Her baby was sitting in a puddle beside her.

Mrs. Suds dragged a hand through her gray hair. "If it's been several days, then it's already too late," she said, voice shaking. "They've figured it out. Not enough time now to respond before—"

"Enough talking!" Cook bellowed, storming into their midst. "Back to work!"

She banged a ladle against the side of a metal basin. The sound echoed throughout the sweltering cavern.

The baby started to cry. Washers hunched over their laundry, arms pumping above their washboards, while Elia scrubbed furiously, the delicate embroidery forgotten. Mrs. Suds, however, did nothing except stare into her tub.

Cook acknowledged the woman's stupor with a frustrated sigh, not an angry outburst. As if realizing the old woman was long past her usefulness, Cook divided Mrs. Suds's remaining laundry among neighboring workers. "We can't have any delays," she mumbled before lumbering back to her cauldrons.

When their midday meal arrived half an hour later, Mrs. Suds had still not moved. Eating in silence, the other women nervously glanced at her, then at the unclaimed bowl, until Elia got up and brought it over. The watered-down soup was standard fare for laundry workers, the only food the kitchen could supply after first feeding the rest of the palace. It was everybody's one guaranteed meal of the day, and certainly better than what they served in the dungeons below.

"You should eat," Elia encouraged.

Mrs. Suds looked up at her with eyes sunk deep into her wrinkled face. With unexpected strength, she grabbed Elia's wrist and pulled her close, pressing the bone into Elia's hand. "Take this."

Elia recoiled. "I don't want it!"

"You must!" Mrs. Suds squeezed Elia's fingers closed around the bone and its blue ribbon. "And when you leave today, give it to your mother."

"My mother?"

"She'll know."

"This doesn't make any sense," said Elia.

Mrs. Suds frowned, making her jowls sag as if they might melt off her jaw. "What you found is not just a message for me, but for your family as well. It's a warning!" She gave an uneasy chuckle. "Funny that after everything, you're the one to discover it."

Gooseflesh prickled Elia's skin. Surely the old woman's mind was going, just as Elia had seen happen to her grandmother.

"Why don't you eat before the scullions take away the bowls," Elia suggested soothingly. She heard noises coming from the stairwell. "And the donkeys will be arriving soon."

The donkey procession came every day around this time, led by the stable boy and the two girls who hung laundry in the hills. The animals carried baskets strapped to their backs, which had to be unloaded for the workers' afternoon of ironing.

Looking with a start toward the entrance, a flicker of alarm crossed Mrs. Suds's face. Rather than donkeys filling the room, the bulk of an Imperial Guard blocked the doorway.

He stepped inside, ducking his head under the frame. His helmet, polished to a mirror finish, covered not just his head, but his face too, and it was sculpted with the same stern, frozen expression that made Imperial Guards indistinguishable. The two metallic wings protruding from the top of his helmet, however, were unique and showed he held the highest rank.

"Commander Wrasse!" croaked Cook, bending in an awkward bow.

Shock radiated throughout the room. Commander Wrasse was a name everyone had learned to fear, his presence no less surprising than if one of the Twin Emperors had appeared.

"Where is she?" he demanded as other guards filed in behind.

"Who—who are you looking for?" Cook stammered.

The imperial commander flung back his helmet to reveal a face even more menacing than the metal mask suggested. A long battle scar sliced his face diagonally, cutting his nose deep into two separate pieces. He glared at Cook, then moved into the room, scanning faces as the women scurried out of his way.

"I'm over here," Mrs. Suds announced. She rose unsteadily to her feet.

Elia caught her breath.

Wrasse marched toward the old woman. "So this is where you ended up," he sneered, towering above her, air wheezing through his ravaged nose. "Have you been here all these years?"

"Right below you the whole time," she replied, thrusting out her chin.

"I wouldn't have recognized you."

"I've gotten old."

"And hideous," Wrasse snorted, his nostrils flaring.

"As have you," she dared to say.

The commander studied her for a moment, then drove a fist into the old woman's abdomen. Elia cried out as Mrs. Suds dropped to her knees.

"Come on! Stand up. Face me!" mocked Wrasse. "Can't do it?" He grabbed a handful of the woman's thinning hair and tilted back her head. "No matter. Only one place for meddling hags like you."

Cook suddenly appeared beside them. "Leave her, please! She's worth nothing anymore," she pleaded. Never before had she shown any concern for her workers.

The commander flung Cook aside and she toppled to the floor. "Careful, or you'll join her," he warned. He signaled to the guards who had gathered in the entrance and they dragged Mrs. Suds away—to the dungeons no doubt. She didn't resist.

"I want this entire space searched!" shouted Wrasse. "I want that damn thing found!"

The men were quick to follow orders. Piles of clothes were scattered, Cook's cauldrons overturned, and ironing boards knocked down with a crash. When the donkey procession arrived, the guards tore open the baskets and dumped the previous day's clean laundry on the wet floor, leaving it to be trampled by their careless, filthy boots.

Elia hid in the shadows, her throat clenched with fear. *The guards could only be looking for one thing. The bone! So just hand it over!*

No. Too dangerous. If the guards discovered it in Elia's possession, she would suffer in a place far more miserable and inescapable than this wretched laundry room, never to see her family again.

Elia smoothed down the fabric of her apron pocket where the bone was hidden. Whether or not she showed it to her mother, her only choice now was to smuggle it out, though as soon as she could, she'd throw the awful thing away.

Chapter 3

ON FOOT, HOKK WOULD HAVE wandered for a week to find the tree; with the gazelk, he arrived after a long day of steady riding. He could see it standing on the horizon like a lone sentry, its branches bending in the wind.

They had successfully outrun the Torkin warrior's bison, and while the gazelk was in dire need of a rest and Hokk's legs would be rubbed raw if he didn't dismount soon, Hokk wouldn't stop. Not yet. He was eager to cover the distance to the tree so he could replenish his supplies. Everything he had been carrying was stolen the previous week.

They had come at night. One assailant held Hokk down, pressing his face into the dirt, as the other snatched the few things Hokk relied upon to survive: his dagger, a flint, some rope, and a blanket. Before knocking him unconscious, they kicked out his fire, stole the skewer of mice he had been roasting over the flames, and took his precious bag filled with items that had dropped from Above. He awoke to Nym licking his throbbing forehead. Only his father's compass remained, which he found in the grasses. Everything else, he had no hope of retrieving.

Hokk never carried all his possessions with him at one time for this very reason. Kalus had taught him that early on. Instead, he had stashes in two locations, spaced a great distance apart, where he kept his collections and extra supplies well hidden. He hadn't been to this particular tree for over a year, and now, standing beside it, he traced his fingers over the symbols he had carved into the bark during his first visit. Five strokes of a blade—one vertical cut with four horizontal gouges above. Only he could understand the instructions to walk forty paces in the direction indicated.

Counting the necessary steps, Hokk spotted the upside-down bottle with its neck in the ground. He pulled out the marker, tore away the grass matting, and began digging into the soil. He remembered the last time he had been standing over this very spot, knowing that someday he would return. But that was supposed to be when his period of exile was over, when it was time to collect everything and return to Ago.

Hokk dug furiously, not needing to go as deep as he had expected before the top of a sack was revealed. He ripped it from the earth.

The bag was empty.

Hokk raised his face to the sky and roared as he flung the sack as far away as possible. Nym froze, staring at him. It was pure mockery, reburying the bag and leaving the bottle marker sticking out.

Kalus! He was the only person present when Hokk originally chose this location, all those years ago. Hokk should never have trusted the man.

An outcast himself, Kalus had been on the prairies for nearly ten years on his own before their chance encounter. He had ridden by on his gazelk and nearly trampled Hokk, who was sprawled in the grasses. Hokk, not much older than eleven, had collapsed, weak from starvation during those first few weeks after being banished from the city, when the burns on his hands and arms were still oozing.

Kalus had stopped only because he thought the boy on the ground was dead and could be scavenged. Hokk didn't stir until Kalus turned him over with his foot.

"You seem too young to be an outcast," Kalus had said.

"Please," Hokk had groaned, pointing feebly to his mouth.

"I don't do charity. Got anything to trade?" he growled, eyeing the ring on Hokk's finger.

Hokk nodded, and Kalus wasted no time twisting it off, letting Hokk's limp arm drop to the ground. In exchange, he gave Hokk water and a bit of food.

From then on, since Hokk had nothing left to trade except the compass that he kept well hidden, Kalus never shared food again. Fortunately, the man let Hokk travel with him after recognizing his family name, and Hokk quickly learned the basic skills for hunting, finding shelter, and predicting the weather.

Hokk had tried to figure out exactly what crime Kalus had committed to receive the Board's standard ten-year sentence, but his stories always changed. Was he exiled for his drunken brawls, kidnapping his neighbor, or his vicious tirades against the Board? Or was it his multiple wives who finally got him expelled when they figured out they had competition?

It was difficult to believe Kalus had so many wives. His body odor was choking, and he was always scratching a crusty rash that ran from his neck to his chest. Half of his teeth were missing, causing him to whistle when he talked, and his scruffy black whiskers poked through skin as pale as Hokk's.

One morning, five months after they met, Kalus woke up in a surprisingly cheery mood. "Well, that was my last night!" he declared. "My sentence is complete."

"You're done? Just like that?" Hokk asked as Kalus packed his belongings.

"The ten years are up today."

"And what about me?"

Kalus shrugged. "You're not my problem."

Hokk had been stunned, yet there was nothing he could do to stop Kalus from riding off, leaving Hokk alone to fend for himself.

And now here was Hokk once again, alone on the prairies with next to nothing.

He relaxed his fists as he looked at Nym. He knew exactly what was necessary. He had made a commitment to himself six years ago when Kalus left that he would do whatever it took to ensure his survival, no matter the price.

You're a criminal, he reminded himself. Act like one.

Chapter 4

WORKERS SHUFFLED TOWARD THE EXIT where Cook dropped a single coin into each open palm. Normally, she would grumble, as if forced to pay everyone from her own wages. Today, not a sound. Nobody had uttered a word since Mrs. Suds's arrest. After trashing the laundry, the guards had left without finding what they were looking for, but the trauma of their visit was written on every worker's face. The women would lose sleep tonight over Wrasse's parting words. *We won't stop until it's found. Our dungeons can hold as many of you as it takes.*

Elia cut to the front of the line. As soon as the coin was in her hand, she darted up the wide staircase, dodging the slower workers. She continued past the level where her mother, Sulum, worked as a seamstress, past the multiple floors of the kitchens, climbing higher and higher toward increasing brightness.

She was panting when she burst into the open. Fresh air! Light!

But the sun was only a few hours away from setting—they had been forced to work much later to catch up. The Grand Bridge behind the palace was empty, except for Elia's mother, who had already collected their bicycles.

Sulum did not resemble her daughter. She had the same blond hair and dark skin, but she was shorter, more delicate, and she walked with a limp because of a birth defect that left one leg shorter. Only when pedaling could Sulum move with no sign of disability, and for this reason, she loved to bicycle.

Sulum's smile faded as Elia approached. "What's wrong?" she asked.

"Let's get home."

Elia released the coin into her mother's hand, and Sulum held it close to her face, squinting to confirm its value. Elia looked away and tried to ignore a pang of pity. Though Sulum had been an expert with needle and thread all her life, her eyesight was getting worse. Aging seamstresses who could no longer see—and therefore no longer sew—had only one direction to go. Down. With time, they all ended up in the laundry room, finishing their lives where they had started as children.

For years, Elia had been diligently practicing her sewing skills by candlelight late into the evenings, keen for an opportunity like her mother's, but her stitches were atrocious. She had little chance of being promoted, and most certainly no hope of pursuing a job outside washing or mending clothing. Sons and daughters were assigned to the same industries as their parents. Tradition was broken only by the few lucky young men recruited to the ranks of Imperial Guards.

Elia and Sulum pushed their bicycles across the massive cobblestones to the crest of the Grand Bridge. The bridge was never used by the Royal Court, but instead offered access to the back of the palace for staff and tradespeople from the City of Na-Lavent. Wider than five roads laid side by side, the bridge deck spanned the top of strong, curved support beams that arched high over the sea of clouds swirling beneath. It joined two floating islands—the Isle of Kamanman, which was the mainland, and the much smaller Isle of the Noble Sanctuary, where Elia worked in the palace. From its apex was a view of the city on the opposite side of the expanse, and much farther beyond, the countryside and the forest fading into the shadows of Mount Mahayit. Across that distance sat Elia's home, little more than a shack built between the edge of the trees and a rugged cliff that dropped away to nothing but mist lapping against the rock.

Descending to the other side of the bridge, Elia and her mother approached the patroled gates where Imperial Guards controlled access to the palace grounds.

"Stop!" A guard grabbed Elia's arm.

Elia froze, feeling instantly lightheaded.

"What's the matter?" asked Sulum.

The guard waved a hand in front of Sulum's face. "You wait."

Elia did not look at the man directly. Ever since she was a young girl, she hated seeing her reflection distorted on the curves of the guards' faceplates.

The guard tightened his grip as he brushed the hair off her forehead with his other hand, revealing a purple tattoo above Elia's eyebrows. Received at birth, it was the seal of the Twin Emperors, marking her as palace staff. Sulum had one too, though hers was a symbol from the Empress Mother's reign. The tattoo should have been all he needed to see, yet the guard was not satisfied. "Sneaking anything out?"

Elia was struck dumb with fear. She had never been questioned before.

The guard began to search her, patting his hands along her thighs and waist.

"Lift your skirt," he instructed. Elia timidly exposed her lower legs. "Higher," he demanded, then roughly slid his hands up her bare skin, feeling past her knees. Elia let go of her bicycle and it crashed to the ground.

"What's changed today to warrant this humiliation?" Sulum challenged, though her voice still quavered.

"New orders."

A second guard's hands began exploring Sulum's body in the same manner. Though her face was defiant, she looked so vulnerable. Elia wished she could race over and pull the man off.

Feeling a small lump in Sulum's dress, the guard tore open a pocket and the few coins inside fell to the ground. "You're a rich one!" he sneered.

As her mother bent to pick up the money, the man searching Elia pulled the bone out of her apron. He dangled it from the ribbon. "What's this supposed to be?"

Elia's pulse pounded in her ears. Her tongue felt fused to the roof of her mouth. Didn't he recognize it? Isn't this what the guards were looking for?

"Something to nibble on later?" he asked.

"It's nothing," Elia sputtered, noticing the shock in her mother's eyes.

"It's only table scraps!" said Sulum, lunging to snatch the bone, then hurling it over the side of the bridge. "It should have been thrown out with the rest of the garbage!"

The other guard snorted. "There goes your dinner." Both men laughed as Elia imagined the bone falling end over end through the clouds, to be found by the Scavengers of Below.

"Are you done with us?" asked Sulum with her head bowed.

"Keep moving," the first replied, shoving her along as other laundry workers nervously approached the gates.

Legs trembling, Elia tried to match her mother's determined, albeit unbalanced, steps as they hurried away. Only when they mounted their bicycles and started pedaling could Elia catch up. "I'm sorry," she said as they rode toward the market.

"They've never stopped us before," Sulum replied. "It's not your fault."

"No, I mean they weren't supposed to find that bone."

Sulum aimed a troubled gaze at her daughter. "Where did you get such a thing?"

"I found it in my washtub. In a pair of dirty trousers."

"You should have left it there."

"It was supposed to be important. I was told you would know what it means."

"Who told you that?"

"Mrs. Suds."

Her mother's eyebrows pinched together. "I don't know that name."

"She's the oldest one still working there. Suds is just a nickname."

"Oh." Sulum frowned, trying to remember. "Perhaps I worked with her as a young girl before I was promoted." Sulum anxiously glanced around and lowered her voice. "But my goodness, Elia, I thought you had stolen food from the kitchen. You could be imprisoned for that!"

"I know. When he pulled out the bone, I was terrified they'd take me away like they did Mrs. Suds."

Sulum's bicycle lurched to a halt. "Who did?"

Elia stopped as well. "Imperial Guards. Commander Wrasse, actually. They took her to the dungeons, then tore up the laundry, looking for something."

"What?"

"That bone. Or so I thought."

"You really are a foolish girl," said Sulum, looking at Elia as if she didn't recognize her own daughter. "To take such a risk for something so ridiculous. I can't understand you."

"I'm sorry," said Elia, shrinking with shame. "I didn't know what else to do."

"This old woman, this Mrs. Suds as you call her, has done something to get herself in trouble and you should not get involved. You should know better." Sulum reached forward and firmly tapped her knuckle against Elia's breastbone. "Just worry about yourself and this family. Do you understand?"

"I do."

Sulum's expression softened. "And don't be so naive. Try to remember what your grandmother was forever saying to us." She squeezed her daughter's arm. "*Perceptions deceive. Things are often not as they seem.*"

Elia nodded. Even now, she could hear Omi telling her to always question what she believed to be true. How ironic that advice had become once Omi started losing her mind to dementia, living in her own distorted version of reality. "I'll be more careful," said Elia.

"Good." With a huff, Sulum heaved herself up onto her bicycle seat. "Now let's hurry home before it gets dark."

Elia looked toward the heart of the city. "What about the market?"

"Tomorrow," Sulum replied as she pedaled off.

Tomorrow? But Elia was hungry today. They never missed the market when they had money, even if their few coins could only purchase whatever bruised fruit, expired eggs, or stale bread was left at the end of the afternoon. And what about Elia's father? Their routine was to ride around the marketplace, peering down lanes and into dark, recessed doorways until they found him. Usually, no more than a soiled foot or a scrawny shoulder sticking out gave him away. Elia always held back while her mother approached with a small bundle of food, her father's ragged hands cautiously reaching for the package.

Sulum's earlier words repeated in Elia's head. *Just worry about yourself and this family.* For Elia, that didn't apply to her father. She grieved for his former self, a man full of vigor who could work for hours and still chase Elia into the forest at the end of the day, climbing up the trees after her, then sitting on the limbs and sharing stories about the many islands he had visited in the System. That was before he abandoned the family for whatever unforgivable reason he had for leaving. Like the skin shed by a snake, he was now nothing more than an empty shell.

Would her father even realize they hadn't come today? Elia didn't care. Let him starve.

Chapter 5

ELIA'S RICKETY BICYCLE, WITH ITS bent frame and rusty gears, struggled over potholes as she and her mother left the city's center, riding through the outlying regions of Na-Lavent. Here the people lived crammed into rundown neighborhoods that smelled of smoke, boiled cabbage, sewers, and thatched roofs. It was the stink of poverty and despair. As children grew up and had families of their own, they were forced to build ramshackle rooms stacked precariously on top of their parents' homes. These wobbly towers stood only because they were so tightly packed.

Elia detested these areas. She felt burdened by the crush of people and was always glad to leave the city for the quieter roads where they could ride toward Mount Mahayit in the distance. Biking home at the end of the day, however, was a grueling, uphill trip, and after long hours at work, the forest seemed so far away. Heading back into Na-Lavent each morning was much easier, with the slope of the road allowing Elia and Sulum to coast down the hills, their legs kicked out as their dresses ballooned with air.

The road narrowed, winding past glistening dew farms, lush orchards, and crops ready for harvest. Sheep and cattle grazed, and yellow flowers bowed in sweeping waves across the landscape. The sun was just setting when they finally turned off the road into the darkening forest, but the moon was up too, light reflecting off its many pieces. Generations ago, it had been a solid disc, floating just like the sun, but now it resembled a shattered plate trailing debris across the sky.

Elia led the way, knowing every curve and bump of the path. The air was chilly and the leaves whispered secrets in the treetops. They rode deeper and deeper, her bicycle rattling in protest as it bounced over roots.

Rounding a bend, Elia suddenly swerved, stopping only inches from her grandfather standing in the middle of the trail. Opi was wringing his hands, his legs braced as though he didn't know whether to return to their shack, or proceed farther into the forest.

"Omi's gone!" he exclaimed.

"Not again!" said Sulum. "How long?"

"We had a nap. I didn't hear her get up."

"When was that?"

"Could be several hours."

Elia's mother surveyed the forest. "Several hours?"

"And I didn't know if I should go after her with the light fading," said Opi. He nervously clutched his throat. "I've never seen her in such rough shape."

Sulum put her arm around his shoulders. "Did something upset her?"

"We had visitors," Elia's grandfather said gravely. "Unexpected visitors."

Sulum tensed. "Who?"

"Imperial Guards."

"Oh no. What did they want?"

"They wanted to talk to her. I don't know about what. They took her inside, but she couldn't have said anything that made sense. She was distraught, rambling pure gibberish by the time they left, so I just put her to bed."

"Thank goodness they didn't take her away," said Elia, thinking of Mrs. Suds. She looked back along the route they had taken through the forest. "We saw nothing along the path and her legs are too weak to travel far. I'll go find her."

"We'll both go," said her mother.

They headed in different directions, the spongy moss dampening the sound of their footsteps. With her limp, Sulum would stay closer to home, leaving Elia to search the outer areas of the forest on her own. Elia didn't mind. She was used to making things as easy as she could for her mother.

"Omi?" Elia shouted. "Omi? Can you hear me?"

She listened carefully for a response, but heard nothing except Sulum's distant voice calling out like an echo. The only light now came from the shattered moon, its glow slicing through the trees and casting long shadows that resembled the bars of a darkened jail cell.

"Omi?"

Still nothing.

After covering more terrain than her grandmother could have traveled, Elia turned back for home. But then something caught her eye. A short distance away, Omi's white blanket hung from a branch like a luminous ghost. Elia ran to retrieve it and called out once more. "Omi?"

Up ahead, the moonlight seemed brighter, the woods less dense. Excited and sensing her grandmother was near, Elia sprinted toward the clearing, leaping over fallen trunks. As she broke free of the trees, the edge of the island suddenly dropped off in front of her. Though she jolted to a halt, some of the ground crumbled away and one foot dipped into the clouds. She yanked back her leg and quickly reached behind for a branch.

She was terrified to look down. Was a claw reaching up? Had her commotion summoned a Scavenger the way a bug struggling in a web attracts the spider?

The Scavengers of Below were horrendous, pale creatures that clung to the islands with their claws, waiting for the chance to snatch people and add them to their collection of corpses. Their spines were curved, and their limbs scrawny with knobby elbows and knees. Most horrifying of all, Scavengers had no eyes, just bulging foreheads above two holes for nostrils and white lips pulled taut over toothless gums. Everyone knew to stay back from the edges where the Scavengers lurked when they came up from the mists.

With her heart still drumming in her chest, Elia spotted Omi farther along the edge, where she was stretched out, asleep on a patch of moss.

"Omi! What are you doing there?" she called out. Her grandmother didn't stir.

Elia inched along, and as she got closer, saw that Omi was lying face down, her arms stretched above her head.

Dread coursed through every vein as Elia crouched beside her grandmother. Her mind fought the obvious. Choking back tears, she rolled Omi over, and was shocked to see fear so clearly etched on the old woman's frozen expression.

She was dead.

Elia sat in the moss and cradled her grandmother's head in her lap. She closed Omi's eyelids and gently coaxed her lips together to make her appear more peaceful. Elia wanted Sulum and Opi to see a serene expression when she brought them here later. As she unclenched Omi's fists, she saw dried blood on her bony hands, and dirt under her fingernails. In the moonlight, Elia could make out deep scratch marks on the mossy ground. It was clear her grandmother had desperately clawed at the earth as she had been dragged by a Scavenger. But why did they fail to pull her over the edge? Did the Imperial Guards return and scare the monsters off, though not before she died of fright?

Elia's body trembled with grief, her cheeks moist with tears, as she remembered her final conversation with her grandmother the previous night while making their way home.

"Omi, it's hard on everyone when you wander off," Elia had said. "Especially for Mom."

"Yes, I worry about her. I want you to take good care of your mother when your grandfather and I are gone," said Omi, never guessing she only had one more day of life.

"Don't talk like that," Elia had replied, hugging her tighter. "We're just trying to look out for you."

Omi patted her granddaughter's cheek. "No, it's the other way around. I'm the one looking out for the family."

Chapter 6

"I'VE RETURNED," HOKK CALLED OUT from his perch atop the gazelk. The solitary tree was a full night's ride behind him.

No response came from inside the tent. All around, the flat landscape was an undulating bed of grass and drifting litter. With its corners pinned to the ground, the tent clung to the earth like any other snagged piece of garbage fighting the wind.

"I've come back as I promised."

Actually, Hokk hadn't promised the old man inside any such thing. He had been undecided about returning the gazelk.

Over the past few months, Hokk had made numerous visits to this meager camp, hoping to combat his solitude. The old man was a hermit, not a criminal banished from the city, and Hokk first heard about him years ago through Kalus, though he had only recently sought him out. As a recluse, he posed no threat, and provided company whenever Hokk felt his mind was struggling, when he couldn't trust his ability to distinguish hallucinations from reality. Hokk was desperate the first time he showed up here, and having not spoken to another person for so long, he had felt self-conscious to speak. The feeling still lingered.

"Are you in there?" Hokk asked.

He could hear shuffling within. Hokk slipped off the gazelk's back and started untying the tent's opening. "I'm taking some stuff. Everything I had has been stolen."

Pulling open the front flap, Hokk recoiled and covered his mouth. In the dim light, he could make out the old man lying flat on the ground, his bulging eyes gazing up at Hokk from two pits in his gaunt, sweaty face. His lips were purple, his breathing rapid. Trembling fingers picked at the frayed collar of his shirt.

"What's happened?" Hokk gasped.

The hermit mumbled, spit bubbling from his lips. "Infection."

He was being consumed by it. Hokk had seen the cut several days ago, thinking the sore would scab and eventually heal. The man had mentioned he had a fever, but Hokk had not offered any help. What could he do? Hokk had only shown up because he needed the gazelk to find the rest of his things, whether the hermit agreed to it or not. He had agreed. And now the man was dying.

"I need a knife. Something to start a fire," said Hokk, pinching his nose against the stink. The hermit simply stared at him, so Hokk stepped back into the fresh air and scanned the camp. The area was empty. Had another outcast already been here? Would they be back for everything else?

Whatever Hokk might be able to use was probably hidden inside with the hermit. Hokk moved to a corner of the tent and pulled a peg from the soil. He went to the other side and yanked out the pin there too, then disassembled one of the supporting poles which made half of the tent collapse.

"No," a feeble voiced protested underneath the fabric.

Wrenching open the front flap, Hokk grabbed the man under the armpits and dragged him outside. As a blanket covering him slipped away, Hokk saw a sack of supplies wedged between the man's legs. Hokk seized it, but the hermit tried to sit up, clinging to the bag. "You can't do this," the hermit moaned. "It's mine."

Hokk clenched his jaw and wrestled the sack from the man's grasp, pushing him back to the ground. The hermit's swollen body shuddered in pain. One leg started twitching and Hokk noticed the large rotting wound eating away the old man's ankle.

Ignore it!

Drops from a light drizzle began to splatter the side of the tent as Hokk removed the last of the pegs and the remaining pole. He rolled up the fabric with all the hardware inside and tucked the bundle under his arm. With the sack of supplies clutched to his chest, he walked back to the hermit's gazelk— no, Hokk's gazelk now. Nym was waiting where Hokk had left him, his furry face tilted sideways as if perplexed. Hokk quickly tied the sack and tent around the gazelk's neck, then launched himself onto its back, all the while hoping not to hear a sound from the man he was abandoning.

No sound came.

Hokk did not look back, but the beating hooves couldn't drum out the thoughts in his mind. He wasn't supposed to be like this anymore. Even his brother would not have been this ruthless.

Before long, he had to stop the gazelk and get off. In the persistent rain, he sunk to the wet ground on hands and knees, his head hanging down. He wanted to vomit, to rid his stomach of the horror he felt inside. He gagged and his eyes watered, but nothing more. The horror could not be expelled. He would have to carry it with him.

Chapter 7

ELIA HAD FINALLY SUCCEEDED. HER mind was dead as she worked. Unfortunately, it took the loss of her grandmother, an empty stomach, utter exhaustion, and arriving to see Mrs. Suds's abandoned washtub to numb it completely. She told no one about Omi's death, and somehow she got her laundry done; somehow she found herself staring into her soup at lunchtime. Revived by the sight of food, she fished out the carrots and chewed them slowly before tipping back the bowl to sip the salty broth.

The donkey procession arrived as she was wiping her mouth with her sleeve. The animals stood calmly, their bodies steaming in the humid heat, while their baskets were unloaded and the laundry neatly stacked. Today was nothing like yesterday's mayhem—everything was back to normal. Back to the endless routine. Elia felt her mind slipping away again, preparing for the afternoon ahead.

But then Cook stood before her. "I'm switching things up."

Elia looked around as if the woman couldn't possibly be talking to her.

"I can't have you down here anymore," said Cook with a frown. "Not after what's happened."

Please, no. What horrendous task had she come up with?

"You're hanging laundry."

But, wait—that was wonderful! Elia sat up straight, now fully alert. "Really? Outside? Today?"

"From now on."

Workers sitting around Elia began to murmur. This was a coveted assignment. Elia couldn't believe it was true, even as she listened to Cook tell the girls who had just arrived about the new arrangements. They both looked crushed, their eyes welling up as they scanned the laundry room that would now become their daily prison.

Cook guided a donkey toward Elia. "Best to start loading baskets right away."

"Thank you," Elia replied with utmost sincerity.

Cook appeared awkward, as if not used to gratitude. She scowled and pointed to Naadie. "You. The blind one."

"Me?" Naadie piped up, adjusting the patch covering her one wounded eye.

"You're useless down here. I want you to join Elia at the clotheslines."

Elia was stunned to hear Cook say her name. Cook had never used anybody's first name before.

"Finish down here, then the stable boy will show you the route." Cook turned and spoke to Elia directly. "If anything happens out there, you be sure to let me know."

Elia squirmed. "Like what?"

"Anything!" Cook bellowed. "Can't be certain what's going on around here anymore with all these bones turning up. That's right," she added, seeing Elia's reaction. "I've seen them too. Best to be ready. And more importantly, be careful. You never know who's up to no good."

•   •   •

The sun was overhead when they emerged with the donkeys. Elia's eyes struggled to adjust to the dazzling light. The stable boy stayed at the front, and Elia and Naadie brought up the rear, following the swishing tails of the donkeys who were so familiar with the path.

The trail passed by the stables before climbing into the hills. With the midday heat, Elia was soon sweating through her gray dress. An extremely pregnant donkey walked steps ahead, the last in line. As Elia wondered how the beast could cope with the burden of her load, both the laundry and the baby, Naadie reached out to touch Elia's arm. "Look!"

Hills of luscious green rolled out before them. Row upon row of empty clotheslines waited for the morning's clean laundry. Beyond that, Elia could see the rocky edge of the island and white clouds to the horizon.

Whatever Cook's reason for choosing her, it was a blessing to be here. Working outside was what her brother—and their father before him—enjoyed each day in the dewfields. She delighted in the fresh air, the brightness, the grass between her bare toes. Peaceful solitude. Virtual freedom.

Elia didn't hurry to hang the clothes, stretching the hours as long as possible. She would love to stay in these hills forever and never have to deal with what was waiting for her at home.

• • •

Elia was thankful the funeral preparations for Omi were almost complete by the time she and her mother arrived home. Her brother, Rayhan, had shown up earlier to help their grandfather wrap Omi's body in pieces of cloth. The final layer was made from strips of Omi's white blanket, bound so tightly around her body that no distinguishing features remained.

Elia could not stay. She left the house, tracing her hand along its side as she walked around the building and sat down with her back against the wall. She watched the clouds pressing against the edge of the rock and kept her legs pulled in, ready to jump at the first sign of a claw reaching up. The vigil kept her distracted from what was happening inside.

Their home sat at the edge of the island, but it hadn't always been that way. Ever since Opi's own grandfather built the house, chunks of the forest had been breaking off and drifting away. Slowly, over time, the land had disappeared, foot by foot, until the home was left where it stood now, balancing on the brink. It was always a worry, but the family was too poor to abandon the place. Who would buy it?

"El, we'll be heading out soon." It was her brother, Rayhan, standing by the corner of the house.

"I know," Elia murmured.

Rayhan stared at the setting sun with its fingers of peach-colored light stretching across the clouds. "I'm sorry you were the one to find her."

"Someone had to."

"I wish I could have been there. I mean, to help bring her back."

"It was late. We didn't know if you were in the dewfields or out training."

"I was in the fields." Rayhan sat down cross-legged beside her. A few moments passed in silence. "I had to go see," he said quietly.

Elia looked at him. "See what?"

"On my way here, I went to the spot where you found Omi. I needed to know where she took her last breath. I hope she was asleep when it happened."

"There were scratch marks in the moss and soil," Elia said sternly. "It looked like she was attacked and dragged!"

Rayhan stiffened. "By who?"

"Isn't it obvious?" Elia hadn't discussed the details with Sulum, wanting to spare her as much grief as possible, so it was a relief to finally discuss this with her brother.

"Wait," said Rayhan, immediately defensive. "You can't blame the guards. They left much earlier, and if she overreacted to their visit—"

"Not guards!" Elia almost shouted. "Scavengers! I found her by the edge of the island!"

"Right by the edge?" Her brother pushed himself up against the building. "But why would Scavengers leave her behind?"

Elia shrugged. "I don't know."

"I hate to think those were Omi's last moments."

"Me too."

Elia's shoulder was touching her brother's. It felt good to be close. Familiar. Safe. Like when they were younger, when stories about Scavengers would keep Elia awake and her brother would climb up into her hammock and promise to protect her. It was hard now to imagine Rayhan training to become an Imperial Guard, especially after what happened to Mrs. Suds.

But maybe Mrs. Suds wasn't as innocent as Elia had assumed. *Perceptions deceive.*

"I wonder why the guards were here in the first place," said Rayhan.

"I don't know," said Elia. "But they showed up in the laundry room yesterday to arrest one of the workers. She was the oldest one there. Maybe the guards thought Omi knew her."

"Did she?"

"Not likely. Not if Omi worked in the Royal Stables all her life. I don't know when they could have met."

The shutters overhead swung open and Sulum leaned out. "There you are. We're ready," she said before pulling her head inside.

Elia glanced up. She hoped her mother hadn't overheard their conversation.

"The walk will be long, El," said Rayhan. "Can you make it?"

"I'll have to," Elia replied. As they stood, she noticed

Rayhan's feet weren't bare like her own. "Hey. You're wearing boots."

"Another benefit of my training," he replied proudly. "I'm still trying to get used to them."

Three years had passed since Rayhan left home to work in the dewfields and apprentice as a Shifter, the first step for anyone hoping to become an Imperial Guard. Shifters were volunteer farmers and craftsmen carefully selected for a variety of tasks—building roads, cutting down trees, putting out fires in the city—but they got their name from their primary responsibility. Whenever islands of the System drifted too close, the Drift Master summoned the men to prevent collisions. Using only their long, flexible poles, it seemed impossible they could push anything away, but Opi once explained that a drifting island was no different than a bar of soap bobbing in water—it's easy to maneuver when it's floating.

"The boots get too heavy after a while," said Rayhan, lifting one foot to inspect the sole. "They don't fit very well either."

"Of course they don't fit!" Elia exclaimed, her face cracking with a smile. "Your feet are too weird!"

"Are you making fun of my toes again?"

"No one in the family has second toes as long as yours."

"I swear they're a sign of good luck," he chuckled as he tousled Elia's hair, then headed inside.

Joking with her brother felt good, but Elia's somber mood quickly returned as she waited by the edge of the forest for her grandfather and Rayhan to emerge from the house carrying Omi. Sulum followed. They took the trail back to the main road, then headed toward Mount Mahayit in the opposite direction of Na-Lavent. Few people were on the road, but those they came upon stepped off to the side, bowing their heads out of respect. As she walked, Elia kept her eyes down, dreading to see their final destination.

Covered with shards of rock, Mount Mahayit was

nothing like the lush, green foothills where the clotheslines were strung. The trees were stunted, the underbrush coarse and prickly. No one came here unless they had to.

"I see it," said Rayhan.

Elia looked up. Yes. She saw it too.

The Slope of Mourning stretched longer than Elia remembered. A man-made slide chiseled out of a natural crevice, its sides had been polished smooth and it swooped down the mountain, dropping off where the cliff met the clouds. After carefully climbing the uneven stairs, they placed Omi's body on a stone platform carved at the top.

The group circled around, standing quietly for a few moments until Opi broke the silence.

"I don't know what to say." He looked down the slope toward the horizon. "We'll all end up here at some point, but you never really believe it will happen."

"Until you're standing here," said Rayhan.

"Yes, until you're actually here . . ." Opi's voice trailed off.

Sulum placed a comforting arm around him. "If it was going to happen, at least she died at peace in the forest she loved to explore."

Thinking of her grandmother's terrified face, Elia was glad no one else had seen it. She would happily carry the burden of that image to her own deathbed if it meant sparing her mother and grandfather.

Rayhan stepped up to the platform with a feather he had pulled from his sleeve. As long as his forearm, it was the kind that sometimes drifted down when horses flew overhead. Rayhan carefully tucked the feather into the wrapping around Omi's body. "I discovered this near the spot where El found her. It seemed appropriate, given all of Omi's years in the stables."

"It's perfect," said Sulum.

The feather was a glossy black, like the usual color of stallions ridden by Imperial Guards. So the guards *had* been there, thought Elia. They scared off the Scavengers.

Opi reached into a little bag he kept around his neck, pulled something out, and tucked it into the folds of the wrapping. He did it too quickly for Elia to see the object, but she suspected it was the orange princess jewel Omi loved so much. It wasn't really a jewel, only a piece of colored glass polished by the blowing sands of the Isle of Drifting Dunes, but when Elia was younger, she preferred to imagine it was a lost gemstone from the ring of a princess. Opi had given it to Omi after Elia's father was born.

The thought of her father made Elia wonder if he should be with them now for their final farewell to his mother. But the occasion was sad enough for such an incomplete family—a family that was becoming ever smaller.

"It's time," said Opi, pointing to the clouds below them. "Look. They're expecting her."

The clouds, no longer lit by the sun, were flickering with a light of their own. White pulses, deep within them, flared across the sea of mist, each accompanied by a purring rumble, as though the clouds had an appetite that needed to be satisfied. No one was sure how to explain the lights or the noise, except that they related somehow to the Scavengers. It seemed so bizarre to be sending Omi to Below for those monsters to finally claim her, but it was the only way to appease their desire for more bodies. Better the dead than the living.

Elia held back as everyone placed a hand on Omi's body. Noticing her reluctance, Rayhan drew Elia forward. He kept his hand on hers as she touched Omi for the last time. She felt the body slip away from her fingertips as her grandmother was pushed off the stone platform. Elia caught her breath, and her heart clenched tight like a fist.

Omi sailed out from the edge of the cliff and the white wrapping shone in the moonlight. The body momentarily hung over the clouds as if the air itself was unsure where to take her. Then the body dropped, plunging into the flashing clouds.

And Omi disappeared.

Chapter 8

SHIRTS AND PETTICOATS FLAPPED IN the wind like phantoms tethered to the line. As Elia removed a clothespin, a strong gust snatched a shirt from her hands and sent it tumbling into the clouds. She anxiously glanced along the corridor of laundry to see if any guards had noticed. She saw no one. For three days now, she had felt as though somebody was standing right behind her, yet every time she whirled around, she found herself alone.

Cook certainly didn't help Elia's anxieties, always questioning her and Naadie when they returned each day for lunch. Had the guards bothered them? Had anyone else tried to make contact?

The sunshine warmed her dark skin as she moved down the clothesline, stuffing laundry deep into the baskets tied to a donkey that obediently followed her. The woolly animal's wings were firmly held down by straps, and Elia wondered if he had any sense they could carry him away to freedom.

Above the green rolling hills, the Mirrored Palace thrust into the sky as if to stab the blue dome. It had two towers, one for each of the Twin Emperors who shared power by way of an unstable truce. While the twins were identical, Elia had heard enough gossip to know their personalities certainly were not. Emperor Tohryn was a humorless man who kept only his most trusted advisors at hand, preferring seclusion over dealing with the court. His brother, Emperor Tael, however, embodied compassion and exuberance. Though he could be temperamental, his emotional swings were excused by the loss of both his wife and his sight. Rumors swirled that he had been blinded years ago while trying to save the Empress from Scavengers who snatched her over the edge when the royal couple strolled too close.

Having reached the end of her clothesline, Elia looked nervously over the island's edge. Why couldn't the lines be strung farther away? She hurried to the start of the next row.

Naadie and Elia took the rest of the morning to finish, then helped the stable boy assemble the animals for their journey back to the palace. The shadows of the towers fell upon them as they approached, and Elia's chest tightened with dread at the thought of going underground. As the procession descended into growing darkness, Elia focused on the smells of the kitchens—both tantalizing and revolting—and tried to ignore the unsettling moans and rattling chains of the dungeons below.

Sitting on the floor beside Naadie, Elia ate quickly, hunched over her food as if it needed protecting. Once finished, she spied the extra bowl the kitchen still delivered each day for Mrs. Suds. None of the other washers ever touched it, knowing Cook would make sure to get a second serving into her belly.

A sudden clatter of dishes at the front made Elia turn, but a scullion was not to blame. Something had startled the donkeys, and their frantic sidestepping had knocked over dishes stacked for removal.

"Get some control!" Cook shouted at the stable boy.

"What spooked them?" Elia whispered.

Naadie pointed to Mrs. Suds's bowl on the floor. Ripples

quivered across the soup's surface. Similar shivers traveled up through Elia's bones.

An earthquake. Another one, yet this time stronger than the tremors she had felt the day Mrs. Suds was taken away. Over the past several months, earthquakes had been occurring more frequently, though all had been gentle.

Now the floor was vibrating with force. Clothes suspended on hangers from the ceiling swung as if they were part of a crazed dance. Voices rose with alarm, and Cook lost what little patience she possessed. "Stay calm! You're not going anywhere. Just another earthquake."

A jarring spasm shook the laundry room. Everyone shrieked. The floor heaved sideways. Small pieces of stone broke away from the ceiling and rained down. A cauldron over the fire snapped from its hook and landed in the embers, sending a burst of sparks onto piles of laundry.

"We have to get out!" someone shouted.

Elia was too afraid to move. Instead, she crouched against a wall that seemed to be crumbling under her touch as washers scurried to find cover. Some were hit by falling debris; others were thrown off balance, landing painfully on their knees. Elia was certain the palace would collapse on itself, burying everyone beneath.

But, mercifully, the shaking stopped. Then silence. Everybody held their breath.

"All of you—outside!" cried Cook, her eyes and hair wilder than ever, blood running down her cheek. The laundry workers rushed toward the exit.

The dreadful vibrations started again when Elia reached the stairwell. The washers pressed themselves onto the stone steps, covering their heads. Desperate voices roared from the trapped prisoners in the dungeons. Did one of those voices belong to Mrs. Suds?

After the shaking subsided once more, the women and young girls raced to the ground level, emerging from the palace onto a ghostly scene. Everything was engulfed in a thick fog of rising clouds. People stumbled around in a state of shock, looking like specters fading in and out through the wall of mist. Elia felt completely disoriented until finally the fog started to clear, the sunlight grew brighter, and the clouds settled level with the ground where they were supposed to be.

The crowd of palace staff who had evacuated spilled onto the Grand Bridge, and a number of them had climbed to the crest to look down upon the bedlam. Elia joined them, hoping to locate her mother. From up here, she could also see to the other side, where the gates leading to the mainland were surprisingly unprotected. The Imperial Guards had abandoned their posts to join a growing group of people at that end of the bridge who were waving their arms and shouting. Elia was about to investigate when she heard her name.

"Elia! Thank goodness!" her mother exclaimed. Sulum grabbed her close. "Are you hurt?"

"I'm fine. Are *you* alright?"

"Yes, but my heart's still pounding." Covered with dust herself, Sulum quickly swept her eyes over Elia to make sure she was unharmed.

The ground shuddered again with an aftershock.

"What's happening?" Elia asked.

"We must have been hit," said Sulum, shaking her head in bewilderment. "But with the clouds rising like this, it seems more likely that we've dropped."

"We can't just drop!" Elia exclaimed. "We must have been hit by another island."

"Perhaps. But we dropped once before. Maybe you were too young to remember."

Elia had been no more than six at the time, but she hadn't forgotten. It had happened at dawn, when only the dew farmers, including Elia's father, were up early enough to witness the island mysteriously dip into the clouds moments before the shaking began. The incident was written off as a miscalculation by the Drift Master, who plotted the paths of islands floating in the System's currents, so people soon forgot about it. But not the laundry workers. That quake took the life of one of their own.

Mellyna was a pregnant washer whom Elia had found fascinating to work beside, watching with wonder as the woman's stomach grew more swollen each day. When Mellyna didn't show up for work the morning after the earthquake, everyone assumed she had finally delivered her baby. However, news spread quickly that Mellyna's husband was missing too and that their home, which stood on the island's edge just like Elia's, had broken off and drifted away.

This was of course reported to the authorities, and Mellyna's family argued loudly for days—there was time! They could still be rescued! But the request never made it to anyone who cared. No effort was made. A baker and a washer were not worthy of a search party. For years afterward, Elia's dreams were plagued with images of a shack sitting on a tiny shard of an island, two corpses inside, lost forever to float in the ocean of clouds.

Elia breathed in sharply. "Do you think our home will be all right?"

"I hope so," Sulum replied.

They were interrupted by a loud *crack* that seemed to come from the bridge, followed by more frantic shouting down by the gates.

Several men ran back toward the palace, fear on their faces, and Sulum called out, "What's the problem?"

One yelled over his shoulder, "The bridge is breaking apart."

Together, mother and daughter raced down to see for themselves. A large fracture had split the stone and mortar like a giant lightning bolt stamped into the ground. Sections of the low walls running along the Grand Bridge had completely broken away to leave gaping holes, and pieces continued to fall into the swirling mist that caressed the wounds.

Could it be fixed? If they were fast enough. But Elia didn't want to wait around to test their luck. She grabbed her mother's hand and dragged her through the gates toward the city. No more work for them today.

Chapter 9

THE PRAIRIES WERE EERILY STILL. The morning's wind had died and litter now sat undisturbed on the grasses. The few occasions Hokk stopped the gazelk, he felt smothered by silence.

The tranquil landscape was not the only unusual difference this afternoon. Earlier, two islands of rock had appeared on the skyline, hanging lower than Hokk had ever witnessed. He could have sworn they were low enough to cut through the grasslands. Normally, the islands should have drifted past and disappeared over the opposite horizon, but they were stalled overhead, caught in a huge vortex of clouds that circled them back, again and again.

Hokk was alert for anything that might drop from them. He was rarely fortunate enough to see things as they actually fell from Above; more often, he stumbled across items that had already landed, such as filthy mattresses, ladders, shoes with holes, broken plows, and once, a trail of rotten cabbages.

After several hours of following the islands, Hokk's patience was rewarded. A small wagon emerged from the clouds, falling end over end, its load of apples raining down with it. Halfway to the ground, the fruit and cart passed through the air's band of weaker gravity, appearing almost weightless, before breaking free and continuing to fall. Hokk kicked the gazelk in the ribs and they charged off to investigate.

The cart was demolished. Though much of the fruit had exploded into a pulverized mess, countless chunks of apple were scattered around, and Hokk gorged himself on the bruised flesh.

The flavor was incredible. It had been so long since his taste buds had savored anything sweet and it reminded Hokk of meals from his childhood. His parents had been wealthy enough to buy specialty foods like strawberries or watermelons, which poorer families couldn't afford—the crops were too difficult to grow, the yields too meager to supply everyone. But Hokk and his brother always had plenty to eat, and the neighboring kids often watched enviously. Davim would smack his lips to torment them, though Hokk preferred eating without an audience.

Recalling those delectable flavors triggered thoughts of Hokk's mother, memories he stored in his mind like a prized collection and only rarely took out to view. He remembered her caresses as she soothed him to sleep, her laugh as boisterous as a man's, how she sang softly to herself as she worked.

She and her third baby both died during labor. Hokk's frantic father tried to save her, while Hokk and Davim, two silent, horrified witnesses, helplessly stood by. Seven months later, Hokk's father was dead too. Constantly fatigued and coughing up blood, the man mysteriously withered to nothing and was gone. If they had to die so young, Hokk's one consolation was that neither of his parents had been alive to see him expelled from the city.

Hokk filed his memories away. With night approaching, he assembled his tent, built a fire, and let the flickering light hypnotize him, knowing it would ease his troubled mind so the door to sleep would open.

But as usual, he slipped into a dream world of misery. His brain, like a demented interrogator, tortured him with every disturbing image it could dredge up. Hokk's dying parents, the hermit's exposed body on the prairies.

A tower on fire.

Hokk bursting onto its rooftop as lightning exploded overhead. The wind plowing against his body and pulling his hair. Running from one side to the other, reveling in the sky's fury. Noticing too late the smoke. The flames. Descending the stairs two steps at a time, covering his mouth against the choking fumes.

Birds on fire. Burning feathers fluttering down into the street below. Carcasses littering the stairwell. Parts of the ceiling collapsing, igniting his sleeves while he tried to protect his head. Desperately smothering the flames with blistering palms as the fire cooked his skin.

How many times would his mind replay this? Why could he show himself no mercy?

But tonight, the nightmare was ending differently. The images were evaporating, replaced with sensations instead. He felt tremendous shaking, heard the earth howling in agony.

Hokk's eyes flew open. The ground beneath him shuddered. The prairies sounded as if they were being ripped open. A surge of fear charged Hokk's muscles, causing him sit bolt upright. Nym trembled and Hokk held him close. The gazelk grunted and stumbled outside in a frenzy, its hooves stamping the ground and almost crushing the tent.

After a last shiver, the shaking finally stopped. Hokk scrambled out of the tent, feeling dizzy and nauseous. The gazelk stared at him with bug-eyed horror in the faint light of the dying fire, as though knowing what Hokk felt in his bones: their world had just changed forever.

Chapter **10**

COCOONED IN HER HAMMOCK, ELIA savored the warmth and wished she could drift off again. She had slept so well. In the middle of the night, she had woken to discover her bed swinging on its own, but its rhythm proved too soothing to question and she was rocked into a deep sleep.

Poking her head above the blanket, Elia opened her eyes on their one-room shack. Sulum and Opi were still asleep. The sun was starting to rise. Through the only window, a cool breeze caressed her cheeks, yet she heard no sound of leaves rustling in the forest. Strange. The trees were never silent. Their branches were always restless, whether from fierce gales blowing through as they had experienced last night, or from the gentlest of winds like the one this morning.

Elia climbed out of the hammock, careful not to flip over onto her mother's. She tiptoed across the rough floorboards and opened the door.

A gasp strangled in her throat as she grabbed the handle to keep her balance.

Instead of a view of the forest's edge, Elia saw a rolling expanse of clouds shimmering with the pink light of dawn. Her eyes strained, hoping to see a hint of trees, even just a slice of the mainland to relieve her dread, yet only mist stretched to the horizon.

They must have been drifting for hours.

She staggered back to her mother's hammock. "Mom!" she said, shaking her by the shoulders.

Sulum moaned and covered her face.

"We've broken away!" cried Elia.

Rubbing her eyes, Sulum pulled herself up onto one elbow. "What are you talking about? You've been dreaming."

"Come see! The forest is gone. There are just clouds."

Elia yanked her mother out of the hammock and led her to the entrance.

Sulum's eyes flared as she raised a trembling hand to her mouth. "This can't be!"

The ragged edge of their property was now just a short distance from their door. A few smaller rocks that had also broken away floated farther out in the clouds, trailing them. "We should wake Opi," she whispered in a daze.

Opi woke up with a jolt. As soon as he heard, he hurried to the entrance on stiff legs and leaned out to peer around both sides of the doorframe. Turning back, his face looked sickly. "So is this how it ends for us?"

• • •

As the sky grew brighter, the family sat in grim silence around the table. Remembering Mellyna's fate in the clouds all those years ago, Elia wondered whether it would hurt to die. Would she grow weak from dehydration before falling unconscious? Would she have to watch her mother and grandfather succumb first before she could finally slip away? How long did they have? How many more sunrises would she see before it happened?

Opi's fist banged the table. "I can't believe I didn't feel anything."

"How could we? Any shaking would have simply made

us swing in our hammocks," said Sulum, placing her hand on top of his. "And last night's wind would have masked any sounds."

Elia kept her head lowered, full of guilt that she had woken up yet failed to recognize the significance of her bed rocking side to side. Maybe she could have gotten everyone out.

"Thank goodness we didn't fall to Below," said Opi, gritting the few teeth in his mouth.

Elia turned to her grandfather with a terrified look. "Could that happen?"

"No, it can't," Sulum said, frowning at her father-in-law. "If it was going to, it would have happened when we broke away."

Elia picked at slivers of wood in the tabletop and flicked the pieces to the floor. "At least Rayhan is not with us," she murmured.

Sulum's body slumped. "Yes. I've been thinking of him." She sighed and wiped the corner of her eye. "He'll be shocked to learn we're missing."

"So will Greyit," said Opi with a disheartened chuckle.

Greyit was an elderly man who occasionally dropped by for wild mushroom tea with Elia's grandparents. He had been showing up more regularly since Omi's passing.

Sulum perked up. "Was he going to come by this morning?"

"Supposed to. Unless the crazy old goat forgets."

"Well, that changes everything!" said Sulum as she pushed back from the table. "He will send for help."

Elia was unconvinced. "Whoever he tells, they're not going to care. They won't send anyone. We don't matter."

"Yes, we do. They will send a search party," Sulum declared.

"They didn't for Mellyna!" Elia shot back. "She's still floating out here with her husband and a dead baby in her belly!"

"That was long ago. Completely different circumstances."

"No one will listen to Greyit."

Sulum smiled. "I have full confidence."

• • •

Their shack was extremely hot after baking in the sun for hours. Elia was lying limp on her mother's hammock, drifting in and out of sleep, her dry tongue stuck to the roof of her mouth. Dehydration—it's starting to happen, she thought.

Opi had stayed inside too, but Elia's mother had spent the entire time outside the shack with their one pot, hoping to shine it like a beacon when their rescuers arrived. If they ever did. Elia was surprised her mother was so sure someone would come. However, by the middle of the afternoon, they heard Sulum exclaim, "I see something!"

Wondering if her mother was hallucinating after too much sun, Elia followed Opi to the door, but was too anxious to step out.

Sulum pointed to the horizon. Several dark spots had materialized against the bright clouds. "I'm sure they've spotted us!" She waved the metal pot above her head and called out.

Within minutes, the team of horses was there, a mass of flapping wings and kicking legs cutting through the sunlight. After so many hours of silent isolation, it was breathtaking to hear the shouts of the men and to see the flurry of activity as the tiny property was surrounded.

One of the horses had a second passenger. Elia recognized her brother at the same instant as her mother did.

"Rayhan!" shouted Sulum.

He waved to them as his horse hovered low beside the house. Swinging over a leg, he leapt from the animal's back and landed on the ground, which thankfully held solid beneath his feet. Beaming, Rayhan squeezed Sulum tight and pulled Opi into his other arm.

"We found you," he said.

"Finally!" Opi laughed.

"I didn't expect to see you," said Sulum. "How did you know?"

"Greyit found me after he had this team assembled."

"The old guy pulled it off!" said Opi.

Elia watched the horse with awe, never having been so close to such a magnificent animal. She wished she could touch its glistening coat.

"El!" said Rayhan as he kissed the top of her head with a noisy smack. "You're looking a bit nervous!" he teased, trying to pull her from the doorway.

"No, I'm not," she protested, clinging to the frame.

Rayhan whistled to catch the attention of a fellow Shifter. "Water," he called up, and the rider tossed down a quivering transparent globe. Rayhan caught the waterball and passed it to Elia, where it jiggled in her open palm.

With water so scarce, waterballs were a luxury, even for dew farmers, like Elia's family, who could rarely enjoy the daily harvest. In the past, Elia's only chance for a decent drink was sneaking gulps from her washtub before soapy clothes were dumped in for rinsing. It was the one advantage of working in the laundry. Now, lifting the waterball to her mouth, Elia enjoyed the cool slipperiness on her lips as she sucked just hard enough to break the surface tension. A thick, quenching liquid ran down her throat. When she pulled away, the waterball snapped back into shape without releasing another drop.

A Shifter lowered a bag of tools and Rayhan pulled out spikes, which he hammered into the ground around the house. To each, he then secured lines that dangled down from the horses. Satisfied after testing the strength of his knots, he gave an all-clear signal. "It's ready to tow in!"

The man who had ridden with Rayhan brought their horse close enough for Elia's brother to get back on, but Rayhan had to dive across the abyss of clouds and pull himself up, legs kicking as he scrambled into place. From the animal's back, he turned to his sister. "El, you should be up here riding one of these too."

Elia was surprised by the suggestion. "What?"

"You'd enjoy it."

"You're nuts!" she replied.

"It's amazing, El. I know you must have thought about it before."

"Never."

In truth, she had dreamt about it many times while she sweated over her work or saw members of the Royal Family flying overhead. And she imagined it every day when the wind blew against her face as she coasted downhill on her bicycle.

"Come on! Don't be such a coward," said Rayhan.

"You might never get another opportunity," Opi encouraged.

Elia looked at the horses with longing, but could not bring herself to do it. What if she couldn't jump far enough to grab the saddle and she plunged into the mists of Below?

"No, I can't," she said.

"Your choice," Rayhan replied with a sigh.

His horse rose into the air with its two passengers. Another man blew a loud whistle, and on cue, the animals surged forward, the ropes straining as the little island began to move.

Elia couldn't bear to think of the opportunity she had missed. She knew her grandmother would have been disappointed in her too. Omi had always wished for the chance to fly on one of the horses she had spent a lifetime grooming in the stables.

Elia slid down the side of the doorframe. She pulled her knees up to her chest and wrapped her arms around her legs. As she watched her brother up in the air, she picked at her lip until the flesh was raw, then rubbed her tongue over the sore to soothe the pain.

If only she could be fearless like Rayhan.

•   •   •

It took the Shifters several hours to tow them back. It was amazing to see the slopes of Mount Mahayit and the evergreen forest begin to appear, growing steadily sharper in detail. The mainland, more immense than Elia ever would have thought, extended farther and farther along the horizon—a view of Kamanman the sun saw every morning as it lifted itself from the clutches of Below for its daily journey across the sky. And somewhere along the great expanse of trees was the spot where their home had sat, attached to the cliff.

A man overhead blew a piercing blast through his horn, calling out to a small regiment of Shifters who stood waiting at the forest's edge. The flying horses slowed their pace, but the island continued to move quickly through the clouds. The men on the mainland braced for impact, each holding a long pole that curved with its own weight.

At the last possible moment, the horses pulled up sharply and began treading air while momentum moved the island across the remaining distance. The Shifters lowered their poles, aiming for a direct hit. When contact was made, the men grunted with the strain as their muscles bulged and their poles bent to absorb the force.

Before the island could bounce away, several Shifters pole-vaulted to Elia's side, unrolling a rope bridge that was swiftly tied to the spikes already hammered in the ground. Rayhan dropped down to help them. The dangling tow lines were then hoisted, and with a final rush of beating wings, the horses flew off over the treetops.

"They're leaving too quickly!" cried Sulum. She turned to Rayhan. "We must thank them. How can we thank them?"

"They're not expecting anything. We'll just have to thank Greyit," he replied, pointing to the old man on the mainland who was waving his arms.

Rayhan helped Opi over the suspension bridge. Sulum ventured next, but her limp made the bridge swing precariously over the mist. Elia dreaded every step as she followed, not wanting her brother to see her fear as she inched along, clinging to the prickly rope railing.

Greyit was beaming as he greeted the family. "You made it!" he exclaimed.

"Greyit! You old devil." Opi shook his friend's hand.

"Thank you," said Sulum, suddenly looking so fatigued she appeared nearly as old as Opi. "We are indebted to you once again."

Once again?

Elia thought she saw a silent exchange between her mother and Greyit. Their glances were so fleeting, however, she couldn't be sure.

No doubt, it was a miracle they had been rescued today, but how had Greyit been able to coordinate the effort so quickly? What price did he have to pay to make it happen?

Greyit had always seemed like nothing more than a long-time friend, yet Elia began to wonder about the true nature of his relationship with her grandparents. With her entire family for that matter. And the more she thought about it, the more Elia realized just how many people seemed to care. Not only Greyit, but Cook and Mrs. Suds as well, all looking out for Elia's family, yet doing so as though there was a secret to keep.

But why?

That was the irresistible question Elia now needed to answer.

Chapter 11

AS THE MORNING'S LIGHT STRUGGLED to penetrate the overcast sky, Hokk crawled out of his tent and immediately saw evidence of the previous night's tremors. In the distance, huge mounds of exposed earth rose high above the grasslands like a newly formed mountain range. Only floating islands could have caused such destruction—the very ones that now hung motionless in the sky.

Abandoning his camp, Hokk raced across the prairies and was panting by the time he hiked up the massive hill of dirt. He peered into a gorge so wide and deep it seemed impossible it had been created in mere minutes. On the opposite bank, layers of compressed trash lay exposed after unknown centuries beneath the grasslands, and debris was scattered from one end of the gigantic wound to the other.

Such a catastrophic scene. Probably like nothing the Board had ever heard of before. He needed to warn them.

Hokk laughed at himself. The idea was preposterous. How did he think he would tell them? Return to the city? As an exile? He had to stay out here until his sentence was served.

But if something like this happened over the City of Ago, it would level the buildings. Islands floated above them all the time, so the threat could be very real.

Hokk sucked on his teeth as he studied the view. Could he actually go back? Would the Board believe his story?

Wasn't he perhaps obligated at least to try to tell them?

Hokk began to descend into the gorge. Halfway down, he discovered a band of buried rubbish three times taller than himself. Clinging to the side of the steep slope, he pulled out handfuls of garbage, most of the items unknown to him, and tossed them over his shoulder as he loosened more and dug deeper. Some of the stuff was moist and smelly, some so dry and compact that it disintegrated with his touch.

He worked his way along the bottom of the ravine with Nym following close. He found masses of twisted metal, wooden beams with rusted nails, and chunks of crumbling bricks cemented together, all still half-buried in exhumed earth. Numerous sealed barrels had been ripped open, allowing the thick liquids inside to ooze out. "No, Nym!" Hokk hollered when the fox started to lick one of the puddles.

Picking his way over a graveyard of worn rubber tires and tattered furniture, Hokk wondered if there was anything down here he could take to rebuild the collection he had lost. He stood above a pile of unusual objects and picked up a piece that caught his eye. Like a plank of lightweight wood, it was black, flat, and had six long rows of buttons on one side, with a thin black cord coming out from the end. Each button had a symbol on it, either a number or a letter, though strangely, the letters were not arranged in alphabetical order. What could the Ancients have possibly used this for? Hokk tossed the worthless thing to the ground and kept searching.

He was beginning to give up hope when farther along, he came upon books scattered everywhere. Unfortunately, most of them were shredded or moldy, but he noticed many more of them still wedged into layers in the bank. He pulled them out, flinging them aside, until he found one in decent condition. Its paper was wrinkled and stained, but flipping a few pages in, he recognized many words. Perfect. Finally, something he could actually use.

Although his ability to read was limited, Hokk had always been fascinated by reading and writing. His uncle had taught him numbers, letters, and a few hundred words. Shortly before getting into trouble with the Board, Hokk had started his apprenticeship as a record keeper for the Farmers' Commission, thanks to his uncle's recommendation. Hokk was glad he hadn't forgotten what he had learned.

Encouraged by the successful find, Hokk spent another hour exploring the rest of the gorge, pleased that he was the only person down there. In addition to the book, he found pieces of tarnished cutlery, much fancier than any he had ever seen, a leather belt with a buckle, a dirty pillow, and several thin, rigid discs about the size of his palm, their mirrored surfaces shimmering with a full spectrum of color.

Hokk was thrilled with his discoveries, and he smiled as he and Nym climbed the bank to get back to camp. Reaching the peak, he gazed out one final time, memorizing the details so he could recount them if he returned to the city.

No, he *should* return to the city and do it before anyone else had a chance to discover this place. The Board had to be told and they had to hear it from him first. And then perhaps, after listening to his story and seeing how much he had matured, how much he cared about Ago, they would forgive his past.

Hokk's resolve was cemented when he spotted someone standing on top of a dirt pile at the farthest end of the chasm. He suspected another outcast.

Bristling with territorial rage, Hokk wanted to chase him away. But he resisted. He would start now and cover the immense distance to Ago as quickly as possible, ahead of anybody else.

Chapter 12

ARRIVING AT THE BARN THE next morning, Elia was worried about the questions Naadie might ask. Elia's instincts told her the less information shared the better, at least until she had a greater understanding of recent events.

"You won't believe how upset Cook was yesterday when you didn't arrive at lunchtime," said Naadie as she looped a basket strap through a buckle and tightened the restraint around the donkey's wings. "She grilled me to find out why."

"She must have been mad."

"No. Worried."

"What did you tell her?"

"I said you were probably sick, or something. Was that the case?"

Elia was relieved that word of her home drifting away hadn't yet circulated. "Yes. I felt so horrible, I could barely move," she lied as she forced a grimace and held her stomach. "My mother too," she added, hoping such an excuse would work later when trying to explain to Cook. By the sounds of it, Cook would be happy today just to see her alive.

Thankfully, something caught Naadie's attention. "Looks like we have a new addition to the herd," she said to the stable boy.

"Yes, that pregnant donkey finally gave birth," he replied.

At first, Elia could see only two quivering legs and the foal's small face peeking around his mother's rump, but he soon ventured out, curious to observe the morning routine. Just seeing him, so timid and innocent, boosted Elia's spirits.

"He's going to love exploring along the trail," said the stable boy.

"He won't be coming with us, will he?" Elia couldn't imagine the little donkey trekking into the hills on his spindly legs so soon after entering the world.

"Of course," he said. "His mother will have a load today, so he can't be left behind."

The baby donkey was slow to keep up, but he teetered along the path, enthralled by the smells drifting by. Whenever he attempted to stray, Elia blocked him, and the foal looked up at her with a bewildered expression.

"I know you want to investigate, but you can't," Elia tried to reason with him, though she could certainly understand how he felt. His destiny was to follow the tail of the donkey in front, hauling cargo day after day. Born into a life of service, his reality was no different than Elia's.

The foal flapped his wings as he stumbled to catch up with his mother, not guessing he could use them to fly away. Soon they would be strapped down, and he would never realize their potential. At the moment, however, he found them fascinating, and he twisted this way and that to catch a better view, biting the air instead of his feathers.

"We'll have to call him Twister," Naadie laughed.

The little donkey's unsteady legs became tangled, and he landed in the dirt with a befuddled look on his face. He leapt to his feet and charged after the procession.

Elia smiled. She was relieved to be back at work. Yesterday's fears seemed so far away, as though she had set them adrift in the clouds.

• • •

The bedsheets billowed and clung to her legs as Elia removed them from the clothesline. The sun was blinding, shining against their whiteness, and Elia squinted as she moved along the line.

She jumped when a shadow quietly slipped across a sheet hanging one line over.

"Naadie?" Elia stepped forward and peered down the row, afraid to see an Imperial Guard. Nothing.

Taking a moment to collect herself, Elia parted the next set of sheets hanging in front of her and stuck her head through. She saw the shadow again, this time farther down.

"Is that you Naadie?"

Looking both ways, all she could see was pinned laundry. But she was certain she was not alone.

Elia pulled her head back and—"Oh!" The terrified face of a young woman was suddenly before her. Elia staggered backward into the clothesline.

"Please help me. Please," the woman whispered.

A lady-in-waiting. She wore a flowing dress of the softest blue, and the tight sleeves hugging her arms ended with a cascade of fabric and lace that spilled almost to the ground. Jewels decorated her hair, normally braided in an elaborate fashion, but now unravelled from running in the wind. Looking both elegant and wild, she was very beautiful, even with smudged, red-painted lips and teary makeup seeping down her cheeks.

"They're coming," moaned the woman as she frantically glanced behind.

"No. Please no!" said Elia, backing away with her arms up as a shield.

"I must give you something."

"Keep it," said Elia, her voice a squeak.

"Today's our last chance."

"I don't want another bone!"

"Shh." The woman cocked her head to listen above the wind. "I can hear them!"

Galloping hooves.

The woman grabbed Elia's hand and dragged her through a line of laundry, tearing down bedsheets that got in their way. The sound of the horses intensified. Elia and the lady-in-waiting stormed through another clothesline, nearly running into a small cluster of donkeys, where Twister darted behind his mother.

"Go—you'll have to go on your own," the woman said between gasps for air. "I'm so sorry it has to be you."

"I don't want it to be!"

The lady didn't respond but instead pulled up the hem of her dress. An elaborately carved wooden box was strapped to her calf. With a few quick movements, she removed the box, tossed it into the closest laundry basket, and yanked a sheet off the line, which she stuffed deep into the basket as well.

The sound of hooves kept pounding, growing more thunderous.

The woman turned to Elia, just inches from her face.

"Hide this," she ordered, pointing to the basket. "Take it away from here. The guards will kill anyone for what's inside."

Elia could only nod.

"Your family included."

Elia felt vomit at the back of her throat.

At that very moment, the clatter of hooves stopped abruptly. Elia saw terror return to the woman's eyes. In the sudden quiet, the woman turned her face to the sky.

Elia looked up too, puzzled. The sky had disappeared, now veiled by a thick layer of mist that dampened the sun's rays.

The lady-in-waiting placed a finger on Elia's lips. A familiar *whoosh* swooped through the air, followed by another. "Go now!" the woman hissed. "Protect the box at any cost."

She pushed Elia away and slapped the side of the donkey carrying the secret cargo in its basket. The animal was Twister's mother, and it was so startled it sprung off the ground. The donkey charged down the path between the rows of laundry. Twister followed close behind, and the pair quickly faded into the thickening fog.

The lady-in-waiting ran from Elia and became a spectral vision in the mist. As Elia watched, a large wing, tipped with feathers, sliced through the air like a cleaver, followed by silent, kicking hooves. Within seconds, the sky above the lady-in-waiting was filled with the silhouettes of Imperial Guards mounted on flying horses, all swirling around her.

The lingering donkeys immediately fled. Elia backed away and covered herself with a bedsheet, leaving only a small opening for her eyes.

The lady-in-waiting spun around, trying to keep her attackers in view, yet there were too many. She was lassoed by a rope that cinched her arms at her waist. A second rope caught her around the shoulders. She cried out in pain, but was silenced when the guards tightened their nooses, squeezing out her breath. They lifted her into the air, the lines pulling so hard at different angles that Elia was afraid the woman would be torn apart.

Then suddenly the ropes slackened and the woman fell to the ground like a stuffed doll. An Imperial Guard leapt from his horse and Elia saw metal wings jutting out from his helmet.

Placing his foot on the woman's chest, Commander Wrasse lifted his visor to reveal his disfigured face beneath. He leaned over to pull up her dress and saw the loose straps around her leg.

"What have you done with it?" he demanded, pressing down with the heel of his boot.

The young woman could only moan.

"You'll pay for this, my dear," Wrasse snarled.

He lifted his foot and the lady-in-waiting was yanked again by the ropes with such force her head whipped backward. She screamed as she disappeared into the fog, her desperate cries quickly growing faint.

Elia was too stunned to move. She cowered against the ground as if the fog were forcing her flat. Her head throbbed, blood pounding through her body. Everything was still. The sheets hung limp in the damp air.

The woman's last request echoed in Elia's mind. *Protect the box.*

Wrasse surveyed the area, a predator sniffing for his prey. But did he see her?

As he crept forward, the ground heaved. The commander staggered and fell.

Elia now realized the significance of the fog. She wasn't shaking from fear. The island was dropping again. Her tremors were coming from the earth!

On hands and knees, Commander Wrasse raised his face. Their eyes locked. They both froze except for a wicked smile that twisted his lips.

Elia threw aside the sheet and shot to her feet as Wrasse charged after her. Ducking behind hanging laundry, she zigzagged across the rows of clotheslines. The sound of scraping rocks came from every direction. Incredibly, the island was shaking more violently than during the previous quake, and she feared the soil would tear open beneath her legs.

How far was she from the edge?

As she ran down a row, a clothesline on one side abruptly dropped to the ground with its sheets still pinned to it. A second later, the line on the other side fell too, but Elia didn't slow down and couldn't change directions. Wrasse was surely right behind her!

Twister's mother materialized through the fog. Hitting the donkey at full speed, Elia's breath was knocked out of her as she flipped over its back and crashed to the ground. Pain flashed white across her vision.

Alarmed, Twister scurried to avoid Elia, cutting her with his sharp hooves as he stumbled over her legs. Elia kicked him off and the little donkey backed away.

But the earth was still shaking violently, and Twister flapped his awkward wings to stay balanced. Then the ground disintegrated beneath his hind legs and his weight dragged him backward over the island's edge.

"No!" Elia cried as he fell out of sight.

A crack in the ground chiselled its way toward her, and all at once, hundreds of fissures spread like a spider's web under her body. By the time she struggled to her feet and turned, the edge of the crumbling island had advanced to the tips of her toes, so she lunged forward in desperation, falling upon Twister's mother.

Just beyond, watching her from a safe distance, was Commander Wrasse. Laughing.

On either side, Elia noticed the ends of the collapsed clotheslines hanging down into the clouds, just as the earth around her and the donkey broke apart into countless fragments. Elia threw herself at the nearest line, arms flailing, desperate to grab anything. As the squealing donkey dropped into the mist below, the wind surged and one of the pinned sheets billowed within reach.

Elia managed to grab a fistful of fabric, only to hear the clothespins snap off, one by one. For a moment, she felt suspended in the fog.

Then she fell.

Chapter 13

ELIA WATCHED HER ISLAND SLIP away. For that first split second, it all seemed so close—the floating rocks that had crumbled underfoot, the two clotheslines dangling down.

The wind pulled at her clothing and at the sheet clenched in her fist. The sun's rays grew weaker, the chilly mist thickened, and the air became unbearably cold and dark. Everything vanished from sight as she was enveloped by the clouds.

Then, in a breathtaking instant, Elia sliced through the bottom of the cloud cover. Above her, she could see a heavy, gray-black, churning curtain rolling out on all sides, pierced by two massive shards of rock. The undersides of Kamanman and the Noble Sanctuary.

As she dropped away from the clouds, she realized how quickly she was falling. But falling toward what?

Elia flipped over and the wind rushed into her face, cutting off her breath and making her eyes water. She expected more clouds, but was stunned to see land. A vast expanse of green stretched far into the distance, and slicing through this, a brown scar like a dirty wound. And beside the green, an enormous span of ... polished rock? A huge sheet of glass?

Whatever it was, she was heading straight for it. Elia closed her eyes. The memory of her wrapped grandmother plunging into the clouds flashed into her head, then the faces of her family, the palace, the hills, the donkeys—all streaming through her mind in rapid succession.

The sound of air racing past her ears was a trigger. A picture popped into her mind of her mother zooming downhill on her bicycle, her sleeves caught in the breeze, and the air ballooning her work dress.

Elia's eyes flew open. *The sheet!*

The fabric was twisted. As she struggled to shake it out, the wind tore it from her fingers.

"No!" she screamed, watching the sheet sail free overhead, out of reach.

But then, surprisingly, her descent slowed. The hemline of her dress stopped flapping. The rush of air eased to a mere caress, and her hair hung weightless around her head. She was hovering between the clouds and Below.

The sheet caught up to her, gently drifting down to settle over her body as if she was sleeping in her hammock. Everything was calm—the throbbing pulse of blood in her ears the only sound.

Elia sensed a faint downward tug on her limbs. Slowly, the sensation grew stronger as the buoyant force holding her began to dissipate. Ever so slightly, her hair and dress began to flutter. Air gradually filled the sheet. She quickly grasped the corners, just as the momentary lull ended, and she was falling once more.

An updraft inflated the sheet and jerked her body like a whip. Now falling feet first, she looked down at the immense surface of glass rapidly approaching.

Elia instinctively pulled up her knees to prepare for impact, expecting to see her legs shatter. Instead, her feet disappeared into the glass and then the rest of her body was swallowed up too, her head slipping through last. The pain was immediate, as if her skull had split open.

And then everything went black.

Chapter 14

AN INTENSE, SALTY TASTE FILLED Elia's mouth and trickled down her throat. Gagging, she spat it out.

She was soaked and sprawled on her stomach, trembling uncontrollably. Through eyelashes crusted with sand, she saw she was lying in a puddle that caressed her sides with a steady rhythm. Pain made her reluctant to move, but the unbearable cold forced Elia onto her elbows. Groaning, she crawled out of the water to a dry patch of grass, then slowly pulled off her wet uniform.

Naked, dazed, and oblivious to her surroundings, Elia hugged her legs and tucked her pounding head between her knees. She tried to steady her breathing and force her mind to reorganize its hazy thoughts. Where was she? Suddenly her body tensed as she recalled the fall, the ground racing up, the glassy sheet she had plunged into.

Below!

She squeezed herself tighter. Smaller. Had the Scavengers picked up her scent? Were they circling her?

The wind stirred, bending blades of grass that tickled her bare skin like the touch of a Scavenger's claw. With a shriek, she opened her eyes and kicked out her limbs, ready to fight.

But there were no monsters closing in. Only a vast prairie stretched out before her.

Rising on shaky legs, she was amazed by the sheer size of the grasslands, and equally surprised to see rubbish everywhere, wafting across its surface. The trash appeared to be paper or scraps of cloth; however, Elia did not want to stray farther to investigate. The monsters were probably hiding in the grasses.

Scavengers don't have eyes, Elia reminded herself. And with land so flat, she would notice them approaching. Perhaps she could outrun them. All she had to do was stay alert.

Pivoting around to check behind, Elia expected to see more of the same prairies, but was awed by a different view. She hadn't pulled herself out of just a puddle. A mammoth body of water extended all the way to the horizon, where the border between gray water and gray clouds was indistinguishable. Only steps away, the edge of it lapped against a bed of fine sand that continued as far as she could see to the left and right.

How could there be so much water in the same place? It was unfathomable. The most she had ever seen was a full tub in the laundry room.

Abandoning her uniform, Elia walked forward and stared at her feet as the freezing water touched her toes. The bedsheet that had slowed her fall remained caught in the surf, so she stepped over it and moved deeper until the waves splashed against her calves.

Above the water, in the distance, two masses of rock gouged the clouds like mountain peaks flipped upside down. They could still only be Kamanman and the Noble Sanctuary. The islands appeared motionless, hovering, waiting for her to catch up to them.

A burst of energy had Elia running through the waves. If she hurried, she could reach the floating rocks. She had to somehow climb back up. Warn the family. Make sure everyone went into hiding before the Imperial Guards could find them.

She lifted her legs as high as possible, and pumped her arms, gasping with the effort to get closer. The water deepened, slowing her down, until suddenly the bottom dropped off and Elia went under. The view of the islands vanished, replaced by churning sand and bubbles. Salty water poured down her throat as she took a startled gulp. Her lungs burned for oxygen. With eyes stinging and her ears plugged, Elia thrashed about, but her feet could find nothing beneath them. The freezing current pulled and pushed her, allowing no escape.

Then she felt the ground. Now able to distinguish up from down, Elia gained a foothold in the shallower water to thrust herself skyward. She glimpsed the shoreline and struggled toward it, choking violently as she tried to catch a breath, while grains of sand flowed past her ankles as if to carry her away again.

Elia shivered as she emerged into the cold wind. She bent over and vomited clear liquid. A horrible taste of salt and stomach acid lingered on her tongue. Stumbling toward the spot where her uniform was laid out to dry, she collapsed beside it.

So this was Below. This water. These grasslands. The endless blanket of clouds overhead. Not what she had envisioned from all the stories. It was immense. Cold. Desolate. Empty—except, of course, for Scavengers and the bodies sent to them.

She studied the water in front of her. It looked so flat, so easy to cross. How deceptive. And the two islands, still on the horizon, beckoned her. They had always seemed large, but compared to Below, they were like buttons on the jacket of a very fat man. If the Scavengers had figured out how to scale their craggy undersides, then she would do the same.

Start walking, she told herself. You'll find a way to return.

Elia pulled on her still-damp dress and began to walk, following the shoreline. The feeble light that penetrated the menacing clouds began to fade, and the water grew darker as the end of the day approached. She spotted a piece of blue fabric up ahead, fluttering into the air from the sand. More rubbish? She had already stopped several times to pick up pieces of trash, but it all seemed to be the same—not paper, but some sort of thin material made without threads. It stretched out of shape easily and tore if she pulled hard enough. It was certainly unlike any cloth she had ever seen before.

As Elia got closer, she realized the blue fabric was more than just garbage. She stopped midstride. It was attached to something. A body.

The lady-in-waiting lay crumpled in the sand, her lifeless eyes facing the sky. Rope used by the Imperial Guards was twisted around her torso, and her dress was torn, with one sleeve missing completely.

Horrifying memories of the woman's last few moments amongst the clotheslines flooded Elia's mind. A young life sacrificed for a secret that Elia had failed to protect. As penance, Elia wondered if there was anything she could do now for this broken woman. She was so exposed. Just leaving her here seemed wrong.

And then a dark thought occurred to Elia. Maybe there was something on the woman she could use.

The lady-in-waiting still wore her shoes, although Elia knew she would never be able to walk in them. She inspected the woman's fingers and then searched the folds of her dress. Recalling the jewels in her hair, Elia combed her fingers through the tangled strands and sifted through the sand around the woman's body. She found only one gemstone. It was about the size of her thumbnail and as blue as the torn dress. Even in the low light, the jewel sparkled and Elia marveled to hold something so exquisite. The woman had no further use for such finery, and while it might not improve Elia's chances of survival down here, she could use it to help her family. She tucked the stone inside her pocket, but felt no better than a thief for taking it.

Elia looked down the shoreline, losing hope of finding shelter for the night. Only then did she see the eyes watching her. Like jewels themselves, they reflected the dim light.

A small dog sat motionless. It had pure black eyes, a short, narrow muzzle, and fur the color of the sand. Its ears were extraordinarily long, curving up from its head like wings.

Elia held out a hand. The animal tilted its head and growled.

"Where did you come from?" asked Elia as she stood up. "I've got no food, if that's what you want."

She noticed a subtle movement of its head, the slightest change of focus in its eyes. Realizing a second too late, Elia whipped around.

A shadowy figure loomed above her, its arm raised.

The dog started to bark as something slammed against the side of her head.

Elia landed hard on the ground and her mouth filled with grains of sand before she fell unconscious.

Chapter 15

WHEN ELIA CAME TO, SHE was being dragged face up through the deepest, blackest darkness she had ever experienced. Her wrists were lashed together, her arms wrenched above her head. Moving swiftly through the prickly stalks of grass and across the rough ground, she was certain her shoulders would separate from their sockets and that her flesh would be scraped to the bone.

She was tied to either a cart or a horse. Whatever it was made little noise to give itself away. Elia arched her back with an abrupt thrust, attempting to dig her heels into the dirt, but her feet slipped. She tried turning over onto her knees to then stand, yet couldn't move fast enough. She kicked and flipped and fought her restraints, refusing to give up, even though her wrists burned raw from the rope. "Raahh!" she yelled in frustration.

She was heard. Their progress slowed to a stop. Elia held her breath and stayed still as she listened to the faint crunch of approaching footsteps. A Scavenger. She recoiled as it halted beside her. A hand slid up her arm to inspect the knots in the rope and Elia imagined the monster's long, knobby fingers. She shuddered.

They resumed traveling, though the pace was now slower. She marveled that anything could move in such darkness, then realized the absence of eyes meant a Scavenger would never need light. But where was it taking her? With little strength remaining, she hung limp, saving her energy.

Their second stop was more abrupt. Elia heard a thunk. Something dropped to the ground, followed by a grunt. Plant stems snapped and nostrils snorted. Metal struck metal. Another thud, then all grew quiet.

After several minutes, Elia wondered if she had been abandoned, but a pull on her rope made her bristle. No, she was not alone. Listening carefully, she could hear blades of grass being torn from their stalks and leisurely chewed. It *was* a horse.

Perfect! She could fly away on it.

Using her teeth, Elia tried to loosen the knots around her wrists. They wouldn't budge, so she picked up the slack rope and followed it to the other end. She advanced carefully, not wanting to startle the beast in the dark. She sensed the steamy heat of its body even before she placed her hands on its hindquarters and slid them along to where she expected to find the base of its wings. Its back, however, was completely smooth. No wings. How could that be?

The knots were just as tight at the horse's neck, so Elia crept away as far as the rope would allow and felt around in the grass for something to cut herself free. She reached blindly, feeling as if she was about to fall forward into a void, yet found nothing.

And where was her captor?

The horse settled down in the grasses to rest. Deciding it was best to wait for better light, Elia lay beside it on the cold ground, and squirmed closer to enjoy its warmth. Though utterly exhausted, her sore limbs and her fears of the Scavenger returning kept sleep at bay for far too long.

•   •   •

The light of the morning was nothing compared to the bright sunshine Elia was used to. Seeing the gloomy clouds above, she slumped with the depressing realization that her reality had not changed. She had dreamed of sweeping fields of yellow blossoms, fresh laundry flapping on clotheslines, the comfort of her hammock, and being tucked cozy under her blankets. Normally, Sulum would be waking her up right about now, gently coaxing her daughter to face the start of a new workday. Today, Elia awoke to the gray, limitless dungeon of Below.

How small, how dark, how miserable a prison cell were her family members confined to at this very moment? She pushed the thought away.

Elia berated herself for being captured so easily by a Scavenger. She was supposed to have stayed alert. Her head was still swollen where she had been hit and every part of her body ached. When the horse's muscles flexed to stand, Elia had no choice but to rise with it too. Once upright, though, she paused to let a wave of dizziness pass. Then she turned and gawked in amazement at the beast she had slept beside.

The striped animal was definitely not a horse—wingless, with a small, tapered head and the most unusual horns she had ever seen, like two long, twisting roots growing straight out of its skull. It was astonishing how the beast could balance such things, yet move with a gentle grace as if they weren't even there.

Following the animal as it grazed, she scanned the area. They were in a sparse camp set in a dip in the landscape. A low tent, large enough for only one person, was pinned to the ground nearby. Elia kept her eyes trained on its opening, nervous to discover who, or what, might crawl out.

At long last, a hand emerged, astonishingly white, with slender fingers that were surprisingly not misshapen at all. As Elia hid behind the bulk of the animal, the fingers unlaced the drawstring around the tent's front flap. Another hand reached through, then the arms, just as pallid, except for darker patches above the wrists. Finally, the rest of the body appeared, crouched low as the creature stepped out.

The Scavenger was very tall and had a slim body, but without the curve to its spine that Elia expected. It had hair—another surprise—tied back in a ponytail, but with its head turned away, she could not see the face. It stretched and stumbled on stiff legs, and Elia wondered if it faltered because it had no eyes.

And then the Scavenger turned.

Elia ducked.

Steps treaded softly along the ground. The creature picked up the rope on the other side of the striped animal and pulled Elia around to the front. Terrified, she kept her head down, barely able to breathe as she stared at the Scavenger's pale, bare feet.

It waited. It did not touch her. After a moment, the rope was dropped. Elia braced herself and looked up with dread.

The serious, yet luminous eyes of a young man stared back.

Relief swept through every muscle of her body. This was not the dangerous monster she had been fearing since childhood. This was another human being, only a few years older than herself. And he was surviving out here, despite the risk of Scavengers. So there was hope!

She held up her hands. "Can you please untie me?"

He glanced at her red, puffy wrists.

"It's very painful. I promise not to run," she offered.

Still, he said nothing.

He doesn't understand.

Elia held her hands to her throat. "I'm just so thirsty."

She expected the gesture to be useless and it was. The young man spun on his heels and returned to the tent to begin dismantling it. She waited, yet he offered no water. He did not untie her. Soon they were on the move again, with Elia in tow.

• • •

The flat grasslands offered no barrier against the constant wind as they traveled, her captor riding his beast and Elia walking behind. Debris drifted all around. Occasionally, fluttering pieces snagged in the animal's horns, and if the young man noticed, he picked them off, tossing them aside. Usually, he didn't—too distracted by a small instrument he kept checking in his hand—and the garbage just flapped like a dirty flag until eventually dislodging itself. Much of it appeared to be the same strange material Elia had seen the day before. Whenever it rustled in the breeze, it sounded like fat sizzling in a pan.

They came upon the same shoreline from yesterday, and Elia was surprised to see her footprints in the sand, trailed by a larger set left by her captor. He had stalked her the entire way. They backtracked along the path and reached the spot where Elia had washed to shore, where the bedsheet she had clung to during her fall had escaped the waves and was lying in a dry, twisted heap. Continuing on, they arrived at a gentle flow of water that cut through the grasslands and ran across the rippled sand before trickling into the huge body of water behind them.

While his dog with its oversized ears lapped water from the edge, the young man took a metal cup from his sack and stepped into the stream, soaking the hem of his leather cloak. After several satisfying gulps, he beckoned Elia with his empty mug, but she shook her head.

"No, I can't drink that," said Elia, mimicking her words with sign language.

He looked confused and then held up the cup once more. She grimaced. "It's too salty."

This made him roll his eyes. He dunked the mug into the water and lifted it dripping into the air. "It's not salty," he declared. "This is fine. That," he said, pointing to the ocean, "is salty."

Elia was too stunned to respond.

"Take it!" he commanded.

"You understand my words?"

"I do."

So then why your silence? Elia wondered. She felt growing rage, but forced herself to accept the mug. The fresh, cool water running down her throat was like an elixir, immediately revitalizing her. "Please," she said, "I must get back to my island. It's crucial."

His eyes hardened. He swung his gaze up to the clouds and the island still hanging there, and sucked a breath through gritted teeth. "That's quite a distance to cover."

"My family is in danger. They need me. Is there any way to get up there?"

He scratched the back of his neck. "Maybe. Maybe not."

"I beg you to let me go. I can't be of any value to you."

When he didn't answer, she had to fight back tears. Why was he treating her this way? She nervously crossed her arms over her breasts, worried about what savage plan he might have.

Stepping out of the creek, he walked back to the beast and removed several long cylindrical bottles from his bag. They appeared to be made of delicate glass. Returning to the stream, he held each under the water, and once filled, twisted on their small lids before placing them back in his sack. Elia tensed when one dropped, yet it did not shatter.

"It didn't break," she observed, rubbing the moisture from her eyes with her bound hands, trying to remain composed.

He inspected the bottles, as if for the first time. He didn't seem impressed. "No, these never break." He pulled out an empty one and tossed it up into the air. The wind caught it as though it were weightless. It landed close to Elia and she picked it up. The sides felt thin, and Elia was sure she could crush it in her hand.

"Where do you find these?" she asked, hoping conversation would help her assess his intent.

"Everywhere," he said with a dismissive sweep of his hand. Elia persisted. "In the ground?"

"Sometimes. But usually just sitting on top of the grass."

She noticed him rub the scars on his arms. Several times already, she had caught herself staring at the horrible burns. The Scavengers must have done this to him. Perhaps his mind was damaged too, having to live among such monsters.

The young man noticed his dog intently sniffing his way upstream. "Nym, where are you going?" he called out.

The animal looked back, then dropped his head again to follow the scent.

"Where's your dog going?" asked Elia.

"It's not a dog," he growled.

"A rodent?"

He looked at her as if she were crazy. "It's a fox."

"A fox?" Elia bit her lower lip and then pointed to the creature she was tied to. "And what about that?"

"A gazelk. You've never seen such animals?"

"No. Never."

She could feel his eyes on her, so she looked away. She was glad when the fox barked, diverting his attention. The animal bounded into the grasses.

"He's found something!" he exclaimed, leaping up. He grabbed his sack to give chase, leaving Elia sitting alone at the edge of the stream.

Now that he was gone, Elia didn't waste a moment. This might be her only chance to flee. Gripping the gazelk by its neck, she struggled to hoist herself onto the animal's back. Having tied wrists made it impossible, though, and she tried again and again, grunting with frustration. The damn beast was too tall.

Come on. Do it! Get your leg over!

The gazelk suddenly whipped its head around, startled by Elia's captor charging back toward them. Narrowly avoiding its horns, Elia quickly let go of the animal and feigned innocence.

The young man was out of breath. His glance lingered on her. He knows, she thought. He knows she was attempting to escape. Yet he said not a word before he grabbed the rope, leading her and the gazelk away.

Elia hurried to match his steps. "What did you see out there?" she dared to ask, trying to sound confident.

He turned to look at her, this time with a glint of excitement sparkling in his eyes. "I found another body!"

Chapter 16

ANOTHER BODY? ELIA FEARED IT could only be Naadie. As they arrived at the spot, the young man blocked Elia's view, and all she could see was a laundry basket. But when her captor stepped aside, she saw the basket was strapped to a brown lump lying on the ground. This was not Naadie's battered body. It was a donkey.

Upon landing, Twister's mother had completely crushed the basket underneath. Luckily, the one Elia cared about was sitting on top, still intact. She took an eager step forward and leaned over the donkey to reach in.

"What are you doing?" the young man demanded.

"Nothing," Elia murmured. Her bound hands touched the sheet that had been stuffed inside and her excitement swelled as she removed it. She reached in again, but her fingertips felt only the basket's bottom. The wooden box was missing.

"You're always looking for something."

Elia shot him a suspicious glance. "What do you mean?"

"You were doing the same thing yesterday when I found you searching that other woman."

By the look in his eyes, Elia realized he knew about the gem she had discovered in the sand. Her hand dropped to her empty pocket.

"How could you take that?" she exclaimed. "That wasn't yours."

"Was it yours?"

Elia wished she had an answer ready.

"Did you kill her for it?" he asked.

"Of course not!"

"That's not what it looked like."

"So is that why you hit me? Knocked me out?" she challenged, clenching her fists.

"I had to be careful. I don't know what to expect with you."

"She died from the fall!" Elia shouted.

"You fell too. You survived."

"Yes, but I fell in the water. She didn't."

"And the donkey?"

"Same thing."

"But it has wings!" he said in amazement as he tugged on its feathers.

"Yes, and no idea how to use them. They're tied down anyway." Elia pointed to the basket with a side glance at the young man's bag. "Was there anything in the basket when you arrived? You were here first without me. Did you already take it?"

"I didn't look."

"I just need to know."

"Why?"

Could it hurt to tell him? "I made a promise to that woman when we were still above the clouds. She wanted me to protect something for her, something she hid inside the basket."

"Well, I don't know where it is," he said nonchalantly, crouching to open his sack. "It could be anywhere."

He was right. And if the carved box had slipped out in midair, it would have smashed into many pieces or sunk in the ocean.

A question suddenly flickered in her mind. What had happened to Twister? Where had he crashed to Below? The little donkey had fallen over the edge first, and Elia remembered his panic as the island disappeared beneath him. Not wanting to see him splattered like his mother, she hoped the breeze would never carry the foal's scent to the fox's nose.

After fumbling in his bag, Elia's captor pulled out a large, folded knife with a jagged blade. He squatted beside the donkey to inspect the carcass, then held up its back leg with one hand and placed the knife at the animal's hip bone.

"Grab this," he snapped, holding the leg toward Elia.

"I'm not—"

"I can't do this with one hand," he said impatiently as he glared up at her. "You'll have to hold it for me."

"My hands are still tied together!"

"Just hold it," he ordered through clenched teeth.

Elia clutched the donkey's leg and closed her eyes as he started sawing through the hide. The knife cracked through the bone and the leg trembled with every scrape of the blade until it eventually sliced through the remaining flesh. "Are you done?" she asked.

"I'd take more, but it would be too difficult to finish eating before it goes bad." He wiped his knife on the donkey's coarse hair. "Now to wrap the end." He scanned the surrounding terrain, then raced into the nearby grasses to catch a piece of garbage floating by. He shook out a large bag with handles as he came back to her and nodded at the severed leg. "Lift that into here."

Elia didn't move. She balanced the weight of the shank in her hands. It felt like a club. She eyed the knife now tucked into the young man's belt. That's what she needed.

"What are you waiting for, girl?"

Anger triggered her reflexes. Elia lifted the hunk of meat into the air and swung. He raised his hands to block her, but Elia caught him on the side of his head. Enraged, he wrestled the donkey leg from her grasp, and as she let go, Elia reached to steal his knife. Realizing her intent, he flung her viciously to the ground, and held the leg above his head. Elia braced herself for the blow.

But then she felt a gentle touch on her hand. She looked over to see Nym gingerly licking her fingertips, attracted by the lingering fragrance of donkey meat.

Seeing this, the young man hesitated before lowering the shank. He rubbed the blood, bits of hair, and smudges of animal fat from his cheek and forehead where she had hit him. It took a minute or two before he could speak. "That will *not* happen again," he said fiercely, stabbing a finger at her. "Understand?"

Elia nodded.

"I don't need any added grief from you."

"Then what do you want with me?" she pleaded. "Just let me go!"

"That won't be happening. Besides, you'll never survive out here on your own."

"You're concerned for my safety?" she scoffed.

"You should be glad I found you."

Elia wasn't glad, but she had to admit his skills would probably come in handy, especially to ensure their survival against Scavengers.

The young man placed the meat into the bag, leaving the hoof and most of the leg sticking out. He leapt up and stood on the back of his gazelk, holding on to the horns for balance and stretching as tall as possible for a better view. "I need a place to cook this meat," he said, jumping back to the ground.

"You can't cook it here?"

"Too exposed. The smoke will drift and get noticed."

With the flat expanse of the grasslands and the water behind them, Elia couldn't imagine a spot where smoke would not be a problem. "Where can we go?"

"We're going to a spot that didn't exist before yesterday."

Chapter 17

DRIVEN BY HIS RELENTLESS HUNGER and the prospect of a meal, Hokk kept the gazelk at a steady trot, even if it meant dragging the girl. So far, that hadn't been necessary. He was impressed she could run behind and keep up. Whenever she tripped, she quickly got back to her feet without slowing them down, but it still took over an hour of punishing travel to reach the second gorge.

Before leading the girl and the gazelk over the plowed-up mountains of dirt, Hokk dismounted and caught two more bags drifting by. He stuffed each with green grass. Assuming they had arrived, the girl lowered herself to the ground; however, Hokk yanked the rope to make her stand. "No, you can't rest yet," he said. "We're almost there."

As they descended into this latest scar on the prairies, the soil was loose under their feet and the girl lost her balance several times on the embankment, cringing with every pull of the rope on her swollen wrists. Watching her, Hokk felt a growing cramp in his gut.

"This is all new," he said, but she ignored him. Her jaw was clenched tight.

The gorge was immense, even larger than the ancient garbage dump Hokk had seen previously. It was formed after a second occurrence, only days after the first, and he had seen the same odd response from his compass—its needle spinning one way, stopping, then spinning in reverse—just before the islands dropped. Hokk glanced at this girl from Above. The Board would certainly believe him now.

"This entire expanse was dug up in minutes," he tried to explain again as the slope began leveling off.

The girl was now able to scan the chasm without stumbling. "How?" she asked coldly.

Hokk pointed to the sky where a solitary island of rock was suspended in the dark clouds. It was not the one she had fallen from. "When an island comes down low enough, it carves through everything, leaving these massive gouges."

Her brow wrinkled. "Why do they drop?"

Hokk shrugged. "Don't know. Until recently, I never would have thought it possible. Yet this is the second time now."

They reached the bottom of the chasm. The air was heavy with the smell of freshly turned dirt.

From around the gazelk's neck, Hokk untied a bundle of driftwood they had collected before leaving the ocean. "We need to find flat rocks to build the base for a fire. Then I can cook my meat." He pointed to a gaping hole in the dirt where a massive boulder had rolled down the embankment. "See what you can lift, and pile the rocks over there in that hollow."

"What about you?"

"I'm going to climb back up for more of this stuff," he said as he emptied the two bags of grass. "But I'll be watching you."

The girl scowled as she pulled the gazelk over to a pile of rocks and struggled to pick up her first stone. He knew it would be a difficult task with her hands bound, but under no circumstance would he untie her. She wasn't as innocent as she appeared, even if she was a girl. He had already seen her trying to climb onto his gazelk by the creek, then she attacked him with the donkey leg. And he still wasn't sure—was the other woman on the beach already dead when she found her or had the girl finished her off? She could be capable of anything. He had to remember what he had learned so often in the past: people can never be trusted.

•   •   •

The girl had assembled rocks just as Hokk requested. "That's plenty," he said when he returned and saw the pile.

"You didn't say how many you needed," she replied, sounding annoyed.

Though leery of the girl, he liked listening to her speak. She had an unusual accent and her voice was lighter, her words crisper than he was used to. It also felt good to talk to someone again. It meant he wouldn't have to fear his brain spoiling from loneliness.

Hokk stacked the driftwood on the rocks and plugged the holes with grass. Sparks flew as he dragged his blade across a flint, while he held his breath, waiting for that first flicker. When a faint ringlet of smoke spiraled up, he gently blew life into the feeble flames.

His body came alive too, like his soul had awakened and all his problems had vanished. Since he was a child, he had loved to watch a fire burn, and always found building one revitalizing, as if he were a creator, bringing something new into a world where before there was nothing.

Smoke rose into the air on the back of the shimmering heat. By the time it reached the height of the grasslands, it would be unnoticeable. Hokk didn't want to attract anyone—he couldn't risk having this opportunity, this girl, stolen from him.

He noticed her inch closer to the flames. She wore only a thin, gray dress that offered little protection from the cold, which advanced on them from the shadows at their backs.

Hokk still couldn't believe his luck in finding her alive. With her dark skin and fair hair, he knew exactly where she was from, but he had never heard of any *living* person from Above actually coming to Below. Their dead bodies, for sure, even if it was the landing that killed them, but certainly never one still breathing.

The wood burned down to glowing embers and the rocks became red hot. Hokk added handfuls of fresh grass, and the blades sizzled and curled in the intense heat. Next came the donkey shank, another thick layer of grass, then water from a bottle trickling down to the embers. As it hissed, Hokk quickly packed fresh dirt around everything to trap the steam.

The smell of the cooking meat took a long time to emerge, but once it did, the fragrance made Nym whimper. The fox watched Hokk with pleading eyes, licking his muzzle as if his tongue could taste the air.

"You'll have to wait," said Hokk as he scratched behind Nym's ears.

The girl sat staring at his makeshift oven, her knees pulled up to her chest. Hokk found her hard to read. At times, she seemed shy and anxious, but then she would catch him off guard by summoning a fiery spirit from within—it was that volatility he had to be careful of.

"What are you called?" he abruptly asked.

The girl jumped. "What am I called?"

"Your name. What do people call you?"

"Oh. Elia."

Just as he expected, Hokk saw her blush. "Elia what?"

"Just Elia."

They sat in silence once more. Hokk was curious if she would ask him in return. After a few minutes, she spoke up. "What about you?"

"Hokk," he said. "Hokk Feste. From the City of Ago."

She hugged her knees closer. "And you've been able to survive out here all on your own?"

"I have."

"Though you must always stay alert."

"You're right. I never know who might be tracking me to take what I have."

Hokk noticed her staring at the burn marks on his arms and hands. He covered them with his cloak.

Her eyes darted to his face. "So what do you do when Scavengers attack?"

"What's a Scavenger?"

Her expression flashed with surprise. "They roam these grasslands searching for bodies."

"Then I suppose you could say I'm a Scavenger."

Elia bristled. "You collect bodies from Above?"

"Collect them? Why would I do that?"

She looked at him as if this was the most obvious thing in the world. "Because that's what Scavengers do."

Hokk frowned. "When I come across a body, I search it for something I can use, yes, but no more than that. Otherwise I just leave them where they landed."

She sighed with exasperation. "I'm talking about monsters. With no eyes. Curved spines. They cling to the sides of the islands and snatch people off the edges."

"Monsters! Don't be stupid," Hokk exclaimed, which made Elia shrink back. "There's no such thing. Is that what you were expecting?"

Elia pinched her lips together. "Yes," she replied quietly.

"I don't know what stories you've been hearing, but they're lies. Sure there are outcasts and criminals out here, but really, none of them are worse than me." Wait, that didn't sound right. "What I mean is, there's danger, absolutely, but you just have to stick to yourself and stay within the proper boundaries. That's how you survive."

Elia seemed sad, as though finding out that monsters didn't exist was a bad thing. She stared up at the sky with longing and Hokk followed her gaze. The floating island was still overhead, silent and menacing.

"That's a different island than yesterday's," said Hokk.

Appearing lost in thought, she did not respond.

"That's not where you fell from, in case you're wondering," he said, trying again.

She concentrated her gaze on him as though playing his words back in her mind. "Didn't think so," she finally replied, her voice trembling.

"I've seen yours a few times before. Always two of them, side by side, but they never touch. The small one seems to follow the massive one."

She swallowed hard and cleared her throat. "That sounds right." She was regaining her composure. "And do you recognize this one now?"

"It looks familiar. But I can't always identify them. There are just so many that drift by."

"How many are up there?"

Hokk thought for a moment. "Hundreds?" he wondered out loud and then decided that sounded a bit much. "At least a hundred anyway."

"Yes. I always knew there were a lot in the System. I've never actually heard how many."

Nym whined impatiently beside them, unable to wait any longer for food. He balanced on his hind legs while pedaling his front paws to get Hokk's attention.

"You think the time's up, do you?" said Hokk. As he stood, Nym dropped to all fours and scampered around his ankles.

Hokk pulled apart the oven to uncover the shank and the mouth-watering fragrance intensified. He lifted off the steaming grasses, and the heat seared his fingertips. Holding the donkey's leg steady, he sliced through the meat with his knife.

Nym and the girl watched, both mesmerized, as Hokk cut off a piece and bit down, chewing with his eyes closed. He savored the gamey flavor as a drop of juice dribbled from his lip.

He sliced off another hunk and flung it at Nym. Catching it in midair, the fox swallowed it whole and barked for more.

The next piece was much larger, and Nym dragged it off as if protecting it from the rest of the pack.

Hokk could see the girl was eager for her share—desperate even—observing his every move. He would make her wait as payback for hitting him on the head. He continued to eat, feeding pieces to himself and Nym while he watched her out of the corner of his eye.

With his stomach full, Hokk cut deeper into the shank and removed a gristly, undercooked piece. Just enough for the energy she would need. He chucked the piece toward her, knowing it would fall short.

The meat fell at her feet. She snatched it from the soil and stuffed it into her mouth, not even pausing to brush it off.

Listening to the dirt and bits of cartilage crunch between her teeth, Hokk felt a twinge of regret. "You're hungry," he said, knowing the feeling all too well.

"Always."

He cut a better piece. This time, he tossed it directly at her and she caught it.

"If you stop trying to run away, I can promise you more," he said.

The girl held up her bound wrists. "Do I have a choice?"

No, you don't, thought Hokk.

Chapter 18

"WE'LL HAVE TO STOP AND make camp," Hokk called out. He had been riding his gazelk for hours, while Elia followed him again on foot.

The food he had shared had given her much-needed energy, but her legs were exhausted and ready to give out. Now, feeling the tension in her rope ease, Elia knew she was safe from being dragged, and she sunk to the ground as if melting into a puddle.

For all of their traveling since leaving the gorge, there had been no change in the landscape. Nothing on the horizon. "Where are you taking me?" she asked as he unpacked his supplies and began setting up his tent.

"My city."

"Why?"

Hokk shot a worried glance at the black cloud cover, appearing reluctant to answer. "I have a plan," he eventually answered.

And what plan was that? Elia wondered. Did any part of it include helping her?

She stared hopelessly at her bare feet sticking out past her dress. They were filthy and scratched, and soil was shoved deep under a cracked toenail. Her wrists were bruised, oozing, and scabby too, with dried blood on the rope. Yet none of that mattered. Her thoughts kept going back to her family. Her worries were like a plague of parasites eating away at her, beginning their feast from that first moment she woke up in Below, now devouring her more ferociously after learning that Scavengers were not real.

But they had to be! It was better they existed, otherwise what had happened to Omi had far worse implications. Because if she had not died of fright from an attack by Scavengers, then it could only have been the Imperial Guards. Elia pictured the guards ambushing her grandmother from the air as they had the lady-in-waiting. What had Omi done to be attacked on the same day as Mrs. Suds's arrest?

A water bottle landed beside her and Elia looked up with a start.

"Drink," said Hokk, "but ration it. We won't have enough for the distance we still have to—"

The sky suddenly flashed a blinding white, quickly followed by a loud explosion in the clouds that reverberated from one side of the horizon to the other. Elia flattened herself and dug her fingers into the roots and dirt.

"What just happened?" she called out in horror.

"Lightning," Hokk answered.

"That can't be lightning!"

Another flash, much farther away, appeared as a line of light that split the air between the clouds and the earth, yet it was gone before she could focus. More of the same exploded in the sky, though Elia couldn't guess where the next strike might appear. These were not the gentle, silent pulses of light she had often seen from her view above the clouds. Below's lightning was violent and frightening.

Low-hanging clouds swept across the landscape like surging horses. A furious wind raced ahead of them, determined to level every blade of grass. With it came a roar and a pounding deluge of water from overhead that Elia's mind could not comprehend. Her clothing was instantly soaked. She looked at her dripping arms in bewilderment.

Water from the sky? How was that possible?

Elia felt desperate as the cold, stinging droplets pummeled her skin. The water ran down her face; her hair and clothing clung to her body. Just when the torrent seemed as if it could fall no harder, the sound intensified, drowning her ears with its noise.

In a panic, she whirled around, looking for shelter—anything to escape. And where was Hokk? He had disappeared into the tent with his fox.

Frustration forced tears to her eyes, tears that were overwhelmed by the downpour. As Elia pulled the rope, trying to make the gazelk move closer to Hokk's refuge, her foot slipped on the discarded water bottle and she fell face-first into a puddle. More water! In a fit of rage, she picked up the container and flung it toward the tent, where it hit the side and rolled off.

"What about me!" she screamed, charging forward and ripping up one corner of Hokk's shelter.

A hand emerged to undo the front flap, but already half of the tent had collapsed as Hokk scrambled out.

He grabbed her hands and yanked the material from her grasp. "What do you want me to do?" he shouted, flinging his arms up in exasperation as water poured down his face.

Elia looked around helplessly.

"What?" he demanded.

"I don't know!" she yelled back. "I hate this! What's happening?"

"It's just rain. I thought you'd be used to it!"

"I've never even heard of it!" She shoved him in the chest. "How could you leave me out here in this?"

Hokk unhooked the clasp around his neck, letting his leather cloak slip from his shoulders. He flung it at Elia, and it landed at her feet. "Take it."

She didn't move.

"Take it!" he bellowed above the sound of rain. Chin jutting out, he wiped his forehead and viciously flicked the water at her in sheer frustration. "I must be crazy. You better be worth all this trouble."

Chapter 19

HOKK KICKED ELIA'S HUDDLED BODY. It was gentle enough, but a kick nonetheless. "Get up," he said. "We've got to get going."

She was lying on the ground, buried under his leather cloak.

"Get up," he repeated, peeling it back. "Enough sleeping."

Her eyes cracked open. "Sleep? I'm lying in a puddle," she hissed.

As she stood, Hokk saw her dress was drenched even more than his own clothes. The storm had moved on, and the only way they would get dry was to keep moving.

She handed back his cloak.

He took it, paused, then gave it back. "No. You wear it for now."

They headed out across the grasslands. Hokk kept the gazelk moving at a much slower speed and the girl trudged behind. Nym was carefully balanced on his front paws between the gazelk's two horns, turning his nose to catch each new scent. At one point, the fox barked with excitement when a herd of wild gazelk leapt across their path. Otherwise, the plains were void of life as usual.

Hokk looked back a few times to make sure the girl was

all right. She was keeping pace. After a while, Hokk was surprised to see her run by him and start walking in front. He didn't care. He could understand her not wanting to be always following somebody else in control. Whenever she drifted off course, she knew by the pull in the rope to change direction, but he would still call out to her each time, "Wrong way!" Clearly irritated, she would stomp past him to resume the lead.

It was late afternoon when Elia's stride began to slow. The gazelk caught up and was soon ahead of her again.

"Stop! I can't!" she finally shouted from behind.

Hokk turned.

She staggered on wobbly legs. "Please. My legs won't work anymore."

Hokk stopped the gazelk and jumped to the ground to walk back. Elia dropped to her knees as he approached, his cloak settling around her. She pulled it off as though even the leather was too heavy to lug any farther.

"You can drag me for all I care," she said.

He ran a hand over his long, black hair. "You're too slow." He paused and glanced at the horizon.

Why was he resisting? He knew he was treating her like a prisoner, just as Kalus used to treat him during their early days together, always keeping him down, removing any doubt about who made the decisions. And though Hokk wished to stay in control now, it was obvious they couldn't continue like this if he also wanted to return to Ago as soon as possible.

"Stand up," he said with a sigh, picking up his cloak and fastening it around his neck. "You'll have to ride with me."

She seemed stunned. "Really?" She held up her bound wrists. "What about this?"

"Don't push it." Hokk took the rope and led Elia to the gazelk. With Nym watching from his perch atop the gazelk's head, Hokk cupped his hands. "Put one foot in here and I'll lift you up."

She didn't weigh a lot, but she was awkward, and her knee buckled as she pushed off, forcing Hokk to heave with a grunt.

"Shift forward," he said, and once she had, he vaulted up behind her. The space was tight, yet doable. He wrapped his arm around her waist. She instantly grew tense, and leaned away, but as the gazelk moved forward with a jolt, Hokk kept his grip firm.

The gazelk had no problem carrying another person, though at first, Elia bumped out of rhythm with its steps. Only after allowing herself to relax against Hokk, to take advantage of his warmth, did they finally move in unison.

It was remarkable to feel her sitting this close. After so many years, he had forgotten the sensation of human touch. His attention focused on all the spots where he made contact with her body—the palm of his hand against her stomach, his thighs pressed against hers, his arm tucked under her own, his chest supporting her back.

He should have had her riding up here sooner. They covered the prairies quickly. At this speed, Hokk would be well ahead of anybody else returning to the city to tell their story of dropping islands. As the afternoon wore on, Hokk grew excited, but also nervous about what to expect when they arrived, especially since the Board's lookouts could have him arrested and kicked out before he had any chance to explain. To be safe, the best time to enter the city limits would be early morning, when they would attract the least attention. He'd slip in and make his first stop at his uncle and aunt's.

They wouldn't recognize him. Just thinking about it made Hokk grin. He would be proud to show them how much he had grown, to see the relief in their eyes that he had been able to survive. Uncle Charyl was devastated when Hokk was first charged, and he had fought the ruling right up to the moment his nephew was hauled away. Auntie Una was upset too, but more because the whole mess was just another sad incident in the family's history.

Yes, he was definitely looking forward to seeing them both. Hokk's older brother, however—not in the least. Davim had despised him for as long as Hokk could remember, so it was no surprise when Davim testified against him in front of the Board and then celebrated his younger brother's sentence. All these years later, Hokk hoped to avoid Davim completely. He certainly couldn't count on him for help when he returned. Only Uncle Charyl would make sure the Board listened to Hokk's story.

And what would his uncle and aunt think of Elia?

Her hair now blew in his face, and her head was tilting as if she had nodded off. Her body leaned to one side, and she could have tipped over completely if not for his firm hold.

He gently shook her.

"I was just looking up at the sky," she murmured.

"I thought you fell asleep."

"I almost did. But then I got thinking. Is there ever a break in the clouds?"

"I don't think it's possible."

"They're just so low, it's almost suffocating. I could never get used to that."

"It's all I've ever known," said Hokk. "But this is nothing compared to what you must come from. I've always wondered how you can endure the constant fog living within the clouds."

"There's no fog," Elia said with surprise, turning her head and brushing aside the hair that caught in her eyelashes. "And I don't live *within* the clouds. Why would you think so?"

Hokk gazed at the sky. "Because the cloud cover is endlessly thick."

"But we float above it."

"Oh," said Hokk. His forehead wrinkled as he thought for a moment. "So what's above you then?"

"Nothing."

"Nothing?"

"No, not nothing. There's air and blue sky. And of course the sun. It's bright and warm all the time. Certainly not freezing like it is down here."

"What's the sun?"

Elia's eyes widened. "You've never seen the sun?"

"I don't think so. But perhaps I have. Maybe we call it by a different name."

"The sun is a big ball of fire."

"Oh, well I've seen fire."

"Yes, but the sun's in the sky, traveling from one horizon to the other every day."

Hokk thought this sounded preposterous. "I can't picture it."

"It'd be difficult if you've never seen it. And I can understand. I've never seen clouds *above* me before. It's the strangest sight."

They rode in silence for a short way while Hokk struggled to visualize Elia's description of Above. Kalus never would have talked so much with a captive, but Hokk was filled with questions. "So, is it dangerous? The sun, I mean. You definitely wouldn't want to touch it or anything."

She laughed. "You've got it all wrong. It's too high up in the sky to touch."

"But if the sun is in the sky, it must fall down."

"It doesn't."

"Impossible!"

"Why would that be impossible?" Elia pointed to the underside of the island floating above them now. "That stays up."

"The clouds hold it there." His comment seemed to stump her, but he continued. "You say the sun moves from one horizon to the other?"

"Yes." Elia swung her arm in an arc across the sky to trace the sun's path. "And it sets each evening directly opposite from where it rose. Its light is so intense you can't look at it directly or your eyes will burn out and you'll go blind."

"Really?"

"Haven't you ever wondered where the light comes from in the morning?"

"The clouds."

"No, the sun. It's the sunlight that shines through to Below, like you see now." Elia looked up to the choking gray blanket and sighed. "Well, whatever light can actually penetrate such heavy mist."

Hokk frowned. From what he had been taught, the Ancients lived in a time of much greater light. The sky had darkened as the cloud cover grew thicker. But the more he thought about it, the more he realized the error in logic. If the clouds emitted their own light, then their thickness shouldn't matter. Perhaps there really was a light source above them.

"So if it rises and falls every day," Hokk asked, "does the sun set fire to the land when it gets too close?"

Elia sighed as if trying to teach a young child who was refusing to listen. "I just told you. It's too far away. It's much farther out than even the moon."

Another new word. "What's the moon?"

"The moon floats in my sky just like the sun."

"So it's on fire too."

"Definitely not. People still live on it. That's where we trace our ancestry to."

"Do you go there to visit relatives?"

"Unfortunately, we can't," said Elia. With her bound hands, she started petting Nym, who was tucked in her lap. "We've been separated from them for centuries and we have no way to cross the distance. However, our islands, all the ones you've ever seen drifting in these clouds, were once part of the moon. Before it broke apart."

"Well, that simply can't be true." He half-chuckled. Now she was starting to sound ridiculous. She obviously didn't understand.

Elia stopped petting Nym. "You would be foolish not to believe it."

"I'm sorry, but I can't."

She stiffened against him. "That's because this is the first you've heard about it. But before the moon broke apart, it was solid and round like the sun. After it shattered, pieces drifted away until they were trapped in the clouds." She twisted around. "You don't believe me?"

"Your ideas are interesting, and yes, I admit, I've never seen the moon," he said. "But I know for sure the islands floating above us come from where we are now. From Below."

"And how's that?" she asked incredulously.

"When the magnetic poles switched, it caused eruptions that broke the earth apart and propelled pieces of the crust into the air. They've orbited there ever since."

"I can't understand a thing you're saying," said Elia, tight lipped.

"Just like me listening to you."

"Your ideas are all wrong."

"And not yours? You were the one expecting to see monsters down here, scavenging for dead bodies."

Elia scowled and faced forward. They rode on without another word.

Chapter 20

ELIA WAS DOZING, LULLED BY the steady movement of the gazelk, when she felt Nym pop up. The fox growled.

Yanking back on its horns, Hokk immediately stopped their steed. He pulled Elia tight against his chest and wrapped his cloak around her. The leather smelled of earth and smoke, and she peeked over the top edge, following Hokk's gaze. All she could see were two motionless bulks in the distance.

"What are they?" she asked. They looked like mounds of dirt.

"Bison," he said quietly.

One of the bulks shifted and Elia could distinguish a massive, shaggy head, small horns, and powerful shoulders. "Are they dangerous?"

"They can be. It just depends," said Hokk, inspecting the landscape on both sides. "As a stampeding herd, they can crush you, but with only two of them—" his voice grew strained. "Well, that usually means something different."

A man suddenly appeared, rising above the grasses. He was bald and bare chested, with black designs painted on his skin. The man grabbed a bison by its shoulder and swung his legs over its back, just as another man appeared and climbed onto the second animal.

Elia turned to Hokk. He was looking down at the spinning dial cradled in his hand. His eyes were raging.

"This is my territory now," he snarled.

"Who are they?"

"Torkins. They don't belong here."

The two Torkins were unaware they were being watched and their animals sauntered through the grasses.

"Off," he said sternly.

"What?" Elia asked with surprise.

"Get off. It's too dangerous to have you with me." Hokk let his arm fall away from Elia's waist and he shifted his hips forward.

Was she supposed to jump?

She had no time to protest. Hokk gave her a hard shove and she toppled to the ground. The gazelk started to move again. Still tied up, Elia was terrified she would be dragged if the animal broke into a gallop. "Stop!" she yelled after Hokk, scrambling to her feet as the rope stretched out.

Hokk spun around, his knife already in his hand. The blade sliced through the rope, and it dropped to the ground like a decapitated serpent, freeing her from the gazelk

An instant later, Hokk let out a war cry and the gazelk shot off. As she watched him draw closer to the men, his cloak flailing wildly, the two startled riders and their bison galloped off in retreat. They rode across the plain and disappeared into a gully. Hokk followed, slipping from her sight.

She was alone.

And free.

She took a few steps—it felt incredible to move about on her own. With her hands still bound, Elia slowly swung her arms around her body as she walked, letting the grasses gently tickle her palms. After a short distance, she wondered which way Hokk had gone, and suddenly, the shock of her isolation hit. In a panic, she turned around and around, fearing she had completely lost her bearings. Then she saw something that drew her to an abrupt halt.

Were those large birds?

As Elia squinted, a large piece of the strange, fiberless fabric splashed across her face, blocking her vision. Startled, she sucked in her breath, and the fabric sealed itself around her lips, creating a suffocating suction. She clawed it away.

Standing on her tiptoes, surrounded by the vastness of the waving grasses, it was difficult to gauge at such a distance, yet Elia was certain she saw a cluster of flapping wings, as if vultures were converging on the carcass of a dead animal. Against the gray clouds, one of the animals stood out from the others. It was pure white. Then the rest of the pack broke up and several more took to the air.

Elia threw herself to the ground. There was no mistaking the powerful strokes of the stallions' wings, and the reflective glint of the Imperial Guards' mirrored helmets as they advanced toward her.

Chapter **21**

THEY'RE HUNTING ME!

Elia hid in the grass, her mind spinning. Once the Imperial Guards were close enough, they would spot her from the air.

What if they're here to rescue me instead? The very idea contradicted her instincts, yet she could not deny that being rescued was a possibility. Help had been sent when their home drifted away. Why not now? What if her mother or Greyit had made arrangements for a search party? She should stand up then, wave her arms, do everything she could to attract the guards' attention so they could take her home.

But what if Commander Wrasse was with them? The box he sought was lost—destroyed. From what she had witnessed among the clotheslines, the consequences would be severe. Elia feared the guards had made prisoners of her family, and the men were now here to finish the job, to account for every missing body—hers the last to collect.

She peeked above the grasses. The Imperial Guards had split up across the prairies. One guard stayed farther back, flying high as a lookout. His horse's legs moved as if galloping, though the animal only hovered in midair, rotating for its rider to survey the landscape.

The sight was still so inconceivable! Imperial Guards following her to the very place everyone had been told to fear. A place for only the dead! Yet here they flew, descending from Above like masters of this desolate, supposedly unknown realm.

Suddenly, from outside Elia's field of vision, a guard appeared and landed alarmingly close, his stallion folding its wings no more than a hundred feet away.

Elia flattened herself, sweating through every pore in her skin.

"Just wait," the guard called out to his squad. "I've got this last spot to check."

Footsteps shuffled through the grasses, moving ever closer. They stopped.

Elia couldn't help glancing up. He was almost standing on top of her. Though his helmet did not have protruding wings like the one Commander Wrasse wore, it was still unique, with a spike centered over his forehead. His faceplate reflected the grasslands and the gray sky.

Another guard's voice in the distance was too faint for Elia to make out.

"Nothing here!" this man shouted back.

How could that be? She was sure he had just looked down at her, pausing for a second as if registering her gray lump on the ground. He had parted the grasses, shook his head ever so slightly, and then turned away as Elia swallowed the stomach acid burning a path up her throat.

The guard stepped out of sight, and moments later, Elia heard galloping hooves, followed by the whoosh of an airborne horse. The underside of a stallion sailed overhead, its wing tips skimming the tops of the grasses.

Man and beast were gone.

Reeling with disbelief, Elia cautiously rose from her hiding spot and saw the guard's horse rejoin the group. The pack of flying stallions flew up in a curling procession until they reached the dark, boiling belly of the clouds. They vanished into the mists of Above.

●　●　●

The night was a black void, but Elia knew she was not alone. If pieces of the moon were scattered across the sky, like Above, their blue hue would have cast enough light to see her stalker, but down here—nothing. Crouching, Elia held her breath and listened.

She heard the *crack* of stems, then silence. The guard with the spiked helmet must have returned, concealed by the night to track her down and claim her for his own bounty. He was the only one who knew her location, and he was on the ground now, circling in on her.

Elia shrieked when something grazed her knee. She shot up and ran blindly, stumbling, swinging her tied arms to keep her balance. If she fell, she knew the man would be upon her in a second.

The guard was shouting now, and each time his voice grew louder, she veered off in a different direction. Then, unexpectedly, his voice was directly in front of her, almost coming from overhead. Was he up in the air again, entertained by her panicked attempt to flee?

He wasn't in the air. Elia ran straight into his arms.

"No! No!" she shouted, swinging her fists and kicking her legs. "*No!*"

The man held her in a firm embrace. "Stop it!" he commanded. "Stop. Quit kicking me." Elia heard a dog start barking. "Shut up, Nym," the man ordered.

For a confused instant, Elia froze, then relaxed in his arms. *Hokk. Praise the sun!*

"It's you!" she gasped. Elia reached up with her hands to touch his face in the darkness and recognized his features. "You came back for me."

"You sound surprised."

"I didn't think you would."

"You'd never survive out here."

"They'll return." With her fingertips lingering on his neck, she could feel a racing pulse beneath his skin.

"I chased them off. This isn't their territory and they knew it."

"Not the Torkins," she said. "Didn't you see the others?"

"There's more?"

"I'm talking about guards from Above. They were flying in the sky, searching for me."

Hokk was silent for a moment. "I saw nothing."

He doesn't believe me, thought Elia. She pushed away from him. "I know it sounds strange," she muttered. "But if the guards have been here once already, they'll be back."

"Wouldn't you want them to find you?" he asked.

"Not these ones. They're looking for something of value and they think I have it."

"What?"

"A wooden box. That's why they killed the woman you found me with by the water. And that's why they will kill us too, even if we don't have it."

She told him everything: what had happened in the laundry room, at the clotheslines, the smuggling attempt, how it all seemed linked to Mrs. Suds's arrest and her grandmother's death. Though Elia couldn't see him, she felt Hokk's concern like an aura around his body when she finished her story.

"You're thinking it's better just to leave me behind, aren't you?" she said. Hokk did not respond. It was enough of an answer. She stepped away and tried to muster strength in her voice. "Doesn't matter. I can continue on my own."

"No." He paused, as if still not sure. "No, it's better we stay together. We can help each other."

A spark of hope rekindled within Elia. "Then we have to keep moving. You have to take me to your city."

"I will."

"How long?"

"We'll be there in about two days."

Two more days! How could they last that long, without cover, on the bare prairie?

Elia heard a click. "What was that?" she whispered.

"That was me," said Hokk, pulling her arms forward. She felt cold metal against her skin and heard the rope drop to the ground. Her hands were finally free. They felt almost weightless.

"Thank you," said Elia, tenderly massaging her wrists. She then reached through the obscurity of the night until she touched him, her hand firmly grasping his leather collar. "But they'll return," she warned him again. "And we'll have little chance in the daylight."

"Then there's no time to waste." Hokk took her hand and led her through the darkness. "We'll leave now and travel only at night."

Chapter **22**

"CLIMB UP THERE," HE SAID, "and wait for me."

Elia looked up at the solitary tree. Its bark was smooth and the trunk split at shoulder height before dividing multiple times. Leaves grew in tufts like big mushroom caps at the end of each branch.

"Will that give us enough cover?" she wondered aloud.

"It will have to do."

Hokk had said he wanted to find this tree by daybreak, that it was his second stash out on the prairies and he needed to collect the rest of his stuff, whatever that meant. They had ridden for hours in the darkness, and Elia had marveled at his ability to navigate.

"How can you see?" she had asked when they first started off. "It's completely black out here."

This had surprised him. "Not completely. Can't you get a faint sense of the surroundings?"

"No," she had replied. Was he seeing something her eyes couldn't?

Sure enough, they spotted his tree shortly after dawn, the silhouette of its branches in the distance. It would be their shelter during the day until they could resume traveling that night.

Hokk boosted Elia to the first fork, and she climbed higher into the tree's leafy dome. He didn't follow.

"Aren't you coming too?" she asked as he passed up his tent and bag for Elia to keep with her.

"I want to find my stuff first. I'll be fast."

Hokk circled the tree trunk, inspecting its surface until something caught his eye. Elia watched as he turned and then walked away with his eyes fixed on a point straight ahead. He seemed to be counting his paces.

Nervously watching the sky through the leaves, Elia kept glancing back at Hokk where he was hunched over in the grasses. Nym was beside him and the gazelk grazed close by.

"Hurry," she whispered.

When Elia saw the stallions in the sky, she almost slipped from the branch. Gliding on outstretched wings, they flew in tight formation, moving rapidly across the prairies toward the tree.

"Hokk!" she hissed, praying the wind would carry his name to his ears.

The stallions were very low when they flew overhead a few moments later. The surrounding leaves were dense, and in her plain, dirty dress, Elia hoped she was well camouflaged. Thankfully, the guards did not hover above the treetop, but circled the gazelk instead.

Trembling, Elia shifted on her branch to get a better view. To her astonishment, Hokk had disappeared. Nym too.

"This is it?" she heard one of the men call out. "This is what we've been tracking?"

"It's a dead end," replied another. "Let's give up."

"We have our orders."

"Forget the orders. She either drowned or died from the fall just like that woman we found by the water. Wrasse is being obsessive."

"Then who left the smaller footprints in the sand? We've tracked this animal all the way from there."

"We should have followed the other tracks that led into the mountains. *That's* where we'll find her."

"What about the rope we found a distance back? Isn't that the rest of it tied around the animal's neck?"

Elia and Hokk had not thought to take the piece of rope when Hokk finally cut it off.

"Did anyone check the tree?" someone suggested.

Elia's stomach knotted. This was it.

"Leave that to me," said one of the guards as he turned his horse around and flew back toward her. He hovered over the tree, looking down, so near that his horse kicked some of the smaller branches. Leaves and twigs fell onto Elia's face. The horse then dropped lower, level with Elia, almost close enough to touch. She wished she could disintegrate and blow away with the wind.

Although the guard's face was covered, Elia felt the dead, reflective stare of his mirrored helmet bore into her. She pressed herself into the tree trunk as if to become one with it, yet she was unable to look away.

Then Elia noticed the spike protruding from his metal forehead.

The guard swung back to his group. "All clear," he said. "You might be right about those tracks heading toward the mountains. Let's check them out so we can finish this nonsense."

His horse flew off. The others followed, except one straggler who circled the gazelk again, sweeping in close for a last look. This time, the gazelk threw back its head, threatening the horse with its horns. The guard kicked his heels into his steed, and the horse beat its wings to catch up, struggling for a moment against the wind.

Elia could not move. No doubt this time—the guard with the spiked helmet had definitely seen her. He could have reached out and pulled her from the limb. Why didn't he?

She stared into the sky, but could no longer see any trace. She then glanced back to the spot where she had last seen Hokk. Below the gazelk's belly, where it had longer, shaggy hair, something dropped to the grass.

Hokk!

It was the perfect hiding spot, clinging to the underside of the animal. He had the mind of a survivor.

Hokk double-checked the sky first before crawling out. He looked up triumphantly toward Elia in the tree and waved. She could tell he couldn't see her through the foliage.

"You still there?" he called out.

"Yes."

"What a sight! I thought I was hallucinating again!"

Hokk returned to the spot where he had been earlier and started digging. Before long, he pulled something from the ground and shook off the dirt. It was another bag like the one already hidden in the tree. He walked back and stood below her. "Those flying horses were incredible! Just as you described, but until you actually see them in person—wow! And now I can understand why you were afraid they'd find us." Hokk tossed the second sack up to Elia.

"What's in here?" she asked. *He won't tell me,* she thought.

"Stuff."

She was right. "Just stuff, is it?"

Hokk didn't answer. He hoisted himself to the first limb and settled on a branch a little lower than Elia's.

Elia tried again. "What's inside that you would want to bury?"

"Things I found a long time ago. Things I didn't want stolen, but that I want to take back with me now."

"Like what?"

Hokk shrugged. "I don't know. Scraps of leather. Tools. Interesting pieces of plastic."

"Plastic?"

"Like this." Hokk unhooked a piece of debris snagged in the branches. It was the same material Elia had seen drifting everywhere.

She studied the flimsy substance. Plastic. "I thought it was some sort of stretchy fabric."

Hokk considered this description. "I suppose you could look at it that way. Indestructible fabric."

"You . . . collect that?"

"No," he said, tossing it away. They both watched it float to the ground. "That type of plastic is garbage. I collect things that are useful. Like those water bottles."

"That's plastic too?"

"There's no plastic up there?" he asked, nodding toward the clouds.

"No. Where does it come from?"

"It's everywhere."

"So you don't grow it."

"Of course not. It's man-made," he said. "The Ancients made it, lots of it. It's easy to find and it lasts forever. But most of it is useless."

Elia held up the sack. "Can I look inside?"

"No." Hokk held out his hand, and Elia knew she had to hand it over. He tied it around the branch and let it hang beneath him. He used the other sack as a pillow and stretched out along the limb.

Elia looked down at the bag swinging like a pendulum. "They might spot that."

"They're not coming back."

"I think they will."

Hokk had closed his eyes, but opened one briefly to look at her. "Try to get some rest."

He seemed so relaxed, but could he really sleep and remain balanced on the branch? Of course he could. He had already impressed her with his ability to build fires, endure the wet and cold, and travel day or night across a barren landscape knowing exactly where he was going. He was made for this environment.

As Elia looked down to judge whether she could survive a fall herself, she saw Nym wander out from the grasses with a mouse clenched between his jaws. He used his front paws to hold it down as he pulled it apart with his teeth. She envied the fox's ability to find his own food so easily. Another survivor. Elia wished she could do the same. She was hungry. If she could just have some water.

"Do you have water?" she blurted out.

Hokk shook his head, his eyes closed.

"Will we find some tonight?"

"It won't be long," he said.

Elia noticed Hokk glance at the festering clouds in the sky, and knew what it meant. She dreaded the thought of more rain.

Chapter 23

THE CITY OF AGO LOOMED out of the rain and mist of the dismal dawn. Pinpricks of light winked from a few buildings, but there was no other sign of welcoming warmth or life. This city appeared dead, more so than Hokk remembered it.

Outlined against the sky, its buildings looked like crumbling pillars, and the tallest of these were located in the center. Surrounding them was a swarm of other structures that diminished in size the farther away they stood.

Hokk could tell Elia was not impressed. "It's too early," he said. "Most people will still be sleeping."

Quite a distance remained before they would reach the city. Elia sat behind Hokk on the gazelk as she had all night. When they first started out, he had again sensed her reluctance to touch him, but as the hours wore on and fatigue set in, she slipped her arms around his waist and rested her head against his back. Hokk had wrapped his cloak around them, but raindrops from the ceaseless downpour had been dribbling down the neckline the entire journey. Only Nym was dry where he napped under the cloak, curled up in Hokk's lap.

"We've almost reached the boundary," Hokk said, pointing ahead.

Elia peered around his shoulder. "The buildings still seem so far off."

"See where the grass ends?"

The carpet of grasses stopped at the edge of an extremely wide band of dirt that had turned to mud with the rain.

"It's so bare," she said.

"The city maintains it. It completely circles the city for protection."

"From what?"

"Lightning strikes can cause grassfires, particularly when it's been dry for too long. When the flames get whipped up by the wind, they can race across the plains incredibly fast. If they ever reached the city, the damage could be horrendous."

"Wouldn't the water from the sky be enough to stop them?"

"Yes, but it doesn't always rain when there's lightning."

Reaching the mud, the gazelk struggled to cross, its hooves sticking in the mire. As each leg was pulled free, the holes left behind quickly filled with water.

"We never try to cross when it's wet like this."

"Maybe we should wait."

"No. I want to arrive while it's still early. It'll be quite a while before the rain lets up."

"How can you be so sure?"

Hokk looked up at the clouds and shrugged. "I can just tell."

The onslaught of water was pulverizing the muddy ground, leaving small craters in the muck and weighing down the plastic debris so it couldn't blow around.

"Can plastic burn?" Elia asked as the gazelk mashed a piece of it into the sludge.

"Not really," he said. "It just melts. Why?"

"If plastic burned, it could carry fire across this barrier to the city."

"The dirt barrier is wide enough to stop anything like that."

Elia thought for a moment. "So what if the fire was to start within the city limits?"

Hokk's back straightened as his muscles tensed. "We hope that's never the case." He wondered if Elia could hear the strain in his voice.

"But what if it does?"

Hokk remained silent, staring straight ahead.

"It's happened," she decided.

He hesitated. "Yes, it has." He hoped that was the end of her questions.

With the mud finally behind them, Hokk pointed to large, grass-covered knolls that dotted the terrain. "Those are ancient homes ahead of us," he said. "There's very little left of them now, but every mound you see used to be a building. Most of them have rotted in the rain and collapsed to be reclaimed by the prairies. And look there," he added, pointing to a rising column of crumbling red bricks. "A chimney." It leaned precariously, rising from the grave of the building to which it was once attached.

"It's hard to believe these used to be homes," said Elia. "And to let them just rot. People could still live in them."

"There's already plenty of space for everyone."

The gloom slowly faded as the morning aged. They traveled along roads overgrown with grass, and the gazelk picked its way through debris that had spilled into them. The shapes of old buildings became more obvious the farther they went. Though roofs had caved in, some walls had endured the impact of time and the elements.

"They've seen us by now, I'm sure," said Hokk.

Elia looked around. "Who?" She followed Hokk's gaze to the tops of the highest structures in the city center. No one was visible.

"Lookouts," said Hokk. "They might be expecting us when we arrive."

The streets remained deserted as they traveled. The

buildings now towered overhead and vegetation clung to their sides as if nature was lapping at the edges, ready to devour them back into the earth. Along the roadway, trees grew in the same, now-familiar mushroom shape, and faint blue layers of smoke drifted in the air. Nym emerged from under Hokk's cloak to balance between the gazelk's horns.

Few of the towers in the center of the city had outside walls. Fully exposed, the multiple floors were stacked one above the other, held up by internal columns. Scattered about, small fires burned on various levels, and runoff from the rain created waterfalls that fell from floor to floor, cascading over the edges.

On the second floor of one building, a stout man sat beside his fire. His hair was as dark as Hokk's, his skin as pale. The man steadily gazed at them, and Hokk knew he was focused on Elia's unusual appearance.

"Why don't the buildings have walls?" Elia asked.

"They used to. If you can imagine, the walls of these scrapers were once made of glass. Over time, however, they were all either broken by storms or earthquakes or removed for recycling."

"You call them scrapers?"

"*Sky*scrapers. They were built so tall, people at first thought they could scrape the sky."

Up ahead, a group of men emerged from the ground level of a nearby building. Hokk immediately slowed the gazelk's pace. Fortunately, the group lowered their heads as little waterfalls showered down from the floors above.

Elia must have noticed his reaction. "I don't think they saw us," she said.

"Hopefully not." He hadn't anticipated being so nervous, and couldn't help feeling as if he had some obvious marking that flagged him as an outcast. The few people they had already come across numbered almost as many as he had observed on the prairies since being exiled. There will be more, Hokk thought. Many more. Prepare yourself.

They carried on, street after street. Up ahead, a herd of gazelks huddled beneath another soaring structure that was open to the wind and rain. Hokk stopped beside them.

They had arrived.

Hokk remained sitting on his gazelk, unsure if he was ready to proceed. He could feel tightness in his throat and his stomach was queasy. Since crossing the dirt barrier, he had considered reversing direction several times to return to his peaceful solitude on the grasslands. Perhaps he was back too soon. Perhaps his reason for coming to the city would be unacceptable.

He just hoped he wouldn't have to see his brother.

Eager to get down, Nym whimpered softly. Hokk ran his hand along the fox's back as if rubbing a good luck charm.

"This is it," he finally said, jumping to the ground. Elia did the same and Nym squirmed until he was lifted down.

The fox led the way, clearly familiar with the area and excited to return. Stiff from the long ride, Hokk trudged behind with the two sacks slung over his shoulders. Elia carried his tent, tucked under an arm.

The building looked deserted. The ground floor was overrun with weeds. Hokk and Elia didn't enter, but moved along the side to a wide ramp—a tunnel—that spiraled down underground. It was devoid of vegetation, covered instead by a flat, rock-hard surface. Overhead, smoke curled along the high ceiling as it escaped from fires below.

"This isn't where you live, is it?" Elia whispered.

Hokk kept walking.

How often had he climbed this ramp as a young boy, racing other children to the top, or ducking inside to avoid the rain, eager to get home? He remembered helping his father bring loads of produce down to sell to the others who lived underground, and straining to prevent the cart from slipping out of his sweaty hands and rolling to the bottom. After that, the equally grueling task to push it back up.

And then there was that day. People had lined the sides of the tunnel, heads down, as his mother left the building for the last time. Such a spectacle of mourning for those who died was rare, but his father was influential, the family respected. Hokk's father and uncle helped carry the casket with his mother inside. Davim and Hokk followed behind, dragging their feet, dreading the moment when—

Don't think about it. Returning is hard enough.

Farther ahead, a faint light glowed from a torch on the wall. They were moving toward muffled commotion, as though a crowd awaited them. Hokk's anxiety grew.

Along the curving wall, they came upon a child sitting on the ramp with a ball between her legs. The little girl let go of it just as she looked up at Elia, her mouth hanging open with surprise. Another young girl was at the bottom, waiting to catch, but she too stared as Hokk and Elia approached. Her hands missed the ball as it rolled inside the entrance. Hokk followed it in, then stopped to take in the scene.

It felt as though he had never left.

The space was immense. And crowded. It was filled with adults and children, plus all their belongings stacked high, wherever they could find room. Row upon row of evenly spaced stone posts held up a ceiling that had disappeared behind a hovering blanket of smoke, woven from hazy threads that trailed up into the air.

At first glance, everything seemed to be in a state of disorder, but this underground community was organized. The square pillars marked off territories for each family. Neighbors were less than a foot away, but ropes were tied between the columns and hung with sheets and clothes for privacy. Crates lined the edges of properties, creating a cramped inner courtyard where food could be cooked and bedding laid out at night. As Elia passed each family unit,

Hokk noticed the children watching her with fascination. The parents often looked up too, trying to mask the shock on their faces.

Not everyone was allocated the same amount of floor space, and not every spot accommodated a family. A wizened old man sat alone in one roped-off area with a lifetime's worth of possessions piled around him. The man's silent, clouded eyes followed Elia, but Hokk wondered if he could actually see her features.

"How long since you've been back?" Elia asked, walking slowly to absorb it all.

"Quite a while."

"Like what? A couple months?" She stopped when Hokk didn't answer and looked at him. "Longer? A year?"

"Six," he mumbled.

"You haven't been back for six years?!"

"That's right," he sighed, lowering his head.

They walked farther before she continued. "And where does your family live?"

"At 358 to 367."

Elia frowned. "I don't understand."

With his foot, Hokk pointed to faded symbols painted on the floor. "Each spot is numbered."

She shrugged. "I can't read what those say."

"You can't count?"

Elia blushed. "Yes, I can count. I just can't read numbers."

"That's 77," he said, and then moved down to the next symbol, where he tapped his foot. "And that's 78. We still have a ways to go."

Hokk led Elia down the middle of the cavernous space. At the far end, a second ramp sloped downward, and Elia turned a puzzled face toward him. "There's a lower level," he said.

It was identical to the one above. They moved closer to the back corner. As the numbers on the family plots climbed,

Hokk could feel himself standing taller, his face steeling its expression to conceal his nerves and excitement.

Hokk stopped in front of a dwelling larger than any of the others. While most families occupied two sections, this one stretched over ten, an obvious sign of wealth.

With his back to them, a man crouched beside a central fire pit, stirring dying embers.

Hokk stood silently, waiting for his uncle to turn around, yet the man seemed unaware of their arrival. Hokk took a deep breath. "Blessings, Uncle," he said.

The man stopped moving. Slowly, he rose to his feet and turned.

Hokk flinched. "I . . . um," he faltered, looking at the markings on the floor, and then back at the man. "I thought . . . 358 . . . I was sure . . . I'm trying to find Charyl Feste."

The man knew the name. "You won't find him here."

"Where is he?"

"Dead."

"Dead!" Hokk staggered back a step and felt Elia grasp his arm. "He can't be!"

"It's been about two years now," the man said, grimacing. He now noticed Elia and did a double take.

"What about Una Feste?" Hokk blurted out.

The man pulled his gaze off Elia. "Alive," he said.

"Thank goodness. And where is she?"

"The next level up."

"Really?" Hokk was concerned. "She's moved up? Do you know where?"

The man shrugged. "I'm not sure. Maybe 27. Or 26. Somewhere in the twenties for sure." He considered it another moment. "Maybe even the early thirties."

"I can't believe it," Hokk muttered, pressing his hand against his forehead. "Simply can't believe it," he repeated as he spun and headed back toward the ramp. Elia followed close. "How could this have happened?" he asked, stopping and staring at Elia as if there was any possibility she might know.

"We'll just go find her on the first level then," she said gently. "We must have walked right by her."

"She should be down here. She belongs on the second level."

"They're both the same."

Hokk shook his head. "She's lost status," he said with dread in his voice.

"By moving up one level? Wouldn't that mean she's better off?"

"But he said 'or.' That she's at 26 *or* at 27. Not both. She has just one plot."

Surely it was all just a terrible mistake. Her wealth couldn't have been ravaged so much that she was now forced to live in the poorest section. If true, why hadn't his brother stepped in to restore the family's position?

Climbing back up, Hokk and Elia checked all the stalls in the twenties, but did not find Auntie Una. Families didn't live in these sections, not even couples. Individuals here were allocated only single plots, and most were occupied by lone men, probably old bachelors, surrounded more by piles of garbage than meaningful possessions. In a few spots, the men were so ancient they were restricted to lying on decrepit beds, either balanced on empty crates or stretched flat on the cold floor. A few had placed a small basket on top of their number, where free food could be tossed, but usually someone stole the donated morsels if the recipient was too frail to get out of bed. Hokk had always wondered how these men managed to survive. Would anyone care when they finally died, or would people walk by without even noticing? It was so easy to walk by now and ignore them.

In fact, Hokk very nearly passed Auntie Una without recognizing her. Chewing an empty pipe, now with short, scruffy hair, she looked like many of her bachelor neighbors.

And she seemed almost as feeble. But something about her caught Hokk's attention, and then he recognized her one-eared ginger cat. Auntie Una was sitting on the floor of stall number 33 with her back against a crate. Her cooking firepit was as cold as the pipe hanging from her lips, and rather than preparing any sort of meal, she simply sat there, eyeing passersby with vague interest and lazily picking at the fur of the cat sprawled beside her.

At first, the woman was more interested in the fox than the people who accompanied it, but then her eyes moved from Hokk's feet up the rest of his body. She squinted to see his face.

"Auntie Una?" murmured Hokk.

There was a flash of recognition in her eyes. She scrambled to her feet with a surprising burst of energy and stepped outside her assigned plot.

"I hoped to be dead before you ever returned," she spat between prune lips.

Chapter **24**

"WHAT DO YOU WANT FROM me?" hissed Auntie Una, her hands clenched into fists. Elia saw hatred burning in the old woman's eyes.

Hokk shook his head. "Nothing."

"Because I've got nothing. There's nothing left for you to take from me that hasn't already been taken."

"I'm just glad I found you," said Hokk.

This seemed to catch his aunt off guard. She glared up at her nephew who towered above. Her face was deathly white. Her matted hair was just as white, and her eyes were pale too, as if aging had drained away their color. The only contrast to her pallor was her red, receding gums around yellow-stained teeth.

"You're thin," she said.

"I'm fine."

"You probably don't eat out there. What's there to eat?"

"I eat," replied Hokk.

"You haven't eaten that mangy fox yet, I see."

"I've always gotten by."

"On what? Mice?"

"Sometimes."

"That's disgusting."

"But it's not always mice. Nym and I have actually become quite good at hunting."

"Humph," said Auntie Una with an indifferent wave of her hand. "I don't really care. Anyway, I'm stunned you would dare to show your face around here."

"Circumstances have changed and I've decided to take the chance to return."

"Humph," said Auntie Una again, turning her back on Hokk to rearrange a few tattered blankets, which Elia guessed to be the woman's only bedding.

"Auntie Una, what's happened since I last saw you?" asked Hokk in a careful tone. "I've just heard Uncle Charyl died. How did you end up here?"

"It's the curse of this family," she said, facing Hokk again. "It started with you and your mess, and then everything got worse. Davim went wild with it, raging over it, obsessing about honor and such nonsense. Of course his plans for marriage were destroyed, and your uncle and I were left to pay the price."

Auntie Una stopped to catch her breath. "I wish your mother had abandoned Davim years ago when she had the chance. Then I wouldn't have had to deal with either of you."

"He's not here, is he?" Hokk asked. Elia sensed his immediate concern.

"No, of course not."

"Where is he?"

"How should I know?" Una grumbled, turning away from them again.

Hokk looked back at Elia, his shoulders sagging. He appeared to be wilting, as if his aunt, this building—in fact, this entire city—was changing him.

Elia was losing hope too. Could anything or anyone in this ruined place help her get back home? Everybody here seemed to ignore each other, which was probably their only way to survive living so close together. The one exception Elia had noticed was an elderly man with a stall right beside Auntie Una's. He had been watching and listening with great interest. Elia could tell he found her particularly intriguing, making her wish she could be invisible.

"Who the devil is that?" growled Auntie Una, as if having read Elia's thoughts about remaining unnoticed. Elia lowered her face.

"She's the reason I've returned," Hokk said.

"What's wrong with her? She's so dark. And the hair!"

"I found her."

"You're a fool. You should have left her behind."

Elia felt her face flush. She couldn't bring herself to look up.

"She's not one of us, is she?" snapped Hokk's aunt.

Elia was startled when a bony hand came into view to grab her chin and lift her head.

Auntie Una's face contorted. "Ugly," she spat. "Dark and scrawny and ugly. Did you set fire to her too?"

Elia was stunned to hear such cruel words coming from a woman so old, with a face so marked and ugly itself. Elia glanced at Una for just a moment before looking away.

"Her eyes!" Auntie Una exclaimed. "Have you seen her eyes?"

"What about them?" croaked the old man from the neighboring stall.

"Shut up and mind your own business, you crazy old jackass!" bellowed Auntie Una. She turned back to Hokk as she grabbed Elia's jaw again with clawlike hands, holding her head still. "Have you seen them?" she asked again.

"Of course I've seen them."

"They're so strange. Why do they do that?" asked Auntie Una.

"I don't know," Hokk replied.

Why do they do what? Elia blinked and tried to pull away.

"There! They just did it again." Auntie Una sounded both thrilled and horrified at the same time.

"Enough!" Hokk stuck an arm between his aunt and Elia

to separate them, but the woman maintained her tight grasp on Elia's face.

"She's definitely not one of us," said Una.

"No, she's not. She's from Above."

Auntie Una shoved Elia's head away. "And you bring her here?" she cried as she stormed back into her marked territory. She narrowly missed colliding with a boy carrying a handful of live chickens by their legs. The youth glanced at Elia, and he too was startled by her appearance. He hurried away, looking back at her twice.

Hokk followed his aunt into her stall, where Una angrily began stuffing empty plastic bags into a container. Her cat was stretching on a crate beside her, but with a quick swipe of her hand, the cat was thrown to the ground.

"I *am* cursed!" she moaned. "I can't believe you would do something so senseless. If she's really from Above, she should be dead."

"Well, she's not."

"Exactly, that's my concern. She should be." With her frantic motions, Hokk's aunt knocked over a small stack of metal plates and they crashed to the floor. Both the cat and Nym jumped out of the way.

"They are going to find out you've returned. Don't think they won't," Auntie Una sneered.

"I know," said Hokk. "And I want to see the Board as soon as I can. I want to show them what I've found."

The Board? Elia's eyes widened.

"You're stupid. The Board won't be interested," said Una.

"They must meet her. I'm sure she will be of great importance to them."

"They'll have you banished again, just you wait. And double the time too, I bet!"

"We'll see."

"Well, like I told you before, I have nothing to give you. Not even food. So you might as well leave."

Hokk ground his teeth. "And like I said before, I'm not looking for anything!"

With that, he whipped around and marched off, pulling Elia by the arm.

The curious man in the adjacent stall strained to catch a glimpse of Elia's face, to see whatever made her eyes so surprising, but to no avail. She never gave him a chance.

Chapter 25

HOKK AND ELIA EMERGED INTO the pouring rain.

"The streets are busier now," Elia observed, trying to draw Hokk out of his sullen mood.

Hokk looked around and sighed. "Yes. Unfortunately."

"Where are they going?"

"Most are heading out to the crops," he replied. "The others to tend animals."

"Really?" said Elia. "I've seen neither since we arrived."

"I'll show you. We're headed there anyway."

Hokk hugged the sides of the buildings as they walked, studying both the people on the street and those tending their small fires in the towers. Occasionally, he would pause, holding up a hand for Elia to stop before deciding it was safe to proceed. "I don't want anyone following us," he said as he quickened his pace.

Elia preferred being outside where people were busy and more likely to ignore her. Thankfully, the tower they were approaching looked abandoned, but Elia still frowned. The remains of the scraper were charred black as if flames had once consumed it. Was it even safe to enter?

"Don't worry," said Hokk, noticing her concern. "It looks worse than it is."

"Are we going underground?"

"It's blocked," said Hokk as he pointed to the barricade across the ramp's entrance.

With Nym leading the way, they entered the first level of the building. Once again, there were no outside walls. The floor was overgrown with vegetation, and Elia found it strange to see plants growing under cover. The ceiling and surrounding support beams had the same burnt look as she had noticed from the outside, and a faint smell of smoke hung in the air like a lingering ghost.

"There doesn't seem to be anything here," she said.

"There isn't," replied Hokk. "But we will be safe and left alone for a while. And it will be a chance for us to sleep."

Elia realized just how exhausted she felt. A safe place to sleep was exactly what she needed.

Hokk tied the gazelk to a post beside a set of stairs in the middle of the main floor and then they climbed, one level after another. Elia's legs began to ache. How high did they have to go? After several more flights of stairs, Hokk stopped. The eleventh floor. Covered with grasses, it was no different from the others.

"This stuff grows everywhere!" said Elia, panting.

"The grass? It's always grown here, even before the building was abandoned."

"Inside like this?"

"Most of these towers have crops growing within them, or animals grazing. It just depends on what the farm produces."

Elia's forehead wrinkled. "The towers are farms?"

"Yes." He raised an eyebrow. "Let me guess. They do it differently in Above."

"They do. In fields. Fields that stretch out in the countryside."

"Sounds inefficient," said Hokk as he tossed his two sacks to the ground. "Doesn't it make more sense to grow them together like this, all clustered in one area?"

"I suppose so," Elia replied. She dropped Hokk's tent beside his bags and walked toward the edge of the building to observe the neighboring towers. "We don't have any other options, though. There aren't old buildings we can use this way."

"Not too close," Hokk warned. "We don't want people to see us, remember."

Lying flat on her stomach, Elia pulled herself closer to the edge. She stuck out her head and water droplets dripped down on her from the floor above. Looking over made her feel dizzy, and she clung anxiously to the ledge. When something pressed against her arm, she jumped. "You startled me," she gasped, realizing Hokk had crawled up beside her.

"Do you see what I was saying?" He pointed to the nearby towers. "There, in that one. Herds of sheep."

Focusing across the street, Elia was surprised to see sheep grazing on several floors. On one level, a small fire was tended by a shepherd sitting against an outside column, dangling his leg over the side.

"Only the one person to look after them all?" she asked.

"Sheep never attempt the stairs."

"So why have a shepherd?"

"To keep people out. To be on the lookout for anyone trespassing."

"Are we trespassing now?"

Hokk shifted uncomfortably. "No, we're not," he replied as he started massaging his neck. "This building has been abandoned. There's nothing left to protect."

Though intrigued by his unease, Elia did not question further. Instead, she shifted her attention to workers in a different tower who were bending over low-growing plants, pulling them out at their roots. "I can't see what they're harvesting."

Hokk followed her gaze. "It looks like the potatoes are ready." He pointed to another building where tall, stiff stalks grew on each floor, creating a dense mass of green leaves. "Do you know what's growing over there?" he asked.

"Looks like corn."

"Yes, that's right. I wondered if they grew that in Above."

"I've seen corn. But I thought it needed lots of sunshine to grow. It looks too dark in there. Same with the potatoes. How does anything get enough light?"

"Not all plants can grow well in these conditions," Hokk explained, "but these particular ones have been modified to thrive in areas of low light."

"I don't understand."

"They've been *altered*—changed so they can grow where they would never have survived in ancient times."

"How can they be changed?" Elia asked.

"It's a mystery. The Ancients devised a way to manipulate the characteristics of many things. Apparently, this became very important as they realized the sky was growing darker. Now, the city's Seed Keeper has a carefully guarded collection of countless varieties, both natural and redesigned, but whenever it comes time to plant or rotate the crops, he always recommends the seeds that have been altered."

"It sounds . . . disturbing," Elia decided. "Makes me wonder what else they might have modified."

Hokk grimaced. "I've wondered about that too. When it's all you've ever known, how can you really tell if something is natural or not?"

"Exactly."

"Yet sometimes you come across things that are so unusual, you just know they must have been modified."

"Like what?"

Hokk looked at her and then glanced away.

"Like what?" she repeated. Why did he keep things from her?

"Like your eyes, for example," he said quietly.

"My eyes!" Elia exclaimed. "Why is everyone so astounded by my eyes?"

Hokk hesitated. "It's the way—they kind of—" He sighed. "It's when you blink."

"When I blink?" She pushed herself up on her elbows. "And what about the way I blink makes you think I've been *altered*?"

Hokk took a deep breath. "I've just never seen anyone with a second set of eyelids before."

Chapter 26

HOKK WAS UNSURE WHETHER ELIA'S cheeks were turning red from humiliation or anger.

"I-I-I'm stunned," Elia finally sputtered.

"It's nothing bad," he reassured her. "It's just something I've never seen before. You seem to have inner eyelids that close, even though your eyes are still open. It's like there's a transparent layer, or . . . a membrane, I suppose, that tints them darker. Usually, it's not obvious because both blink in unison. But sometimes, the inner eyelids close separately on their own and you're looking at me with your eyes shaded." Was he making himself clear? It was hard to tell from her expression. "It only seems to happen when you are mad at me," he added with an uneasy laugh.

Hokk stopped talking and waited. He rolled onto his side to face Elia, watching as her eyelids blinked, one set after the other.

"You probably don't know what I'm talking about," said Hokk. "You probably don't even know you do it."

Elia slowly nodded her head. "No, I know exactly what you're talking about," she said in a measured tone. "Of course I've seen this."

"Oh, you have?" Hokk marveled.

"Yes. Everyone from Above has these same eyes."

"But you looked so surprised when I mentioned it."

"What stuns me is you think I was *modified* somehow to be this way. This is how I was born. We all were. And no one has altered us. Maybe *you're* the one who has been modified."

Hokk picked at blades of grass, searching for something to say to break the awkward silence that had settled between them. "I bet it's useful for something," he eventually blurted out. "Something that benefits your people in a way that would offer no advantage to us. I just can't think what it could be."

"I can," said Elia as she too rolled onto her side to face Hokk. "Protection for our eyes. The sunlight gets too intense."

"It really gets that bright up there?"

"Every single day."

Hokk half-chuckled to himself. "Amazing, isn't it? The variety. That whether it was natural or not, your people would develop in a certain way, but not us. We start from the same place, but we change or can be changed to suit the different environments we end up living in."

Elia sat up. "When you say it like that, it sounds like you still think we share the same origins."

Hokk quickly placed a hand on her shoulder, pressing her to lie flat again. "Don't let them see you."

"They can't . . ."

"Just do it," he insisted as he started to move away from the edge.

The two of them crawled back until they were safely out of view. Once standing, Elia glared at him. "You do think that, don't you? That we have the same origins."

"Does it matter?" Hokk replied, turning away to walk back to his tent and supplies.

"We are *not* like you," Elia insisted as she followed him. "We're not like anyone from Below, because we're not from here. It's obvious just looking at the two of us."

Hokk held up his hand to stop her. "Yes, I know." There was obviously no convincing this girl. "Look, we are both exhausted and we just need to sleep," he said as he unrolled his tent.

"Sleep won't change what I'm saying!"

"Fine!" Hokk spun around, his face just an inch from her own. "I'm from Below and you're from Above, from the moon, or whatever you call it. But explain this then"—Hokk's eyes narrowed—"If our homes have always been separate, and we were never one and the same people, then how is it we speak the same language? How can we understand each other's words?"

He stared her down, but Elia could only stand with her mouth open. She had no answer to offer.

Chapter 27

HOKK HAD LEFT HER SPEECHLESS before crawling into his tent without another word. Now Elia sat alone, her back against a pillar.

Her thoughts gave her no peace. Her grandmother's advice played again and again in her mind. *Perceptions deceive. Things are often not as they seem.*

She wanted to shrug off Hokk's frustrating comments but couldn't. They made her feel troubled, as if something inside her, normally undisturbed, had been shaken awake. For all she had ever believed to be true, Hokk had said enough for her to start doubting what she knew. Or thought she knew.

Speaking the same language was easy to take for granted, but Elia could not deny it was remarkable. How could people from two separate worlds have the same words for everything, or at least for the things shared in common?

But his idea of people from Above and Below sharing the same origins? The concept was mind-boggling—completely opposite to what she had always been taught. Her ancestors came from the moon. That was a fact, wasn't it? She did sometimes wonder how the people of Above had survived the moon's destruction, but surely an accurate account of the

System's history had been passed down through the generations. Elia could think of no reason to deceive people. Besides, her beliefs didn't have to crumble because of a few naive remarks from Hokk. What did he know anyway? He had never even seen the sun!

Yet Elia had never seen rain before. Nor clouds overhead. She had been taught to be afraid of Scavengers with no eyes, who collected the dead. And look how wrong that turned out to be.

Elia stretched on her side and rested her head on her arm, staring at Hokk's tent. How would she ever be able to find out the truth?

• • •

The barking was incessant, tinged with the frantic shrill of outrage and fear. A man yelled and cursed.

Tucked tight against the base of the pillar, Elia awoke from a deep, dreamless sleep.

Nym sprang back and forth, challenging the intruder with snarling fangs as though he were a much more ferocious animal.

"Get out here, Hokk, you miserable bastard!" the man yelled as he pulled at the tent.

When Nym charged to bite his heels, the man swung his foot, kicking the fox in the ribs. Nym yelped but did not back down.

Elia cowered against the pillar. The man was taller than Hokk, heavier, but just as pale, with a goatee braided into two points.

"I know you're back, Hokk!" the man shouted, and then turned to Nym. "Shut up!" He tried to strike the fox again with his swinging foot, but missed. "Shut up, damn it!"

With the tent coming down around him, Hokk struggled to get out. When his arms appeared, he was hauled into the open, but the man's hands were choking his throat before

Hokk could get to his feet. Gasping, Hokk reached up to loosen the vice on his neck.

The man jerked Hokk close to his face. Saliva spit from his mouth. "You made a huge mistake returning here."

Pushing against the man's chest, Hokk broke free from his hold, and stumbled backward.

The man looked disgusted. "And to find you here of all places. I can still smell the stink!"

"I knew you would find me, Davim," said Hokk with contempt. "But why did it take you so long?"

"You're back too soon," said Hokk's brother. "You're not welcome and they won't stand for it."

"We'll let them decide that."

"The Board gave you their sentence, which you now choose to disobey."

"So be it."

"So be it?" Davim sneered. "Brave words coming from a fool. There's no future for you here. I'll make sure of it."

"You don't have the influence," said Hokk. "You might think you do, but you don't."

Nym silently crept forward; his stealthy approach, however, had not gone unnoticed.

"The Board may decide your fate," said Davim as he reached down, catching the fox in his large hands. Nym yelped as Davim lifted him high above his head, threatening to throw him outside. "But I'll decide his!"

"No! Don't!" Elia shrieked without thinking.

Davim paused, allowing the whimpering fox to wriggle from his grasp. He turned in the direction of Elia's voice and saw her shrinking against the pillar.

"Ah, the girl!" he said. "Yes, I heard about the girl!"

Elia trembled as Davim moved toward her. She tried to dive behind the column as he lunged, but he grabbed her legs, bringing her down. He pulled her through the grass by the ankles, her dress bunching up to her hips, and pinned her with his body.

Although Davim's features resembled Hokk's, up close he was too frightening to look at. Elia squeezed her eyes shut. She could feel his breath on her face. His odor filled her nose. He stunk of alcohol.

She flung her head to the side, but he grabbed her face, as Auntie Una had done, although with hands much larger and stronger. Elia felt his chest and stomach vibrate against her body as he chuckled.

"Well, she's ugly," laughed Davim. "But is she a freak? Let's see those eyes, girl."

Elia twisted her head away again when his fingers touched her eyelids.

Suddenly, there was a cracking sound, followed by a grunt. Elia opened her eyes and saw Hokk standing over them. He held something solid in his hands.

His knife.

The heavy handle had struck Davim hard, cutting open one side of his brow. A few drops of his blood dribbled onto Elia's cheek.

The dazed expression on Davim's face did not last long, and he touched the wound. Seeing the blood enraged him. Pressing his hands painfully against Elia's chest, he pushed himself off. "I'm going to kill you," he said to his brother with a seething voice.

Hokk stood his ground, the blade of his weapon still closed.

Breathless, Elia used the pillar to haul herself to her feet and watched Davim and Hokk circling each other with hate in their eyes.

"Get out of here," Hokk commanded.

Elia didn't realize he meant her.

"Elia, go! Get out!" screamed Hokk.

She hesitated. Could she desert him?

Hokk charged his brother. Davim stepped to the side, then swung around, pushing Hokk against the pillar where Elia was standing. She moved out of the way just in time, but her gaze remained locked on Hokk's face pressed up against the rock-hard surface.

His eyes flared at her. "Go!"

Elia ran. She bolted down the staircase, spiraling around and around until she reached the main level. She darted past the gazelk, out into the open air, then quickly stepped back against the building, afraid someone from the floors above would see her.

She inched along the side, glad the street was empty, until she reached the barricaded entrance of the ramp. She wouldn't have to descend all the way down. The shadows near the top could hide her while she waited for the victor to come out.

Chapter 28

ELIA DIDN'T KNOW HOW LONG she had been waiting. It felt like an hour. Neither Hokk nor Davim had emerged, though she could have missed them leaving from any other side of the burnt tower. She bit a dirty fingernail as she peered around the ramp's barricade.

The rain had stopped and the street was empty. Cautiously stepping into the open, she kept her head down, and with a few quick strides and twice as many rapid heartbeats, she was back under the first-floor ceiling.

Hokk's gazelk was gone. Some of the rope was still tied to the post where the animal had been tethered, but a knife had sliced through it. Elia imagined Hokk being chased down the stairs, desperate to cut the gazelk free so they could escape—likely without a second thought about Elia. He had abandoned her in this abandoned city.

She ran her hands through her hair. Where should she go now? She didn't want to wander through the city attracting curious stares. She needed food, water—all the essential provisions. Perhaps Hokk had left something behind in his haste.

Elia climbed to the eleventh floor, but Hokk's supplies and tent were gone. The grasses were trampled and the pillar had a shocking splash of blood on it. She stepped back into the stairwell and noticed for the first time drops of blood on the charred floor, trailing down the steps she had just taken.

A shuffling sound came from the stairs above.

Flattening herself against the wall, Elia expected to see Davim's feet come rushing at her. Instead, she saw paws, and then the rest of Nym descend, warily stopping halfway down to stare at her.

Elia patted her thighs, coaxing the fox to come closer. "Come on. Come here."

The fox was hesitant and kept glancing back up the staircase.

Elia understood: she was to follow. As Nym bounded ahead, he looked back frequently to make sure she was still behind. Elia was sweating by the time she reached the top floor. The staircase ended within a small enclosure, as blackened as the rest of the tower. It no longer had a door and opened directly onto the roof.

Stepping out, Elia was awed by the view. Most of the other scrapers were well below her, and the panoramic sky extended on all sides as it had on the grasslands. A massive expanse of rock, however, had emerged through the mist, looming above the City of Ago, impossibly weightless.

An island of Above.

Home.

Well, not quite her home, since only the one dagger pierced the clouds. But certainly more her home than where she was now. It seemed so close, as if Elia could just reach up and grab the island's rocky tip.

Nym barked. He sat on his haunches, glancing from her to something behind the staircase enclosure.

As Elia approached, she noticed an object poking out from around the corner. Hokk's tent. A few steps more and she saw a sack, then a second one. Elia came around the side and her heart surged. Hokk was sitting, leaning against the enclosure's wall with his arms across his knees and his head tucked under.

"Hokk!" she exclaimed. "What are you doing up here?"

His neck seemed sore as he slowly lifted his head. He had a black eye, and a battered nose that had bled over his lips and down his chin.

"Oh my goodness!" Elia gasped, kneeling beside him.

"Are you all right?" Hokk asked in a croaky voice.

"Of course I am. But what about you?"

"It's nothing," he groaned.

"You look dreadful. I can't believe you climbed all the way up here in your condition." Elia placed a comforting hand on his arm, and used the other to gently brush away the dirt on his cheek. "Let's get you clean."

Hokk turned his head away. "No, don't bother."

"Do we still have water?"

"It's not necessary."

Elia ignored him and picked up one of the sacks.

"No. No, don't . . ." Hokk protested.

"Don't worry. I won't snoop," Elia replied as she reached inside. She noticed his anxious eyes relax when she removed nothing more than a crushed bottle half-full of water. "See. I thought we had a bit more."

"It's the last one."

"Shh," said Elia as she untwisted the cap and held the bottle to his lips.

Hokk gulped eagerly, drops spilling around the edges of his puffy mouth.

"There." She poured the last of the water into her hand, and carefully washed away the dried blood around his lips.

Hokk watched her intently. Her eyes met his for a fleeting moment. She blushed and lowered her head, wiping her hands on the top of her dress where it seemed the cleanest. "That'll have to do," she said.

"Thank you."

Elia sat back on her heels. "I thought you had left. Your gazelk's gone."

"It's gone?" Hokk sat up straighter. He slouched again just as quickly. "Of course it is."

"The rope was cut with a knife. I assumed it was you."

"I don't have the knife anymore."

"Oh." Elia paused and picked at a loose thread on her dress. After a few minutes, she said quietly, "Was it bad?"

"Yes," he whispered.

Elia glanced up and saw his eyes were closed. "He's horrible," she said.

"Davim's crazy, even without alcohol," Hokk replied, his face grim. "He's actually gone mad over the years. I hope I don't follow the same path."

"Why would you say that?"

Hokk didn't answer. Instead, he rested his forehead on his crossed arms.

Elia leaned against the wall beside him and waited in silence.

"It's like he's hated me from the start," Hokk finally mumbled, his face still hidden. "And I hate him too." He lifted his head to see her reaction.

"I can see why."

"Do you hate anyone in your family?"

"No."

"Do you have a brother or sister?"

"A brother. He's older than me as well." As Elia said this, she glanced up to the island floating above. Sitting next to Hokk now reminded her of the day of Omi's funeral, when Rayhan, wearing his new boots, joined her at the back of their small house. His presence had given her the support she needed, which was something Hokk had probably never experienced with his own brother.

Hokk's gaze followed Elia's into the sky. "You miss your family."

"I'm afraid for them. For what's happened to them."

"And they seem so close."

"They do." The words came from her mouth as though drifting on the faintest breeze.

"Yet you don't recognize it, do you? That's your island up there again."

Elia spun back to Hokk. "It isn't!"

"It is. Not the same angle as before, so you can't see the smaller one following it. But that's definitely the one you fell from. Though I'm surprised it's circled back so soon."

Elia stared at the island with such intensity her eyes watered. "Is there any way for me to get home?" she asked. "With the Board's help, I mean."

"We'll know better tomorrow. They'll have to convene for certain now that I've returned. Davim will make sure of it."

Hokk stretched his legs and looked at his feet for a long while. "Just sitting here like this reminds me of that day. After everything that's happened, I can't believe it doesn't feel that long ago." He raised his head and stared out past the rooftop, appearing not to be focused on anything. "I was stupid, really, to have come here. It was like I had to see it again, just one last time."

"It makes sense though. It's been so many years, of course you would want to come back to the city."

"I don't mean the city. I mean this building." Hokk turned to face Elia.

She sensed he had something important to say but he was holding back. "You can tell me," she encouraged him.

Nym wandered over, sniffed Hokk's outstretched hand, and began to lick it. Hokk paid no attention. "I was tending chickens. You know chickens, right?"

"I've eaten chicken a few times," said Elia.

"Not that. I'm talking about how they have to be watched, especially when it's time to harvest them."

Elia raised an eyebrow. "I'm not sure what you mean."

"When they first hatch, the chicks are kept in the lower levels of a building, underground where it's warmer. Once they put on enough weight, large flocks are brought up to the fresh air of the higher floors to finish growing. This tower was used like that—as a chicken farm. The time to move them is very important, however, because when the birds are forty-five days old, like clockwork, they start dropping all their feathers."

Elia started to laugh. "You mean one minute the chickens have feathers, and the next moment they're naked?"

"Almost, just not as fast as you describe. It begins with a few birds, which seems to trigger the rest. Within about three hours of the process starting, the birds have completely molted, and there are feathers floating everywhere. Let me guess—your chickens never lose their feathers."

"They do, but only when we pluck them out."

"Really? That would be so much extra work."

"It is."

Hokk pursed his lips. "See, here again is another thing that makes me wonder. Have our birds been modified in some way by the Ancients—as if they were *designed* with a built-in timer to make it so convenient?"

"I don't know. But it must be quite a sight," Elia added with a grin. "Naked chickens flapping about in a sea of feathers."

Hokk gave a half-hearted laugh. "Yes, I suppose it is."

The humor had lightened the mood, but only for a very brief moment. Hokk quickly slipped back into a melancholy state. "If I had just—" he started and then stopped, struggling to explain. "My uncle had warned me that as the chickens neared their time to molt, I was not supposed to have any flames burning. Since we keep careful records, I knew that particular morning was day forty-five after hatching, but because I was cold, I started a fire."

Hokk's face distorted with the pain of the memory and he lowered his voice. "There was a spectacular storm rolling in over the city, and without thinking, I left the fire burning when I ran up to the roof to watch the lightning. Only when I heard people yelling from other buildings and from the street did I turn and see smoke coming up through the stairwell."

Hokk sat silent for a moment, remembering.

"I guess the molt started while I was on the roof. The fire must have ignited the drifting feathers, and they, in turn, started fires in the dry grass that covered the floor. Any birds that hadn't completed their molting probably caught fire too, and in a panic began flying to other levels, also covered with grass, which is how the flames spread so quickly."

Again, he paused to steady his emotions.

"Six floors of chickens on fire. Soon the entire building was engulfed, and the people who lived below had to be evacuated. Many were already tending crops or animals in other towers, but for those still here, most got out. They watched from the street as burning feathers and birds dropped from the sky. I was trapped on the roof and got badly burned, beating back the flames."

Both Hokk and Elia looked at his hands and forearms, where the rippling scars were a lasting reminder. Hokk self-consciously crossed his arms as if trying to hide them from view. Elia looked at her own arms, the skin cracked and red with sores from working in the laundry.

His face twisted with regret, and he couldn't look at Elia as he continued. "There was no rain with this storm, so people below were frantically trying to put out the fires that had started at street level. They were panicking, desperate to prevent the fire from taking over the city."

"But it didn't," Elia murmured almost breathlessly.

"No, it didn't. Yet the flames were able to reach the lower levels underground, and possessions were destroyed. And eight people died. Most were old, but there was a baby and her sick mother who was too ill to escape. They all died from the smoke."

As he recounted this last detail, Hokk grabbed two handfuls of his disheveled hair and pulled, rubbing his palms on his forehead as though trying to squeeze the guilt and grief from his brain.

Elia was stunned. She watched the torment grip Hokk's entire body. Eventually, he released his hold on himself and his limbs fell limp.

"My parents were already dead and were spared my disgrace," he continued. "But of course, there were consequences. The Board wanted compensation. I owned nothing, so Davim had to pay for the damage. It must have been a huge financial drain, enough, I guess, to affect my uncle."

"And what about you?" Elia asked.

"Although it was an accident, it was still my fault. I was banished from the city for ten years."

"Ten years!"

"I was escorted out past the dirt barrier, and I have not been back since."

"Unbelievable," said Elia.

"Does my story shock you?"

"I feel more stunned than shocked. I guess . . ." She struggled to find the words. "I just feel so sorry for you," she admitted.

"Don't feel sorry for me," Hokk said gruffly as he rose to his feet. "That's life. You take what it delivers."

He walked to the edge of the roof. Watching him stand motionless, Elia marveled at how circumstances had changed his life so drastically. People had died because of his carelessness. Such a horrendous burden to bear. One senseless decision and he was left to pay the price for the rest of his life.

"Look at that," Hokk called out, interrupting her thoughts as he pointed up to the sky. "I told you, didn't I?"

"What?" she asked, but knew as soon as she saw it. The island above them had rotated, and now, close beside its large bulk floated another, smaller island. Elia ran over to stand next to him.

"You were right," she exclaimed. "How long do you think they will stay around?"

"Don't know. They don't seem to be moving fast, though you can never tell for sure what the air currents are doing up there."

"They appeared so quickly. I just hope they stay over the city long enough for me to find a way home."

Even as Elia said it, she didn't feel hopeful. The islands would likely be gone by the next morning. She needed more time for Hokk to meet with the Board and figure out what she could do.

Tomorrow, she would know.

Hokk suddenly grabbed her arm, making her jump. "Do you see that?" he shouted. "Quick. Look closely." He pointed into the clouds. "There, against the dark surface of the rock!"

Elia's eye caught the racing image of something white, like a package, falling to Below. Then she realized. "I know what that is!"

The body paused in midair for a few moments before continuing to fall. The white fabric around it began to unravel. It was clearly going to land within the city. Hokk's grip tightened on Elia's arm.

The body plunged past the tallest of the towers and disappeared between the buildings beyond the city's center.

Hokk was ready to bolt. "Come on!"

Elia held back, knowing what Hokk intended to do. "I don't want to."

He was too strong for her to resist and his grip hurt her bruised wrist.

"We've got to get there quickly," he said. "And we've got to be the first!"

Chapter 29

THERE WAS NO BODY. THEY had searched up and down several streets without a trace.

"Where *is* it?" Hokk growled, pacing with frustration. They were too slow getting here—all those stairs to climb down, no gazelk to ride, his body still sore from the fight with Davim. Yet Hokk had been determined to keep moving.

"Someone's already taken it," Elia decided. "We're probably not the only ones who saw the thing fall."

Although the streets in this area were mostly deserted, they had noticed a few people earlier who were clearly on the hunt for something too.

"Is it really that important to find?" she asked.

"Yes, of course it is!" Hokk roared, surprising himself by such an impassioned response. While most city dwellers might consider the body just another piece of garbage to be removed, the more destitute inhabitants would pounce on such an opportunity to scavenge. Raised in a wealthy family, Hokk had never guessed he'd someday be one of them, driven by a competitive survival instinct.

"Maybe we're in the wrong spot then," Elia suggested more cautiously.

"No, this is it," he said. "And if someone already dragged it away, we would see tracks."

"Not if the body was carried by more than one person."

"True," he said, clenching his jaw as he looked around. "But there's no point of impact either. Remember how we found the donkey?"

"We wouldn't see any impact if it didn't actually hit the ground."

Hokk's face lit up. "Of course!" He had assumed the body had cleared the buildings, but not necessarily. One location in particular stood out in his mind, a spot where his mother used to enjoy sitting on the steps. He started running.

Elia ran after him. "In the trees, you think?"

"No. I was looking for that earlier," he replied over his shoulder.

Rounding the next corner, Hokk immediately slowed, not wanting to attract anyone's attention. He headed toward a building they had already passed. It was in the middle of an open plaza, and the surrounding buildings seemed to hang back along the square's border as if out of respect. The main structure looked part fortress, part barn. Its strong stone walls rose high to a peaked roof of aged wood, and it had damaged windows made of colored glass. At the front of the elaborate building stood a tall bell tower and wide, crumbling stairs that climbed to the entrance.

"It's in here," Hokk called back to Elia.

"How do you know?"

"There's a hole in the roof."

Hokk raced up the steps. He pulled on the handle of the large wooden door, and surprisingly, the ancient lock gave way and the rusty hinges creaked open.

Together, they peered into the recesses of the old building that had probably sat silent for over a century. The air was dank and dust clung to its thickness, swirling throughout the cavernous space. The particles in such ancient air should have already settled into place years ago, but this air was freshly disturbed.

A faint beam of light shone through the hole in the roof, filtering between the particles of dust. Row upon long row of benches stretched out in front of them, and at the far end, they could see the body bound in white rags. It had scattered several benches on impact.

Elia held back at the front door, but Hokk and Nym didn't hesitate. "Come on," Hokk beckoned from halfway down the center aisle.

Clearing away debris, Hokk pulled the body free of the mess. He inspected the bundled corpse and removed jagged splinters of wood that had stabbed through the fabric as it crashed through the roof.

Elia joined them but took a nervous step back when Hokk began to loosen the wrapping at the head. He glanced at her quickly. "It's okay," he said, but she kept her distance.

With his back to her, Hokk unwound the strips of tattered, mismatched cloth. There were only a few layers and soon he exposed a bald scalp, then the wrinkled face of a very old man.

Hokk blocked Elia's view. "What are you going to do with it?" she worried.

"I'm just checking."

"You're not going to unwrap it completely, are you?"

"Don't worry." Hokk turned to look at her again, shifting enough for her to finally see past him. "I only go far enough to—"

Hokk saw a flash of horror sweep across Elia's face. Holding a hand to her mouth, she staggered back, blindly reaching behind and knocking over a bench. She fell hard on its upturned edge.

"Elia!" Hokk hurried to her side. "Are you all right?"

Elia's complexion was drained of color. She moved her mouth but no words came out.

Hokk helped her slowly sit up. He tucked a flyaway piece of hair behind her ear and smudged a tear under her eye. "I know it can be a shock to see a dead body," he said.

"No, it's not . . ." Elia was finally able to sputter.

"I should have made you wait outside."

"That's not it," Elia replied, her voice cracking with emotion. More tears welled up in her eyes. "I've seen dead bodies before." She paused, struggling to speak. "I just didn't expect it to be my grandfather."

Chapter 30

LEANING OVER THE OLD MAN'S partially exposed body, Hokk did not know how to proceed. Though tempted, he decided it would be wrong to continue stripping away the fabric with Elia standing so close.

"It's horrible," Elia whispered. She hugged herself tight and watched with hooded eyes. "It's too much of a coincidence. Almost as if I was meant to find him."

Hokk considered rewrapping the head, but worried it would draw attention to another problem. So far, she seemed reluctant to take a second, closer look at her grandfather's face.

Nym had grown impatient, and he snagged a piece of wrapping between his teeth, ripping the fabric as he pulled. "Nym, stop it," Hokk hissed with a swat of his hand. The fox let go and licked his muzzle.

A small bag hung around the body's neck. Hokk lifted it gently. "Do you want to keep this?"

Bracing herself against an upright bench, Elia slowly shook her head.

"Perhaps as a memento," he encouraged.

"Tradition says it must stay with him," she said. "That's how we do it."

"And do people from Above know this is where their loved ones end up?" Hokk immediately regretted the question and wished he could take it back. "I mean, are you sure you don't want anything?" he quickly asked again.

Elia considered it for a moment. "Maybe I'll take one thing." Kneeling, she loosened the bag's drawstring and shook the contents into her hand. A snail shell, some twine, and a coin fell out, as well as a set of stained teeth.

"Are those his teeth?" Hokk wondered aloud.

"Yes." She smiled sadly. "But not his real ones. He carved these out of wood. Somehow, he was able to wedge them between the ones that hadn't fallen out yet." Elia squeezed her fingers around her grandfather's meager treasures. "When he would finish eating, he'd rub them clean on his shirt and drop them into his little bag."

"To make sure they never got lost."

"Actually, he lost them all the time, thanks to my grandmother. It was her ongoing practical joke—she'd sneak the teeth out while he slept so she could hide them for the next morning."

"Did it drive him crazy?"

"Opi didn't mind. It became a game to see how quickly he could find them. And my grandmother loved it too, not only because it was fun to watch Opi on his hands and knees, but later for her to see where the hiding spot turned out to be. She rarely forgot to play the joke, but as her mind deteriorated, Omi always forgot where she had hidden them."

Elia shook the bag again. A shiny orange stone rolled onto her hand. "I can't believe this!"

"What is it?"

Elia gazed up to the ceiling and blinked back tears before speaking. "I was sure he had tucked this into my grandmother's wrapping when she died." She wiped her eyes. "We both loved it. It's a piece of polished glass that he found on the Isle of Drifting Dunes, but I always imagined it to be a jewel lost by a princess."

Elia gingerly picked the stone out from the rest of the collection. She placed it in the pocket of her dress, then tipped the remaining items back into the bag and placed it on her grandfather's bare chest. "That's all I need," she said quietly.

She allowed herself to look at the corpse, as if for the final time, but did a double take. Her eyes flashed.

Hokk had been watching her closely, hoping she wouldn't notice. The far side of her grandfather's face was dark purple with a large scab above his ear.

"Is that a bruise?" she asked.

"I think so," said Hokk, knowing full well.

"From the fall?"

"Probably." He hoped he sounded convincing.

Elia kept staring at the old man. "It'd be a horrendous fall, and then crashing through the roof like this."

"You're right."

Elia looked at Hokk and he knew she suspected the worst. "But that scab isn't fresh."

Hokk frowned and nodded his head, saying nothing.

"And I don't think dead bodies can bruise," she added.

"No."

Elia clawed her dress by her heart and twisted the fabric. "They wanted me to find him."

Her imploring eyes made Hokk's body tense. "I'm sure it's simply a coincidence," he lied.

"No! The guards know I'm down here, that I'm in the city somewhere, and they've sent my grandfather's body as a warning. My entire family is in danger! If I could only return that box, I could end all this."

Hokk bit his lower lip, surprised this carved box she kept mentioning could carry such importance.

At that very moment, Nym growled at an unexpected noise at the front entrance. Before Elia and Hokk could stand, they heard a deep voice.

"You wretches beat us to it!"

A man's silhouette filled the open door.

"That's right," Hokk said loudly, hoping to sound threatening as he stood tall. "We got here first, so we lay claim."

"Perhaps," came the reply as the man stepped through. Two other men followed close behind. While all three were similarly cloaked, the last two were shorter and moved like skittish rodents.

The first man strode straight down the aisle, preceded by a stink of body odor that made their noses wrinkle. His face moved into the light.

"Kalus!" Hokk gasped, unable to believe his eyes.

"Ribs? Is it really you?"

Hokk had forgotten the nickname, but recognized every detail of the man who now stood before them—the scraggy beard, the raw rash on his skin, the stench, the leather cloak trimmed with patchy bits of fur. Hokk pulled at his collar as if his cloak was suddenly choking him.

"You're looking older." Kalus squeezed Hokk's slender arm. "Seems like you got a bit more meat on you too."

Hokk pulled away. He had always hated Kalus making fun of him. He'd put up with it when he was younger and desperate for food, but no more.

"Has it already been almost ten years since I dumped you and returned to the city?" Kalus whistled between the gaps in his teeth.

"Closer to six," Hokk answered coldly.

"So what are you now—seventeen?"

"That's right."

"You're taking a big risk coming back here before your sentence is over."

"Things have changed." Hokk didn't want to offer more. "Who's traveling with you these days?" he asked as the other two men hovered in the background.

"Just a bunch of parasites," Kalus sneered. "It's like I've always got someone following along, leeching off me. You remember how it was, don't you, Ribs?"

"I survive on my own now," Hokk said, though Kalus didn't seem to hear him as his attention turned to Elia.

"Wow! I'm impressed. I've seen plenty like her, but never one breathing," he leered, taking a step forward. "Where'd you find this one?"

Hokk raised an arm in front of Elia to prevent the man from getting any closer. "She's my find," he said sternly.

Kalus glanced at him with mock surprise. "Steady," he scoffed. "Just looking."

"Don't forget what you always made so clear. Nothing gets shared. Whoever finds it, keeps it."

Scratching the scabs on his neck, Kalus seemed to be debating whether to back down. "Nah, she's not worth it," he said after another look at Elia. "I don't need one more empty stomach tagging along." He then turned to the old man's body on the floor. "And he's already been picked clean, I bet."

"There was nothing," said Hokk.

Kalus shifted the body with his foot and noticed the side of Opi's face. "Old guy met a nasty end."

Feeling Elia flinch beside him, Hokk reached for her hand.

"He looks more battered up than you do," Kalus said, observing Hokk's black eye. He pointed to the small bag sitting on Opi's chest. "You left that."

"It's worthless. Just junk," said Hokk, but Kalus ignored him. His foul odor churned in the air as he bent down and grabbed the bag in his large hands. It took only one pull to snap the string.

"Leave it," warned Hokk.

"Why?"

"Out of respect."

Kalus snorted. "You're funny." He tossed Opi's bag to one of his rats as Elia squeezed the blood out of Hokk's fingers. "If you won't take it, then I will. No use leaving it behind." He bent again to pick up the fabric strips used for the wrapping.

He sniffed them and tossed them back to the ground where a few fell across Opi's face.

"Well, I suppose I'm done here," Kalus said, filling his chest with air as he scanned the rest of the scene. With nothing else catching his interest, he gave an arrogant bow and wiped his nose with the back of his wrist. "It's been good to see you, Ribs. But don't start following me again!" He smacked one of his weasels as he turned, and the three of them strutted out the building's front entrance.

Elia sank onto a bench and placed her head in her hands.

"I'm sorry," Hokk whispered.

"Don't be." Elia's words were muffled. "There was no way for you to stop him. Not with three of them."

Hokk sat beside her and they remained silent, staring at the body.

"I don't know what to do now," Elia finally murmured, sounding defeated.

"We'll get things sorted out with the Board. We'll go straight to them tomorrow morning." Hokk stood and picked up the scraps of fabric. "But first, we'll help your grandfather."

"We will?"

"He doesn't have to stay here. Not like this."

Hokk tightened the wrapping around her grandfather's shoulders and then wound strips of fabric over his head. He couldn't do what had been done for his own parents, but he could offer something similar.

Elia was curious. "What now?"

"We bury him."

She reacted as if having never considered this an option. "Really? You mean in the ground?"

"That's the tradition down here. Are you fine with that?"

Elia thought about it. "I guess so." She looked around. "But where?"

"Do you think you could help me lift him?"

She nodded.

"Then you take the feet."

Elia picked up the bound feet and Hokk lifted her grandfather by the shoulders. He was heavy and they staggered forward, careful not to step on Nym or any of the debris in the aisle between the benches.

As they carried the body toward the door, however, Elia abruptly stopped, her mouth gaping as she stared at the large stained-glass panel above the entrance. Hokk looked up too. Even though the light outside was faint, the window still shimmered with a myriad of colors. The images depicted men in robes, some bearded, some with wings of their own. They appeared to be ascending toward a blue sky containing two orbs, one sphere white and the other one yellow with lines radiating from its edges.

"What is it?" Hokk asked.

"I can't believe it." She couldn't pull her eyes away. "In that picture. Do you know what those are, those round things?"

"No."

"They're the sun and moon. Or at least the moon as it used to be."

"Really?" Hokk was equally stunned.

"But how could such an image exist down here? What is this place?"

"They're not used any more, but I think they were once gathering places for the Ancients. There are several of them in this city."

"And do they all have pictures like this?" Elia scanned the other windows. Some images had pieces missing and were hard to distinguish, but one portrayed a tortured man hanging from his hands. Another showed a mother holding her baby.

"I never paid any attention before," replied Hokk. "Not that I would have known what I was looking at."

"Yet to see them here! You said no one from Below has ever seen the sun or moon."

"That's true. But as I also said before, our worlds were once the same."

"Yes," Elia whispered. Her brow wrinkled. "But it raises so many questions."

No, it answers questions, thought Hokk.

Her grandfather was getting heavy in their arms, so they continued to the door. Outside, they looked up at the islands floating over the city, a view so different from the image depicted in the ancient stained glass.

Nym was waiting for them at the bottom of the steps.

"Come on, Nym," said Hokk. "Find us a hole."

Hearing his name, the fox's ears twitched and he tilted his head, perplexed by Hokk's request.

"Go Nym. Find a hole!" Hokk repeated, and this time the fox let out a sharp bark before tearing off.

Burdened with the body, they struggled to keep up. They found Nym one street over, where he sat patiently on his hunches, gazing intently at the grasses. Hokk was glad they were the only people in the street. They slowly lowered Opi to the ground and Hokk crouched beside the fox. "Good boy, Nym, good boy!" he said. The fox rolled over on his back and squirmed with delight as Hokk scratched his belly.

Elia looked down at the ground, confused. "He hasn't found a hole," she declared as if Hokk had lost his senses.

"Just wait." Hokk stabbed his fingers through the grass and grabbed a handful of roots before lifting off a section like a mat. He flipped the grass pad over and began digging down into the soil. The layer of earth was not thick, and soon he hit something solid. Brushing away the remaining dirt revealed a round, metal hatch. It was tightly sealed, but Hokk knew how to grip it. With a twist and pull, the heavy lid came away, revealing a dark, seemingly bottomless pit.

"See," said Hokk triumphantly. "A hole! Will that do?"

"I suppose. How deep is it?"

"Deep enough."

Hokk picked up Opi under the armpits and dragged him forward until his bound feet were dangling over the opening. "No one will find him in here." He carefully lowered Elia's grandfather into its depths but paused with just the wrapped shoulders and head sticking out. Hokk glanced at Elia. She nodded and he let go.

Opi slipped into the black and disappeared from their sight.

Chapter 31

NIGHT HAD FALLEN AND THE eleventh floor was dark. Hokk sat with his legs hanging over the edge of the building. Elia leaned against a wall farther inside. Every time she closed her eyes, her grandfather's battered face flashed through her mind. She imagined his violent death and guards attacking her family's shack at the end of the suspension bridge. Massaging the nagging cramps in her stomach, she didn't know whether to feel some comfort that Opi's body had been wrapped for burial, or to feel worse it was such a sloppy, hurried attempt to bind him, using only dirty, frayed rags.

And what about her mother and brother? Were their bodies similarly wrapped and littering the prairies? Or falling into the city this very minute?

"Wake up!" Hokk called out, leaning forward to look down into the street.

Elia jerked. "I wasn't sleeping," she answered, his words mercifully saving her from her thoughts.

Hokk hurried to his feet. "They've come for us."

"What?" she exclaimed, jumping up too. "Who's come? Your brother?"

"No. It's the Board. I wasn't expecting them tonight."

"But this is better. It beats waiting until tomorrow."

"I'm afraid it's not the *actual* Board." Hokk glanced nervously at the stairwell where Elia saw a faint glow illuminating the space. "They've sent men to arrest us."

"Arrest us?"

The flickering light in the stairwell grew brighter. Nym started to growl.

"Quiet, Nym," Hokk commanded and the fox obeyed, lowering his tail. "I know you need the Board's help," he said to Elia. "But I've dealt with them before. You'll have to let me do the talking. Promise me?"

"Of course. Whatever it takes."

The Board had sent five men carrying torches. They looked like regular citizens except for their red armbands. One of them struggled to control an enormous dog that strained against its leash.

"Hokk Feste?" the leader asked.

Hokk nodded, confidently standing his ground.

The man glanced at Elia and then back at Hokk. "Are these going to be necessary?" he asked, pulling two sets of metal cuffs from his belt.

"No," said Hokk. "We'll follow without a fight." He bent to pick up one of his sacks.

"Leave it," the same man ordered.

"I need this," said Hokk. "I have things in here to plead my case before the Board."

"Let's see it."

Hokk handed over the bag.

"Check this," the unit leader said to another standing behind.

The second man opened the sack and rummaged through its contents. "Seems fine. No weapons."

The first man took the bag back and turned to Hokk. "We'll bring this for you. It will be returned at the hearing."

"But—"

"Either that or it stays behind with the rest of your stuff."
He gripped Hokk's arm. "Now move along."

Hokk shook himself free. "I told you we'd follow." He
stepped behind two men who were already descending the stairs.

"Get going," the unit leader said, pointing at Elia. "You're
coming too."

• • •

The security squad escorted Hokk and Elia through the
empty streets, three in front and two behind, with the dog
leading the way. Hokk didn't resist, just as he promised. Elia
was surprised he was cooperating.

They criss-crossed the city, moving closer to its center. As
on the other avenues, mushroom-domed trees grew beside
the buildings, many of them reaching two or three levels
above the road. In a few spots, clusters of gazelks huddled
quietly beneath their branches. Turning onto another street,
Elia noticed Hokk discreetly glance over his shoulder. She
did the same, just in time to catch a fleeting glimpse of a
bushy tail diving into the grasses for cover. Faithful Nym was
keeping up with them.

Several blocks down, an unusual tower stood out like a
beacon. Its lower levels, dark and desolate, were still open to
the wind, yet farther up, the higher floors were sealed with
solid glass windows and light shone through each one. As
bright as daytime, the light was steady, unlike the flickering
glow from torches or candles.

Elia craned her neck to take in the building's soaring
height, to admire the upper levels shining against the black sky.

Suddenly, the lights blinked off. The tower plunged into
darkness like its neighbors.

Entering the first floor, Hokk and Elia were escorted to
a dead-end hallway in the middle of the building. There were
four sets of double doors, two on each side of the corridor,
and at the far end, a single light attached to the wall. The

fixture was most intriguing. It wasn't a torch, and didn't have a flame. Instead, it seemed to have a bud of light trapped in a glass jar, and its radiance illuminated the whole hallway.

Two men stepped up to the closest of the double doors and forced open the panels with a loud scraping sound to reveal a small inner chamber.

"You'll both stay in here," said the unit leader.

Hokk and Elia entered the space. A cramped, unlit cell.

"The sack?" asked Hokk.

"You'll get that tomorrow morning, after you have been summoned," said the man. He then turned to one of his companions. "Watch the door till morning."

"Yes, sir."

With that, the doors were dragged shut, trapping Hokk and Elia inside. A sliver of light leaked through the narrow gap between the panels. Outside, they heard commotion as the men left. Then silence.

"And now we wait," whispered Hokk, his voice drifting in the dark.

"How long?"

"Until morning."

"We'll be stuck in here all night?"

"Don't worry. I've been through this before. It's tight and it'll get hot, but it could be worse. It's definitely not worth trying to break out of here."

No, don't jeopardize anything, thought Elia.

• • •

Just as Hokk predicted, the temperature in their little space quickly rose, and Elia was soon fanning herself with the neckline of her dress. "I'm roasting."

"Me too," said Hokk. "But if you sit by the door, there's a slight draft coming through the crack."

They sat next to each other to get a little bit of the fresh air, but their bodies, so close together, generated even more heat.

"What is this place?" Elia asked.

"A holding cell."

"No, I mean this building."

"This is where the Board meets."

"On the lit floors higher up?"

"Yes. They have residences in here too, but that's not all. There are rooms where records are kept, spaces where emergency supplies are stockpiled, and most importantly, an area where the Seed Keeper maintains the city's collection of seeds. The Seed Conservatory is a specially sealed room used to protect thousands of varieties—the ones the farmers use all the time, plus the rare ones that are never planted."

"All in this one building?"

"It's the most important building in the city."

Hokk leaned on the door and rolled his head closer to place his ear against the crack. Elia could feel loose strands of his hair tickle and stick to her sweaty neck, but she didn't move away.

"Are you trying to listen?" Elia asked.

"Yes," whispered Hokk. "I'm hoping this guy starts to drift off."

"Has he?"

"I don't think so."

"Let me hear," Elia said, and Hokk moved his head. "I think he's sitting against the opposite wall facing us."

"That's what I thought too."

It was quite a while, however, before their guard began to snore. "Finally," said Hokk. He stood, forcing Elia to pull in her legs to give him more space.

"What are you doing?" she asked.

"Keep listening and let me know if anything changes."

Elia kept her ear to the crack in the door and tried to see in the dim light. Hokk reached up, moving his hands above his head as if searching for something.

"What's up there?"

"There should be a hatch," replied Hokk as he continued to feel around. "In the ceiling."

Elia heard Hokk's fingernails scratch across the surface. He found what he wanted near the back corner of their small enclosure. He grunted softly as he pushed against the hatch. It wouldn't budge.

"It's stuck. It's too old," said Hokk.

"I bet it's locked," Elia replied.

"No, I'll get it. I just have to work at it."

"Why would they have a trap door in a jail cell? Why give us a chance to get out?"

"I'm not trying to get out. At least, not yet. I'm just afraid to make too much noise."

Elia listened outside once more. "He still seems to be sleeping."

"I'll try a bit harder then," said Hokk. He pounded his fists against the ceiling.

Elia cringed when she heard the sound boom around them. "Wait, wait," she quickly cautioned. Taking a moment to listen, Elia murmured, "I think that woke him up."

"Damn," said Hokk softly.

Elia was right. They heard shuffling sounds as the man across the hall got to his feet and walked over. His body blocked the thin slice of light coming in, and Elia and Hokk held their breath. The man cleared his throat, paused, and then stepped away to sit once more against the opposite wall.

Elia waited a moment longer. "Did it move up there?" she murmured.

"Only a bit. I need to hit it a couple more times."

"You can't. He'll hear you."

"I know."

Hokk sat beside Elia once again, letting out a large sigh as he settled on the floor.

"I still don't understand why you are bothering if we aren't going to try to escape," said Elia.

Hokk leaned so close his lips brushed her ear lobes, sending tingles down her neck. "I want to help you, and to do that, we need to see the Board," he whispered. "Escaping now will only make our problems worse. But if things don't go as I hope, I need a backup plan. Will you follow me no matter what happens?"

"You're making me nervous," said Elia. And for more than one reason, she thought.

Hokk placed his hand on her arm, causing her entire body to quiver.

She had never before reacted to a man's touch. Her brother was always more rough or playful, her father more protective. But this . . . this was something different. She didn't pull away.

"Promise me," he urged.

"Yes, of course," she sputtered, still flustered by her emotions. "I probably won't have any other choice."

"No, you won't."

"But still, if the hatch is part of your plan and you can't get it open—"

"I'll wait for my chance."

• • •

Several hours later, the chance finally came when they heard noise coming from the corridor. Leaning closer to listen, they realized their guard had been joined by another.

"Hey, Chotter. You're already here with someone?"

"Yes," replied the man keeping watch. "I got two of them in there. What about you?"

Before the other man could answer, Hokk was back on his feet and standing below the spot in the ceiling.

"I have that drunk from last week."

"He's not looking too good. You'll sober him up here for the night?"

"That, plus the Board said if he ever caused damage again, he'd have to be sentenced. So I got orders to bring him in. Is this one empty?"

"No, they're in that one. Use the next one down. I'll help with the doors."

Thud. It sounded as if the drunkard had been dropped.

As the panels of the next cell squealed and rattled open, Hokk slammed his fists against the ceiling.

Outside, the men grunted as they dragged the drunk into his chamber.

"Did you get it?" asked Elia.

"Almost."

When they started to close the doors, Hokk tried once more. He finally succeeded, and the hatch swung back on its hinges with a crash just as the neighboring cell's panels banged shut.

"These doors make such a hell of a noise," one of the men said.

Hokk sat beside Elia, trying to steady his breathing. "I got it loose," he whispered. "I closed it again to be safe, but next time, it won't stick."

"What's up there?"

"Nothing."

"So what now?"

"We wait."

I'll wait as long as it takes, thought Elia. At this point, seeing the Board was a certainty, though she worried about what exactly they could do for her. She had at first assumed the Board, like the Royal Family, would have its own team of stallions to fly her to Above, but that seemed unlikely if Hokk had never seen winged horses. Still, he seemed sure the Board could help, so she would just have to prove—or let Hokk convince them—she was worth the effort.

Chapter 32

GROGGY WITH SLEEP, ELIA AND Hokk nearly tumbled into the corridor when the cell doors slid open. They scrambled to stand as a different guard from the night before entered their small enclosure. The hallway's only light was still shining, causing them to squint, but Elia could see a set of keys in the man's hand. He stuck one of them into the wall.

With a twist of the key, the chamber came to life, filling with light from the cell's ceiling. Elia was surprised to see the panel doors close automatically and with little noise. Above the key, rows of black circles ran up the wall like the shiny buttons on the front of a uniform. They were flush with the surface, all except for a red one at the bottom.

"They're ready for you," said the guard, pressing one of the top buttons.

A thin ring of light circled the button, and an instant later, Elia felt a strong pressure on her feet. The peculiar sensation traveled up her legs, causing her knees to buckle slightly to absorb the force. The tiny cell trembled gently, and when the vibrations stopped, the floor seemed to momentarily drop away.

Even more strange, as the door once again split open down the middle, the hallway outside had been miraculously transformed. The same two doors stood opposite, but their frames had carvings that Elia hadn't seen previously. And the floors and walls looked cleaner, undamaged, as if they had been instantly repaired and painted. Elia followed Hokk out, turning her bewildered gaze down the length of the corridor. Directly ahead were the sealed windows of one of the upper floors!

Hokk noticed her surprise. "It's an elevator," he explained. "Saves us having to take the stairs."

The guard escorted them down the hallway to an expansive room. The gloomy daylight of Below filtered through floor-to-ceiling windows that looked onto a view of the surrounding scrapers. The same unusual light fixtures were embedded in the ceiling, forming evenly spaced rows from one end of the room to the other. Their light reflected off the highly polished surface of a massive semicircular table that curved toward them like a frown. Seated in the center were three imposing figures who clearly commanded the attention of all.

In the middle sat a statuesque woman wearing a robe made from the striped hide of a gazelk, the front legs of the pelt draped over her shoulders as though the animal were clinging to her back. The woman's creased face was serious, but not cruel. Her hair was pure white, her skin pale, and her eyes a piercing blue that radiated vitality and wisdom. Her very soul seemed to shine through them.

On one side of her sat a heavyset man, also dressed in the same furs, though the top of his robe extended above his neckline and covered his bald scalp with what was once a gazelk's face, with holes remaining where the nostrils, eyes, and horns once were. Tiny spectacles balanced precariously on the tip of the man's greasy nose, and he scrutinized Hokk and Elia over the rims. On the opposite side sat a much younger man wearing similar attire. He was very handsome, and his hair, surprisingly gray for someone with such a smooth face, was whipped up around his head as though a storm had raced through it.

Yesterday's leader of the security squad was also in the room, as well as some of his men, one of whom was walking toward Hokk and Elia, leading away a scruffy prisoner who staggered and held his head as though it ached. When he passed, the alcohol vapors gave him away as the drunk from last night.

As Hokk approached the Board, the woman in the center leaned forward. "I'm intrigued," she said with a gentler-sounding voice than Elia was expecting. "The face looks familiar."

As she spoke, the hum of activity in the room quickly subsided. The more youthful man beside her, who was scribbling on a sheet of paper, put down his pen and looked up.

The unit leader stepped to the front. "Minister Seeli, this is Hokk Feste."

"Remind me, Minister Tollo," said Seeli as she glanced at her colleague and settled back into her seat.

"He's the younger brother of Davim Feste," replied the minister with the wild gray hair, pointing to the side of the room.

Everyone turned. Elia felt a lump catch in her throat to see Davim, apparently there by his own free will, standing among a dozen other men, each with red armbands. His vicious eyes were boring a hole into his brother.

"Six years ago, Hokk Feste was sentenced to exile for arson," Tollo added. "Tower 46C was torched due to the carelessness of this young man who was tending a flock."

"Ah yes, he set fire to those birds," said the fat minister. "Though, I've forgotten now. How long was the sentence?"

"The sentence, Minister Crawlik," replied Tollo, "was for a full ten years."

"Yet only six years have passed?" Crawlik squawked, squinting at Hokk over his glasses.

"On whose authority have you returned?" Minister Seeli asked sternly.

Hokk took a tentative step forward, bowing his head out of respect. "Your Honor, I plead with the Board to hear my case."

"We heard your case six years ago, and we made our decision," Tollo sneered, swinging a dangling leg of the gazelk hide over his opposite shoulder. "And now you choose to blatantly disregard our ruling."

Hokk ignored him and kept his eyes only on Minister Seeli. "I respect the Board's previous decision. However, certain recent events will be of great interest to the Board."

Tollo scoffed. "You've set more fires, have you?"

Seeli held up a hand to silence him. "When did you return?"

"Early yesterday morning," replied Hokk.

"Can this be confirmed?" Minister Seeli asked an aide standing behind her.

The aide flipped through a logbook. "Yes, that's correct. Shortly after dawn, the lookouts in the north sector observed a single steed with two passengers making their way through the ruins."

"Which ruins? The outer ruins?"

"No, the middle ring."

"That was the first sighting? They weren't spotted crossing the dirt barrier?"

The aide flipped back a page in his records and then shrugged. "The report doesn't say anything more."

"This is not acceptable," said Minister Seeli. "Why have lookouts when they allow such things to happen?"

"That's a good question for the Chief of Border Security," said Crawlik.

"Make a note to summon him," said Seeli, but Minister Tollo had already written down the command on a piece of paper, which he passed to another aide.

Seeli turned to Hokk with a raised eyebrow. "You say things have happened that we will find interesting, yet you arrived in Ago yesterday morning and did not come straight to see us. I suspect you never intended to, and you are only saying this now because we took you into custody."

Hokk nervously wiped his palm across his forehead as the ministers glared at him. "My sincerest apologies. It was very early in the morning, before the Board would have assembled for the day, and I wanted to first pay my respects to my aunt."

"You were in exile and had no permission to do so," said Crawlik.

"I had just learned my uncle passed away. I wanted to make sure my aunt was all right."

"Well, you are before us now, Hokk Feste," said Minister Seeli. "I'm interested to hear what you have to tell us."

Hokk took a deep breath. "I'm certain the Board has not yet heard accounts from anybody else that the isles of Above have been dropping lower in the sky."

"No, we have not," said Seeli. "That doesn't happen."

"I've witnessed it!" replied Hokk. "On two separate occasions."

"And how low have they come?" asked Crawlik, seeming reluctant to show intrigue.

"Low enough to tear through the grasslands." Hokk paused to let the significance of his statement sink in. He saw Minister Seeli's eyes dart to Crawlik, who returned her worried look.

"Describe what you saw," she said.

"The first time was at night, so I didn't see anything until the next morning. However, I heard it. The land was ripped open ..."

"How badly?" asked Crawlik.

"At least ten stories deep and twice as many blocks long. It dug up huge walls of earth on both sides of the trench."

"Where did this take place?"

"About a five-day ride north of here."

"Near Torkin territory," noted Minister Crawlik.

"Yes," said Hokk.

"And the second time?"

"Shortly after, early one morning. I was camped close to the ocean, and noticed that two islands had been circling overhead since the previous day. With no storm and none brewing, nothing seemed to be any different except the islands hung much lower and I could see that they were continuing to sink. When the islands made contact, they tore through the grasslands and churned up the ground as I had seen previously, except this time, they created a much longer and deeper gash."

"Though they rose once again?" Crawlik pushed his glasses up his nose with one finger.

"They dragged through the water a bit, but yes, they soon climbed back up into the sky."

"And you traveled close enough to investigate?"

"I did. By the time I got to the spot, the islands had drifted far out over the ocean."

"Incredible," said Crawlik as he turned to Seeli and Tollo. "Almost seems impossible."

"I agree," said Tollo. "Quite a story. And an unlikely one too. Tell me, did you go mad out there on the prairies in your solitude? Did you create these lies to entertain yourself?"

Hokk bristled. "I swear this is the truth," he exclaimed, his voice cracking. Elia noticed his hands fidgeting behind his back.

"It is hard to believe," said Minister Seeli. "Nothing like this has ever happened before. I would have expected we'd at least feel tremors of some sort."

"Which no one has reported. I certainly didn't feel anything," said Tollo. "Do you realize how serious this could be if islands actually started dropping out of the sky?"

"Of course," said Hokk. "And they *have* started dropping. That's why I returned to the city, so I could warn the Board."

"Do you have any evidence to support what you say?" asked Seeli.

"Yes, I do, Your Honor." Hokk turned and pointed to Elia. "I've brought her."

Elia flushed with embarrassment as all eyes shifted to her. Not knowing where to look, she took a timid step back, but came up against the guard, who pushed her forward.

"Yes, I was wondering how she fit into all this," mumbled Crawlik.

Seeli turned to Hokk. "What is the significance of this girl?"

"She's not from here," he replied.

"Of course she's not. Her skin is far too dark," said Minister Seeli. "Was she also a witness to what took place?"

"She's from Above."

An audible gasp rippled through the room. Even the ministers appeared wide-eyed.

The reaction seemed to bolster Hokk. "She dropped from Above when her island plowed through Below," he said. "Whether she jumped off or fell accidentally, I do not know."

"She should be dead!" declared Crawlik, shaking his head. "Another impossible story!"

Tollo banged his fist on the table, making items on its surface jump. "Are you mocking the Board? Because if you are lying, you'll lose your life!" The younger minister started to rise out of his chair. "I'm inclined to break your neck right now for trying to deceive us!"

"No, I assure you. I'm not lying." Hokk pleaded. "You must believe me!"

Elia could see Hokk's nerves were starting to get the best of him. Wringing his hands and sweating, he did not look like someone telling the truth. He shot her a look of desperation. Did he want her to step in and say something?

Seeli again raised her hand to calm Tollo, and he begrudgingly sat down. "What is your name, girl?"

Elia swallowed. "Elia," she murmured.

"Is this true, Elia, what we have just heard? Are you from the isles of Above?"

"Yes."

The room quivered with commotion.

Minister Seeli waited for quiet. "Yet somehow, you were able to survive the fall?"

"Yes, I did."

Hokk pressed forward. "She survived, Your Honor, but another young woman did not. She landed on the beach and was killed. But I believe this one landed in the water and was washed to shore. That's where I discovered them, together on the beach."

"Did you know the other girl?" Seeli asked Elia.

"No, I did not," said Elia.

"Don't believe her," Hokk blurted out. "She's lying!"

"What?" Elia exclaimed, whipping around to face him.

"There's more to her story than she wants to let on," continued Hokk, wiping his forehead once more. "And that's why I wanted to bring her before the Board. *She's* the one not telling the truth."

Chapter 33

ELIA FELT AS THOUGH HER stomach had been dealt a death blow. She couldn't breathe. She could barely stand.

"Not only is this girl from Above proof that islands have dropped," said Hokk with growing fervor, "but I also have evidence to prove she will be very valuable to the Board. I wish to exchange her for my freedom."

"You're crazy!" cried Elia, finally finding her voice.

In unison, the three ministers shifted their scrutiny from Hokk to Elia. Elia saw Hokk flick a triumphant glance at his brother. She dug her fingernails into the flesh of her palms.

"Show us this evidence," Tollo ordered.

"It's in my sack," said Hokk, holding out his hand expectantly toward the security unit leader. "May I have it?"

Lifting the bag, the man hesitated, appearing on the verge of passing it to the Board.

"Give it to me," insisted Hokk.

"That's fine," Seeli said to the unit leader.

Hokk grabbed the sack and crouched over it, pulling out supplies and setting them aside as he dug down. Elia was curious to finally see what he had kept so carefully hidden. When he removed a bundle of crumpled blue fabric, she recognized it instantly.

Hokk shook out the delicate dress of the lady-in-waiting, then turned around for everyone to see it. Even with its wrinkles, torn seams, and missing sleeve, the garment was clearly an exquisite piece of clothing.

"She may be wearing these plain rags now," said Hokk with a nod toward Elia, "but when I first saw her that day, she was wearing this fine dress. From my hiding spot, I watched her change into the dead girl's clothing, which you see her in now. It's clear she's trying to conceal her identity."

"Why would you say such a lie?" shouted Elia, stunned that Hokk would try to twist the truth. "You can't believe any of it!" she beseeched the Board, though every member was now dissecting her with suspicious eyes.

Hokk, too, looked at her with the cold stare of a heartless stranger. He reached into his sack again, and took out something clenched in his fist. Slowly uncurling his fingers, he revealed the blue gemstone Elia had found in the sand. "This is hers too."

"Pass it up here," said Tollo.

Hokk gave him the gem and returned to his bag. "There's one last thing to show you." He grabbed an object tucked deep at the very bottom. "And this," he declared with an air of triumph, "is something that is immensely important to her."

When Elia saw the long, intricately carved box in his hands, the one the lady-in-waiting had died to protect, a fiery rage surged through her body.

"You bastard!" she hissed. She lunged for the box, but Hokk held it away from her, using his other arm to push her off.

"Control her!" yelled Minister Crawlik, and the guard grabbed Elia.

"You had it all along!" Elia screamed, the arteries in her neck throbbing.

Hokk calmly looked back at the Board. "See how passionate she is about it?"

"Bring it here. Let's see that too," said Tollo.

"No!" shouted Elia.

Hokk was clearly pleased as he approached the Board. He passed the box to Tollo, who turned it over in his hands, inspecting it carefully, tracing a finger along the design on the top surface. "Have you looked inside?"

"I have, but I don't know what it is," replied Hokk.

Tollo unlatched a small clasp at the front and lifted the lid. He didn't take anything out, but seemed impressed by the contents. "Look at this," he said as he passed the box to Seeli.

Minister Seeli opened the lid. "Oh!" Her eyes flashed at Tollo in a silent exchange, and Tollo nodded in agreement.

When Seeli passed the box to Crawlik, he examined it through his spectacles, and then looked over the rims at his two colleagues. "Well, well," he muttered.

The three ministers sat silently for a moment before Crawlik finally spoke. "Come here, girl," he said.

Elia slowly approached. She stood in front of the fat minister and waited, her eyes averted.

"Look at me," Crawlik commanded.

Elia reluctantly obeyed and returned Crawlik's stare. She tried not to blink, but her eyes soon dried and she was forced to let her eyelids close.

"Ah, there. Her eyes," Crawlik said with amusement. "She has those odd eyes, just as I expected. Now pull back the hair from your forehead."

Grudgingly, Elia brushed her hair to the side.

"Look at that marking," he said when he saw the tattoo near her hairline. "Turn for the others to see." Elia did as she was told.

"It's the same symbol carved on the box," Crawlik explained.

Seeli nodded. "The Seal of the Twin Emperors."

They recognized the Royal Seal? They had heard of the Twin Emperors? Elia couldn't understand how that was possible.

"So the question now," Minister Crawlik continued, "is what do we do with her?"

"I just want to go home," pleaded Elia. "That's all."

"I'm sorry, but it's not as simple as you might think," said Seeli.

"Is it at least possible?"

"No."

One word, but it was enough to kill Elia's last hope. Now, not just Hokk but the Board had failed her too.

"You were wise, Hokk Feste, to bring her to us. Very wise, indeed," said Minister Seeli. "I'm curious to hear who you think she might be."

"I don't know. I suspect she's wealthy. Certainly someone important. Someone worth searching for if they went missing."

"We agree." Seeli looked at Crawlik and Tollo, who were both nodding. "In fact, we believe she is a member of a royal family from Above, and we are sure they will want to find her."

"They've already started looking," said Hokk. "They came down on flying horses to search for her, but she hid. She's probably a runaway."

"I'm glad to hear she is of value," said Minister Tollo. "It will be best if she remains under the care of the Board."

"And in exchange, I can return to the city," added Hokk.

"Not so fast," said Minister Tollo. "I'm sure the other ministers will agree there is still the matter of your outstanding sentence."

"What?" Hokk exclaimed.

"It was your duty to bring her to us, but nothing more than that. One's duty must be fulfilled. It cannot be rewarded."

"This is insane! I don't deserve this!" Hokk looked frantically at the other two ministers, but their expressions remained resolute. They were in full agreement.

Seething, Hokk stepped closer. "What becomes of me?"

"You will lead a group of men to the sites you described

so they can see the damage for themselves," said Minister Crawlik. "You will then remain on the prairies until your sentence is complete."

"I won't do it!"

"You will. But not right away," said Tollo. "First, you will be confined to quarantine for one month."

"Quarantine?" bellowed Hokk.

"You have been in contact with someone from Above," said Minister Seeli. "We have strict rules for the disposal of their dead bodies, but you have been with someone who is living. We cannot risk having you infect the rest of the population with a contagious disease."

"Nonsense," said Hokk. "I've already been to visit my aunt. I have probably come in contact with lots of people by now, and I don't see—"

"Well, that was very foolish," Tollo interrupted. "If there is an outbreak, you will be held responsible, and you'll *never* be allowed back into the city."

Crawlik spoke next. "You, your aunt, and the men of the security unit who picked you up last night will all be held in separate confinement for precisely one month. No less."

The men with red armbands roared with angry objections.

Hokk smiled wickedly. "If that's the case, you must also include my brother. Since I have returned, he has had the closest contact with me." He pointed to his own battered face. "This is thanks to him. He has even touched the girl."

"Then Davim Feste will also be quarantined for one month," ruled Crawlik without hesitation.

"Damn you, you little maggot!" Davim growled as the guards beside him held him back.

"Silence!" Crawlik's face turned red with the effort to restore order. "The girl herself will be held in quarantine indefinitely until the Board determines if, and how, she can be of use." He gingerly held up Hokk's evidence. "For now, these items will be safely stored. Someone seal them in a plastic bag."

An aide stepped forward to take the engraved box and gem from Crawlik, then dumped them in Hokk's sack with the dress before stuffing everything into a large, white plastic bag.

"Your possessions may be returned to you if you are deemed disease free, but not those of the girl," Crawlik continued. "The box, the dress, and the precious stone are now property of the Board."

The aide tied a knot at the top of the plastic bag and handed it to the guard standing behind Elia.

Hokk looked miserable and his expression was mirrored on the faces of the other men who had just learned their fate for the next month. A few began cursing out loud.

Minister Seeli spoke up quickly. "Order! That's enough!"

People paid no attention.

"The Board demands order in this room!" she said, banging the table. "The safety of this city is paramount and we will not put it in jeopardy. Remember, we do this to protect your wives and children. And to prove it, your families will be compensated double for your lost month's salary. Of course, the Feste family will be charged the expense."

"Wait! That's not justice!" shouted Davim, but the ministers ignored him.

"Now remove these two and lock them up before we are exposed to them any longer," Tollo added. "The rest of you will wait until they have been taken down and away from this building."

The guard standing behind them was eager to follow the Board's orders. With the plastic bag slung over his shoulder, the man elbowed Elia to get moving and used his other hand to shove Hokk hard in the back. Hokk stumbled, but then steadied himself. As he walked, his head down, he ignored the jeers of the other men, not even flinching when several tried to spit on him.

Elia dragged her feet, her body slouching. She didn't care where they were taking her. The Board's verdict was ridiculous. So much had been said, but so much of it twisted lies. Hokk had deceived her from the very beginning—deceived everyone. She had been foolish not to see it coming.

They reached the hallway and their guard pressed a button on the wall. They heard a *ding*, and the doors started to slide apart. Not waiting for them to open completely, Hokk took a step forward but was pushed out of the way by someone within. Hokk stumbled back into Elia, pressing her against their guard.

"Out of the way!" bellowed a frightening voice.

Peeking over Hokk's shoulders, Elia couldn't suppress a gasp.

The imposing bulk of Commander Wrasse stepped into the corridor.

Chapter 34

THE MAN WAS MONSTROUS. WITH a helmet of polished metal and silver wings sticking out from the top, he was like nothing Hokk had ever seen. The man raised his mirrored visor to reveal a mutilated face, his skin dark like Elia's. His nostrils flared with each angry breath through a nose sliced in two.

Hokk felt pressure from the man's hand on his chest and could also feel Elia cowering behind him, clinging to his cloak.

"This way," the ogre in uniform ordered, shoving Hokk aside. His troops followed as he strode down the hallway, showing arrogant disregard for the people lined along its length. Every Agoan shrunk against the walls, and their whispered alarm trailed after him.

"What the hell was that?" said the equally startled guard who was escorting Hokk and Elia. He quickly refocused his attention, however, on the closing elevator doors, reaching forward to hold them open. "Come on. Get in, you two," he ordered. "Enough gawkin'."

Hokk stepped inside, with Elia pushing desperately from behind.

"I don't know what the two of you have started here," said their guard, "but I sure don't like it." When the doors shut, the man touched the lowest black button and it lit up with a ring of light.

"One goddamn month," he growled viciously as soon as the carriage started to descend. "Could this day get any worse?" He turned to Hokk. "Got no answer, boy?"

Hokk stared at the sealed door and said nothing.

In the next instant, the guard raised his elbow and slammed it into Hokk's face. Hokk groaned in agony. Blood gushed from his nose. He thought he heard a satisfied snort from Elia.

"That feels better," the guard snarled. "How about for you?"

Hokk resisted his urge to retaliate. The timing was not right.

Proud of himself, the guard stood with his back to them, staring at the lit display above the door, which was slowly counting down the numbered floors.

Hokk did the same. Sniffing back the blood dripping from his nose, and keeping his eyes on the numbers, he thought about how badly things had just gone with the Board. His plan had seemed so solid. Then he watched in disbelief as it all fell apart.

He had been nervous, which he should have expected. Having that many people around was still so foreign and unsettling. Unfortunately, standing in front of the Board only made it worse, bringing back the same fear and shame Hokk had felt six years ago.

But then, when the Board seemed so ready to lynch him, the lies became necessary. Didn't Elia recognize her life was in danger? Couldn't she play along to convince the ministers she was more valuable to them alive, not dead?

No. She didn't understand. Her expression could not mask her devastation. Hokk had been surprised how crushed he felt that she would believe him capable of such a betrayal. He still felt wretched.

Yet he didn't show it. His face remained blank as he counted down the number for each floor.

Six.

Five.

Four.

When the three appeared on the display, he struck.

Hokk executed his ambush at lightning speed. He lunged forward, one hand smashing the guard's face into the wall while the other hit the red button on the control panel.

The carriage screeched to a halt.

The unexpected jolt caused Elia to lose her balance and she fell against the back wall.

At the same moment, the stunned guard spun around, but Hokk was ready. He pulled the man forward by the shoulders and thrust his knee into his abdomen. The guard doubled over, enabling Hokk to strike him in the face. The man slumped to the floor, moaning, and Hokk finished with a few savage kicks to make sure he stayed down.

With his victim huddled in a ball, Hokk grabbed the plastic bag containing his belongings and stepped on the guard's back to reach for the ceiling. He pushed against the loosened hatch, and it swung back onto the outer hull with a crash.

"Follow me!" he hollered at Elia.

Hokk poked his head through the trap door's opening and tossed his sack onto the roof. Then, thrusting with his legs, he propelled himself upward. As soon as his long, slim body passed through the hole, his head popped back in, and he lowered a hand down to Elia. "Hurry up!" he said, flexing his fingers for her to grab hold.

Elia recoiled from his reach.

"Now!" he yelled. "You want that metal-head to find you?"

She scowled and reluctantly raised her hand. Hokk pulled her through the hatch, then closed the small door, trapping the guard below.

They were standing in a poorly lit, drafty shaft that was not much wider than the space they had just left. And there was no visible means of escape. At their feet, a thick cable, still trembling from the carriage's sudden stop, was attached to the middle of the elevator's roof and it extended high above their heads, vanishing into the blackness.

"You're making things worse!" Elia seethed.

"I'm helping us escape."

"So then, what's your great plan? You're going to make us climb up?"

"Of course not," he said, handing her his sack. "Now hold this."

Facing one of the extremely high walls, Hokk ran his hands over its surface. It had to be here.

"What are you doing?" she asked miserably.

"Shut up!"

He crouched and found what he wanted. Hooking his fingers into a thin groove, he strained against the crack. A narrow beam of light shone into the elevator shaft as the wall became a set of door panels.

But Hokk had not timed it right. Instead of stopping in line with the floor, the elevator had halted several feet below. They were standing now on top of the carriage, and the ceiling of the third floor corridor was only as high as their knees. There was little space to squeeze through.

"Out!" said Hokk.

"I'm not going first!"

"Get out in case these doors close!"

Sitting on the roof, Elia stuck her legs into the hallway and flipped onto her stomach to lower herself.

"Hurry!"

"I am!" exclaimed Elia. "I'm just—"

The elevator shuddered.

"Go!" yelled Hokk as he pushed her off.

Elia tumbled into the corridor.

Hokk began to lower himself through the opening too, but a second later, the elevator started to move again—but it was going up, not down!

His heart pounded as if trying to tear free from his rib cage. He frantically shimmied through the shrinking space as the carriage rose. Only inches away from decapitating himself, Hokk slipped his head through the opening and he crashed next to Elia.

Hokk sprang to his feet. He picked up his supplies and ran down the shabby passage.

"Take the stairs!" Elia called out as she sprinted after him.

"No!"

"So where?"

When Hokk turned the corner, the space opened up as it had on the higher level where the Board congregated. Yet this floor was completely empty and the wind blew through unobstructed. No glass windows.

"Shouldn't we be going down?" Elia challenged.

"No," he said. "They'd catch us easy. We're going out. Straight out." Hokk looked past her across the large, vacant room.

"No way!" Elia said.

"Then they'll capture us," he replied, "and we'll be dead for sure."

"We won't survive the fall."

As if she had dared him, Hokk winked at her, then broke into a full-speed run toward the far side of the building.

"Don't!" Elia screamed.

"Trust me," he shouted back as he sailed out beyond the edge of the tower, his cloak flapping as he dropped.

Chapter 35

HOKK WAS EITHER INSANE OR stupid. Jump out of the building? And *trust* him?

He obviously had no intention of helping her. Elia was stuck in Below whether she followed him or was locked in quarantine. Enough of this madness. Turning back now seemed the most sensible option—anything to avoid making the situation worse.

Yet Elia froze when she heard barking dogs somewhere on the floors above and the muffled shouts of men. They had wasted no time in starting their search and would soon arrive on this level.

She thought quickly. Hokk still had the carved box. And if Wrasse caught up to her, it would be better to have it than not—perhaps she could bargain for her life.

Don't let Hokk get away!

The barking grew louder and more frantic as the dogs reached the third floor. Elia started running toward the open side of the building, wondering if she could really make herself jump. As the edge drew nearer and Elia's heart pounded faster, the leaves of a mushroom-shaped tree growing outside revealed themselves inch by inch. Had Hokk known the tree would be there beside the tower? Of course. He had been working with a plan all along.

The dogs were right behind her now. Elia sprinted the final few steps on the tips of her toes for fear of being bitten on the ankles, then with one last forward lunge, launched herself off the building's edge. Arms spread wide, she flew toward the center of the tree where the soft tufts of leaves below appeared ready to cushion her fall.

The littlest twigs snapped under her weight, but the limbs quickly grew thicker. She tried desperately to grab anything to slow herself down as the branches scratched her skin and pummeled her body like clubs.

The air was knocked out of her lungs by the time she finally stopped. Gasping to catch a breath, Elia opened her eyes. She was wedged upside down where the trunk split in two.

A shadow fell over her and she struggled to look up.

Hokk had waited.

He rushed to untangle her, making no effort to be gentle. "Ow!" Elia yelled as he yanked her hair free from a branch.

"Are you hurt?" Hokk asked after helping her to the ground.

"Only my hair!" Elia shot back. She noticed he was standing oddly, holding one foot off the ground. "What about you?"

"I hit my knee really hard when I landed," replied Hokk. "It's already swelling."

Good, she thought.

Hokk gingerly took a step and winced from the pain. "I think I can still run, though."

"Not now you can't!" Elia could hear the hair-raising howl of dogs three floors up. Soon the hounds would be tracking them at street level. "We have to move fast! Give me your sack so I can carry it."

Tearing into the Board's protective white plastic bag, Hokk pulled out his sack and gave it to Elia without arguing.

He then lifted up his arm as if hoping to rest his weight on her shoulders, but Elia swiftly stepped out of reach and swung his bag onto her back. "Ha! Don't think I'm going to help you," she fumed. "Not after what you said to the Board."

"But—"

"You're on your own." Elia started walking backward. "You're a burden to me now." She turned and hurried away, relishing the glimpse of Hokk's defeated expression.

Elia kept close to the side of the tower, moving quickly. She needed a place to hide—but where? Coming around a corner, she saw a cluster of gazelks. Unfortunately, they were not alone. An Imperial Guard stood nearby and the flying stallions beside him were drawing a large crowd of curious, though very concerned, onlookers. An elderly woman cried out and everyone took a further step back as another horse landed with a fierce guard sitting in its saddle.

Elia ducked behind a pillar and pressed herself against the wall. She couldn't possibly escape in a city so carefully watched! Definitely not on her own. No doubt Hokk would know a way, but she hated the thought.

What would her brother do? Probably something fearless. Create a distraction? Sneak up behind a guard and steal a gazelk? Or a flying horse?

A bark at her feet almost stopped her heart. Looking down, she was relieved to see it was only Nym, wagging his tail. *Where's Hokk?* his eyes seemed to say.

Elia sighed. If the fox found her, the dogs would have no problem tracking her scent. Only one option remained and she would have to take the risk. "Come, Nym!"

She rushed to retrace her steps. When Elia rounded the corner, she saw Hokk hobbling across the street. He had almost reached the opposite building.

Momentary uncertainty stalled her. He could steal the carved box again so easily. He could turn her over to the Board whenever he wanted. However, he could have done that after getting her out of the elevator shaft, before taking the chance to jump out of the building, expecting her to follow. And he had turned over his bag to her without resisting.

Use him as he used you!

On the ground, she noticed the torn plastic bag he had tossed aside earlier. Slipping the drawstring of Hokk's sack over her shoulder and grabbing the plastic bag with both hands, she snuck up behind him. Before he could turn, she lifted the bag over his head and pulled it tight over his face, yanking him off balance. With his knees almost giving out, he clawed to remove the suffocating plastic, but Elia maintained her tight hold. Nym looked up at them and whined.

"You're going to get me to safety," she hissed beside his ear. "You got it?"

Hokk's fingers tore a small hole for his mouth and he gasped for air.

Elia jerked him back again as he tried to rip the bag open across his face. "You owe me that much, you bastard."

"I know. I'm sorr—"

"Shut up," she said. "I keep the box. Try to steal it again, and next time I'll make sure you suffocate." She released her grip, allowing Hokk to regain his balance.

He removed the bag and rubbed his neck. "I really am sorry."

"I said shut up!" She had no choice but to slide his arm over her shoulder. Hokk looked as if he wanted to say more, but Elia's face remained severe. "Let's go. We're wasting time."

With her support, Hokk could move more quickly, and they cut through the building's first level. Dogs bayed in the distance. It sounded as though they were running loose.

"We have to go faster!" said Elia.

"I'm trying!"

Nym ran ahead of them as they swerved toward a different tower, again hurrying across the main floor and back out into the open on the other side.

"Look!" Elia exclaimed. "There's a herd up ahead." She saw gazelks tied together in pairs, clustered under trees farther down the block.

"I don't think this will work," said Hokk. "Those animals look like they were rounded up on the prairies. They're wild. They've never been ridden before."

"We're doing it!" She was in charge now.

Only one man guarded the herd. Elia and Hokk approached from behind and slipped among the animals, crouching low. The gazelks became skittish, and the herdsman tried to calm them with a soothing whistle. "Settle down now. Settle down," Elia heard him say.

After pushing their way deeper into the pack, they were safely concealed. Elia gently placed a hand on a gazelk's rump so it would know she was there. Leaning close to Hokk, she whispered, "We'll take this one."

Another surge of nervous energy rippled through the herd when the echo of barking dogs reverberated between the towering buildings. The sound flowed through the streets with increasing volume like the first drops of a stream that would become a river. Distracted by all the commotion, the herdsman walked to the corner of the building to see what was happening. Elia decided this was their chance.

Though the gazelk was tied to its neighbor, the rope around its neck was not tight. Once it was removed, Hokk helped Elia onto the animal's back and placed Nym in front. With his sore knee, he had difficulty vaulting up, especially since the beast was not happy to have passengers, but he managed to get onto his stomach, and then heaved himself into place.

As the cluster of animals grew even more anxious, Hokk reached around Elia to grab the gazelk's horns, but Elia pushed his hands away and held a finger to her lips. Too soon. Only when she heard a piercing howl alarmingly close was the moment right. As the gazelks danced about with fright, stomping their hooves, Elia started to shout and wave her arms with Hokk immediately joining in.

"What the hell?" the herdsman shouted.

The animals scattered everywhere, bounding and leaping in pairs. They were a blur of bodies, legs, and twisting horns. Elia feared she would be bumped off and trampled in the frenzy, and she squeezed her steed's rib cage with her thighs.

Then Elia caught a fleeting glimpse of something among the chaos so startling that her heart skipped a beat. Though convinced she was mistaken, she leaned dangerously to the side, trying to spot it again. Racing in the same direction, another gazelk darted back and forth, blocking her view, until finally Elia saw with certainty something tied by a rope to its neck. It was an animal too, but a much smaller one in comparison, and its feet barely made contact with the ground, as if it were floating beside the gazelk.

The gazelk changed direction again and—there it was!

A wing! A flapping wing. Then a second wing attached to a woolly, brown body. Surrounded by the stampede, it was learning how to fly and struggling to keep up without being dragged.

The donkey was young. No more than a few days old.

Chapter 36

THE PANICKED HERD FANNED OUT across the street as a horde of snarling dogs charged. Some gazelks bounded down side roads, while others cut through the wide-open main floors of nearby buildings. Twister's beating wings lifted him above them all, but Elia was afraid he would be led away and she would be unable to keep the little donkey in sight.

"There, there!" exclaimed Elia, pointing. "Follow that donkey!"

"We have to stay ahead of the dogs!" Hokk shouted, fighting to control the untamed gazelk as it attempted to buck off its riders. He yanked back on its horns and the animal galloped wildly down an empty street, swiftly taking them away from Twister.

"Turn around! We have to go back!" Elia pleaded. "Didn't you see that donkey could fly?"

"I know," said Hokk. "But it won't help us escape."

Elia wanted off the gazelk, even if it was still charging. She wanted to be off the gazelk, and away from Hokk and away from Below and this miserable, crumbling city. She would wander the streets for the rest of her life if that's what it took to find Twister again.

She struggled to slide from the gazelk's back, but Hokk caught her by the arm. She elbowed him in the chest.

When they had finally outrun the dogs, the gazelk's pace began to slow. Hokk steered the animal away from the main street and they continued down a narrow alley. After stopping, Hokk lowered himself to the ground, careful not to put too much weight on his swollen knee. Elia didn't budge.

"Climb down," said Hokk.

"We're stopping here?"

"We're going the rest of the way by foot."

"Why? What's your twisted plan now?"

"Just get down."

Elia angrily swung a leg over and dropped to the ground. "I'm going back!" she announced.

Hokk blocked her. "For that bloody donkey?"

"Twister's my only chance to get home."

"Twister? Is that what you call him? Have you seen his size?" Hokk looked up to the clouds overhead. "Have you seen how far he would have to fly to get you back up there? The poor animal would never make it."

Elia's eyes flared. "Maybe not now, but someday he will be big enough. It's my only hope."

"Fine. Go back then," he said with a wave of his hand. "Let the Board capture you again, if that's what you want."

"That's not what I want. But I'm sure they can do more for me than you can."

"Don't be stupid. They'll do what's right for the Board, not what's right for you."

"Oh, but you will? I can't count on you!"

"I got you this far."

"Yes, so you could trade me off to the Board for your freedom. You found it so easy, didn't you? That was your plan from the start."

"It was the best way to handle the situation."

"You made it sound like I'm from some rich family. From royalty, for goodness' sake."

Hokk grabbed her by the shoulders. "I wasn't planning to lie! But I figured if there was a reason to keep you alive—like you were wealthy or someone important—then there'd be a greater chance the Board would offer protection and not have you executed. And I didn't expect them to force me back into exile, so I thought I would be there to help you figure out your next move."

"Then explain why you kept the box hidden from me this entire time!"

Hokk bowed his head and rubbed the scars on his arm. "What can I say? I'm a scavenger." He appeared full of remorse. "I wanted the box and that thing inside . . ."

"What's in there anyway?" she demanded.

Hokk frowned. "I have no idea. But compared to the other garbage I collect, it seemed like a prized possession. It was just too tempting. I assumed you were lying about its importance to trick me and keep it for yourself."

Elia pinched her lips together, trying to maintain her suspicion.

"I'm sorry," he said in a softer voice. "I'm sorry I failed you. I'm sorry the Board failed you too."

Elia's muscles relaxed. Hokk's reasoning made more sense than she expected, or wanted. "But running away makes it all worse. Now, no matter what, they're sure to have me killed. I would have been better off in quarantine."

"You would have died there."

"They would have released me."

"And when would that be? Besides, those men in the elevator are here to find you. You might have been safe in quarantine, but not if you were turned over to those Imperial Guards. My gut told me to get you out of there—to get us both out of there!"

Elia clutched her throat. "I can't believe they've returned."

"And in the city no less! It almost seems like they've been here before. Like this isn't their first visit," Hokk added.

"It probably isn't."

"If those guards had arrived any sooner, the Board could have hand-delivered you to them."

"You're right," Elia said, sounding very discouraged. "I know you're right. And that's why I need to find the donkey."

Hokk pulled her closer. "I understand, I really do. But not now. Can you trust me?"

Elia looked up at him, hesitating, trying to read his eyes. "I guess so."

"Good." Hokk stepped back. "So as I said, the rest of the way is by foot." He crouched and his fox came close. "All right, Nym, it's up to you. Find us a hole!"

Elia grimaced. "It's not—"

"No, it won't be where your grandfather is buried," he assured her as the fox took off.

Once again, Nym loved the game, and his nose stayed close to the ground. With Hokk's injury, it was difficult for them to keep up, and Elia kept her eyes on the sky the entire time, looking for winged stallions in case Imperial Guards were searching from the air.

Nym finally found a place several streets over that sparked his excitement, and he circled the spot while he waited for Hokk and Elia to catch up. The street wasn't deserted, but luckily the few people on it were walking in the opposite direction.

"Good boy," said Hokk as he carefully squatted and started pulling out patches of grass. Once he had uncovered a large section of earth, he stood. "Can you get that dirt up?" he asked Elia. "There should be a hole under here like the other one we found."

"What about you?"

"I'll be right back. I have to get a few things," Hokk replied as he limped painfully toward a building with a ramp leading underground.

Elia vigorously clawed at the earth, and Nym, sensing the urgency, started digging too. The soil wasn't deep and her fingers soon touched the metal cover. She cleared away as much of the debris as possible, then sat back on her heels, looking around for Hokk. But why wait? She would get the lid off herself.

She tried to turn it with her hands. It didn't budge. How did Hokk do it the last time?

Elia noticed a small dent in the top still filled with soil. Once the dirt was scratched away, she discovered the dent was really a hole, with enough space to hook through her thumb. Straining to lift the cover, Elia made several attempts before it flipped over. She stood proudly, wiping her hands on the front of her dress as Hokk approached with a burning torch and a pair of pants draped over his arm.

"Perfect," he said, seeing the cover. "I didn't know if you'd be able to get it open." He handed Elia the pants. "Here. Put these on."

Elia was surprised. "You stole a pair of pants for me?"

"Yes, and I stole the torch too. Trust me, you'll appreciate both where you're going."

"Where?"

Hokk nodded toward the hole. "Down there. You'll need light and something warmer than what you've got on."

Having never worn pants before, Elia inspected the garment before slipping in one leg, then the other.

"Tuck in your dress so you can move more freely," Hokk suggested, which Elia did, struggling to fasten the front buttons over the fabric of her uniform bundled up around her waist.

A single bark in the distance made the two of them look up in alarm. It caught Nym's attention too. Whether it was from the pack, or just a stray dog on the street, Elia couldn't tell.

"Hurry," said Hokk. "Climb down and I'll pass you the torch. There should be some sort of ladder."

Elia looked into the dark hole and frowned. "Wait. Aren't you coming?"

"No. They're sure to find this spot, even if I cover it up well. And who knows who's been watching us," he said as he scanned the surrounding buildings. "I want to create a trail that will lead them away from here."

"You'll get caught."

"I won't."

"How can you be sure?"

"I know my way around these streets. Besides, I have to find the rest of my things. I've got supplies we'll need for surviving if we end up on our own."

Elia held out the sack to him.

"Do you need anything in here?"

"That stays with you. For now, it's better to keep it sep-arated from my other stuff so they can't take it all. And I will find that donkey for you. I promise." Elia's forehead wrinkled as she studied him carefully. Could he pull it off? Just a short time ago, he had refused to follow Twister, only to turn around now and make this offer. He certainly knew the city and he might already know where to start searching. Yet, did she really want to be left alone?

"I should just come with you," Elia replied. "If they'll find the hole anyway, they'll catch me."

"There's more than just the hole. There's an endless network of tunnels down there you can follow. They'll never be able to find you, and I'll come for you as soon as I can. It won't be long."

"If they can't find me, then how will you?"

"When you come to a fork in the tunnel, turn left the first three times. Whenever the path divides after that, choose the route on the right and go as far as you can. But keep going. Don't stop until you absolutely must."

Elia stared into the hole and then back at Hokk. She didn't like the plan, yet it seemed to be the only option he would consider.

Another howl echoed between the buildings.

"Go!" said Hokk, searching the street on both sides. "Go now, before anyone gets here!"

Elia started to climb down. The ladder was no more than metal rings attached to the wall, and at its base was a puddle of water that wet her feet and the hem of her pants. The blackness of the space embraced her. She could taste the stale air on her tongue and the cool dampness on her skin.

Hokk passed down the sack and the torch. The light glowed warmly around her, and while the shadows shrank back, a dark void waited only a few feet away.

"I'm going to seal it up. Are you fine?" asked Hokk.

"I'll start walking in this direction," Elia said, pointing ahead of her. "Three lefts and then only to the right for as far as I can go, no stopping."

Hokk nodded. "Exactly. And don't worry. I'll return for you as soon as possible."

"Please hurry," Elia urged as Hokk's shadow fell across the opening.

He lifted the cover and put one edge into place. He started to lower it, but before he lost sight of Elia, he paused. They looked at each other. Elia squeezed the metal rung in her hand until her knuckles turned white. Hokk opened his mouth as if he had changed his mind, and Elia caught her breath, placing a foot on the ladder to climb back up to him. Then Hokk smiled gently and lowered the lid.

As the torch burned, Elia continued to stare at the closed cover, imagining Hokk standing above, looking down. This felt so wrong. They should not be separated.

Elia gazed down the black tunnel. She was utterly alone. Releasing her grip on the ladder, she threw Hokk's sack over her shoulder and began to walk.

Chapter 37

NOTHING WAS WORKING OUT AS planned. Returning to the city was a mistake. On the run, injured, and now obligated to find that donkey—what was he thinking?

Yet Hokk knew his offer to help Elia was the right thing to do. He could understand her desperation to find a way home just as it had been his goal for the last six years. Apparently, she had something to return to, unlike him. He wasn't welcome in Ago and he no longer had any desire to be here.

Hokk now realized why the hermit had preferred a solitary life on the prairies. Again, Hokk felt a stab of tremendous guilt for stealing everything from a man who simply wanted to live alone in peace. Perhaps helping Elia would compensate for some of the bad things he had done.

Kneeling down, Hokk pressed the grass matting back into place as he pictured Elia creeping beneath the city. Or was she still standing right below him? "Be safe," he murmured as he gently patted the ground.

"A bit too obvious, don't you think?" said a voice from behind, making both Hokk and Nym jump.

Twisting around, Hokk was stunned to see Kalus standing above them. The wind was blowing in the wrong direction—no reeking odor to give the man away.

"I know I told you to always bury your loot," said Kalus, looking up and down the street, "but is it wise to do it right here in the open? Someplace more discreet would be better."

Hokk erupted. "You mean like that place I chose on the prairies?"

"What are you talking about?"

"It doesn't matter where I hide things. You'll always return to dig it all up. Or send someone to do the dirty work."

Kalus seemed taken aback.

"Don't pretend," Hokk continued. "I used that plastic bottle to mark where I hid my stuff. You were there."

"Oh that," said Kalus dismissively.

"What are the chances that someone would have accidentally stumbled upon my spot in an area so vast? They knew where to find it! You told them!"

"Nothing of the kind," Kalus replied. "I did not share your secret. It must have been bad luck. And believe me, you had very little to make it worth the effort."

Hokk took several deep breaths to control himself. His eyes were mere slits. "So, are you following me now?"

"Course not, Ribs. Only a coincidence. I happened upon this street and noticed someone bent over and it caught my interest."

"What about your two admirers?"

"I was able to shake them off. They're doing something else for me today."

Hokk frowned. His instinct was to doubt every word from this man's mouth. As Kalus bent down to scratch behind Nym's ear, the fox cowered suspiciously, as if even Nym questioned his intent.

"Is this little guy the same one that used to travel with us? He's still alive?" asked Kalus.

"Same one."

"And the girl?"

Hokk stiffened. "What about her?"

"Wasn't she traveling with you too? Or is she on her own now in the city?"

Hokk shrugged, trying to look indifferent. "She's not with me."

"Ah." Kalus stood up and glanced at the covered hole again.

"Feel free to dig, if you want," Hokk suggested, stepping aside.

"No, not interested." Kalus started to walk away, but then turned around with a thoughtful expression. He looked directly into Hokk's eyes. "So I guess things didn't go well with the Board then."

Hokk was at a momentary loss for words. How did Kalus know? And more importantly, how *much* did he know?

Kalus took Hokk's silence as affirmation, and he scowled. "Those bastards. I'm not surprised. They're a rotten bunch of power-hungry tyrants. They're so corrupt, they'd exile their own babies for not paying taxes in the womb!"

Hokk remembered how enraged Kalus could become when discussing the Board. The man's continual public criticism of the ministers had been one of the reasons for banishing him from Ago. With such hatred toward them, perhaps Kalus would be willing to help him now.

A lone dog howled again in the distance as a reminder that Hokk was being pursued. "Listen, I need you to hide me."

"Hide you?" Kalus chuckled.

"From the Board. Just for now, until things get quieter out here. No more than a day. Then I'll be gone."

Kalus picked at his scabby rash as he considered the request.

"And you don't have to feed me," Hokk added, which was all Kalus needed to hear.

"Fine," he decided. "I'll do anything if it hurts the Board. Follow me."

Kalus swiftly crossed to the opposite side of the road, turning around to see Hokk lagging behind. "What's wrong with your leg?"

"I injured my knee."

"Well, we don't have very far to—" Kalus's eyes flashed with alarm and he instantly recoiled.

An Imperial Guard, his stallion's wings stretched wide, was flying down the street in their direction, carefully checking the lower floors of the surrounding buildings. Hokk hadn't counted on being hunted from the air.

"What the hell!" Kalus exclaimed.

"We have to hide!" Hokk warned.

Never shifting his gaze, Kalus wrapped one arm tight around Hokk's shoulders. "We can't hide. I'm sure he's already seen us." He forced Hokk to face the approaching stallion.

Hokk fought his hold. "What are you doing? Are you crazy?"

"I must be if I'm seeing what I think I see," said Kalus. "Just keep walking straight ahead like you're supposed to be out here."

That was the last thing Hokk wanted to do, though he understood Kalus's logic.

The flying stallion hovered beside the second level of a tower just a few buildings down, and the Imperial Guard peered inside. Directly below, a group of men and women emerged from an underground ramp, and they gazed skyward upon feeling the powerful thrust of air from the horse's wings. The animal flew lower for the guard to inspect them, and the people shouted and scattered, some falling to the ground in their haste, others ducking and covering their heads as they fled. Farther down the street, red-banded security men dispatched by the Board were coming from the same direction, cautiously following the guard's path, but obviously unable to do anything to stop his search.

The Imperial Guard turned his focus on Hokk and Kalus.

With several beats of its wings, his stallion was above them, and the man stared down through a mirrored helmet that had a single metal spike sticking out from the forehead. Kalus stared right back, his mouth open with genuine amazement.

The guard lingered, studying them. Hokk held his breath. Finally, the man kicked the side of his stallion and the beast rose into the air.

Kalus made Hokk turn to watch the guard fly away and disappear around a corner before loosening his grip on Hokk's shoulders. Seeing Hokk's terrified expression was the only clue Kalus needed. "It's not only the Board that's after you, is it?" he asked gravely.

"They're after the girl, but I guess that includes me too."

"And they flew down from Above to find her. That's where she's from, isn't it?"

"Yes," Hokk replied.

"Then that changes everything."

Hokk grew concerned. "Will you still be able to help? Maybe make up for what you owe me."

Kalus cocked an eyebrow and chuckled. "We'll have to be extra careful, Ribs."

"But can you hide me?"

"Of course." Kalus smiled slyly. "I'll have to hide you with one of my wives."

Chapter 38

THE BLACK VOID HOVERED THE same distance ahead no matter how far Elia traveled down the tunnel. Her steps were unrelenting. Although her joints grew stiff and her muscles sore, she was determined to keep trekking through this subterranean labyrinth.

Though she turned left only three times, just as Hokk had instructed, Elia worried she was walking an endless loop. But wading through the many puddles, she never encountered her own wet footprints.

Metal-rung ladders, attached to the walls at regular intervals, led back up to the surface. The holes were covered with lids similar to the one Hokk had lowered to seal her in. She passed so many, she lost count. Water dripped from cracks in the ceiling and she caught the drops in her mouth to quench her thirst. In some areas, she had to duck around roots that were growing down, and occasionally, she crawled over sections where the walls had collapsed, making her appreciate the pants.

She was tempted to stop and pull out the carved box to finally see what it contained, but knew she should wait for a better time and place. The lady-in-waiting had said to *protect* the box at all cost, so that had to be Elia's primary goal, especially down here in these crumbling tunnels.

•   •   •

The torch eventually died. Elia had practically forgotten it was in her hand until it sputtered with a last flicker of light. She shook it, hoping to resurrect its flames, but nothing. The pitch-black consumed her in an instant.

Her mind was black as well, as if her brain had switched off. Exhausted, Elia felt for the wall and lowered herself to a dry patch on the ground. She would stay here. If her torch lasted to this point, then Hokk's would surely burn at least this far too. He was bound to show up soon. And since there was no light anymore to inspect the contents of the box, she would sleep. It would shorten the wait.

•   •   •

Elia awoke when a boom of thunder penetrated the tunnel walls.

She sat up to clear her head. She had been entombed in complete darkness for what seemed like hours already and wondered how many more lay ahead. What if she had days to wait, instead of hours? And what if Hokk had been captured? He might already be in quarantine, or worse, dead. She could be waiting for him down here forever.

Enough of this. Hokk had given her instructions, but she had to take care of herself.

Elia got to her feet and began retracing her steps, feeling along the walls. She would climb the first ladder she came to and try to open the hatch. She'd leave a sign that she had left the tunnel, and then, hiding in one of the buildings, she could keep watch from a safe distance for Hokk's head to pop up through the hole. Perhaps she could even steal some food.

Elia's fingers found a ladder just as she stepped into a puddle that soaked her pants high above the ankles. Water droplets, heavier than before, fell on her from the cover overhead. It must be raining. Not ideal, but at least people would be more likely inside than out on the street.

As she climbed, the raindrops soaked her hair and trickled through her eyebrows into her eyes. Thunder boomed like a warning shot as Elia pushed against the metal lid with as much force as she could. The cover rose slightly, but her arms gave out and the lid dropped with a clang.

She tried again. Lifting it just enough, Elia wedged her extinguished torch into the gap and used it as a lever to pry the cover open. She could hear the roots of the grass tearing. Dirt fell into the tunnel, landing on her head. Finally, the hole's cover flipped over and Elia breathed delicious fresh air.

Climbing farther up the ladder, she cautiously raised her head and was startled by her surroundings. Through the rain, she expected to see a street with scrapers looming on both sides, yet she saw only ruins. The ruins of the city's outer limits. Had she really traveled such a distance in the tunnels?

Elia descended the ladder to grab Hokk's sack and then emerged on the grass-covered street, forgetting all about closing the lid or leaving a marker for Hokk. A few buildings still stood amidst the rubble, promising shelter, and she hurried toward the nearest with a roof, conscious that lookouts might spot her from their distant watchtowers.

The door wouldn't budge when Elia tried its handle. Glass was missing from all of the building's windows, so she reached through one, let go of the sack, and heard it land with a soft thud inside. Placing her hands on the cracked pane, she pulled herself awkwardly over the ledge and lowered herself to the floor. The deep shadows within the building stretched close to where she sat. No one would find her here. It was dry and she could wait as long as it took for Hokk and Nym to track her down.

Elia leaned her head against the wall. She closed her eyes. A gust of wind blew through the gaping window above her.

She heard a sudden and very brief shuffling sound, yet she hadn't moved an inch.

Elia's eyes flew open.

The storm's growing fury let loose a flash of lightning. Its white light lit up the inside of the building, and then faded as quickly as a blink.

The light had lasted long enough.

At least twenty men sat silently in the shadows directly in front of her. The lightning's illumination had seared their images into Elia's mind before they vanished into the gloom.

All were bald, all wore leather leggings, and all were naked above their waists. Black designs were painted on their bare chests and scalps.

Twenty pairs of Torkin eyes, their piercing stares focused only on Elia.

Chapter 39

STAY AWAY FROM THE JUNCTION!

Though Hokk had heard this warning repeatedly as a child, this was going to be his second visit.

It wasn't his fault the first time; he was too young to know any better. He had wandered away from Davim, who was charged with watching him, and had followed the parallel tracks that cut through the streets like thick, metal ribbons. He was soon lost in the maze of wreckage. Scared and confused, he sat by a tree and cried until Davim found him. It took them a while to find their way out, but they succeeded just as their worried father, who had traced them there, arrived to haul them back home. He was very angry and Davim bore all of the blame.

Of course Kalus would bring him here! How appropriate for the man to choose to live in a spot removed from the rest of the population, in an overgrown area of absolute neglect and ruin, where the mentally ill were banished to live among scoundrels and fugitives.

Hokk had learned most of what he knew about the Junction from stories Kalus had shared on the prairies. Ages ago, when the city's scrapers still had walls of glass, the Junction was a working rail yard, a hub of activity, with people unloading cargo and rearranging freight cars to form long, snaking trains that could race through the city on their narrow strips of track. Now, centuries later, the area was just a scrapyard of derailed boxcars with tall weeds and trees growing everywhere—some right on top of the cars, but most in the middle of the tracks the trains once rolled upon.

As Kalus led them along, Hokk saw many destitute men, dressed in rags, using the boxcars for shelter. A few scurried out of sight when they approached, but most peered at them with interest. Some had deformed limbs, while others were clearly insane, muttering to themselves or rocking back and forth. The few who greeted Kalus by name looked like all the other men, scrawny and filthy, but with devious eyes.

Hokk could see how the Junction was a great spot for Kalus to find troublemakers eager to do his bidding, but how had he convinced a woman to join him in a place like this?

And then he met Pree. She was a wife no man would dare to challenge, and certainly not a woman who would worry about anything as trivial as comfort. She had a swollen face, shaggy eyebrows, and a discernible mustache on her upper lip. Her torso was shaped like a box set upon two spindly legs. Her arms were hairy, her fingers thick, and she sat on a stump, legs spread wide, shucking a cob of corn. A roofless boxcar was right behind her, tipped on its side, and within it were the charred remains of a fire, a dirty blanket, miscellaneous bits of clothing strung up to dry, and a stack of cut branches.

Looking up, she showed no spark of interest in seeing Kalus. "You're back," she snorted.

"How you been, Pree?"

"Survivin'." She tossed a handful of corn husks onto a nearby pile and pointed the freshly stripped cob at Hokk. "Who's this one now?"

"This here's Ribs," Kalus replied. "He's the kid who tagged along with me on the prairies."

Pree shook her head. "Don't remember."

"You know, the one I helped out who was starving, but wouldn't eat the fox that kept following him."

Noticing Nym, Pree looked at Hokk. "Has it got fleas?"

"No, he doesn't," said Hokk.

"'Cause I ain't gettin' fleas again. I got enough to itch as it is," she said, scratching her armpit. She turned her attention back to Kalus. "How long you stayin' this time?"

"For a bit. Don't worry. But I'll be coming and going because I got some stuff to deal with. Can I bring you anything back?"

"Nah, I don't need nothin'."

"I'll see what I can find to surprise you anyway, 'cause I want you to do something for us."

"Us?" she repeated.

"Ribs and me. You gotta keep an eye on him and hide him if anyone comes looking."

Pree glared at her husband. "Who's comin'?"

"The Board's after me," Hokk replied.

"And you know how much I hate the Board," said Kalus.

"Fine. I'll do it. And whatever you bring back for me, make it good."

"You'll be all right here with Pree," Kalus said, slapping Hokk on the back. "She'll make sure no one bothers you. Just lay low, and I'll go figure out what's going on in this damn city."

Kalus turned to leave, but Hokk stopped him. "Wait. Maybe you and your men can be on the lookout for something else the Board will be after."

"What's that?"

Hokk hesitated. Should he mention it? If anyone in the city could track it down, Kalus would be the one. "I need you to find a donkey. One with wings. It's very young and quite small."

"Sounds to me like he's talkin' nonsense," Pree piped up as she shucked another corncob.

"You mean to tell me there's a flying donkey somewhere in the city?" asked Kalus. "Where'd it come from? Above?"

"It's the girl's. I promised to return it to her."

"Well, I don't really think . . ."

"There'll be a reward," Hokk hastily added.

"What kind of reward?"

"A jewel," Hokk replied, thinking quickly. "A blue gem that I'm sure the girl will gladly trade."

"I think a flying donkey would surely be more valuable."

"Yes, but you haven't seen the size of the gem."

After a moment's consideration, Kalus made up his mind. "I'll do it. But not just for the fancy stone. I'll also take that carved wooden box she had with her too."

Hokk's mouth fell open. How did he know about the box? Kalus was clearly better informed than he was letting on. And judging by the smirk on his face, he was delighted by Hokk's surprise.

Kalus became very serious. "You good with that arrangement, Ribs?"

"I don't think I can promise the box," said Hokk. "The gem is what has true value."

"You don't really have a choice, though, do you?" Kalus sneered, making Pree chuckle. "Neither does the girl."

"No," Hokk replied quietly.

"You obviously don't have the stuff with you now. She's got it, right?"

"Yes." Hokk's shoulders slumped. "But I can get it. I can go tonight when it gets dark."

"Good. I'll have what you want by the time you return."

Chapter 40

SLIVERS OF WOOD PIERCED THE flesh under Elia's fingernails as she clung desperately to the window frame. After the flash of lightning, and hearing the Torkins moving toward her, she had tried to leap outside. Now they were pulling her by the ankles, tugging so hard it felt as though her arms would be torn off.

"No!" she screamed, trying to kick her legs free. If she could just get herself through the window, the hole of the underground tunnel was only steps away!

The ancient wooden frame cracked and splintered in her hands and Elia fell to the floor, smashing her face. Her forehead and nose raged with pain. Her lower lip split, and she tasted blood in her mouth.

The Torkins staggered back, hauling Elia face down across the gritty floorboards. With arms flailing, she made contact with Hokk's sack lying under the window, but she couldn't grab it fast enough before she was dragged into the dark recesses of the decaying building.

When the men released Elia's ankles, she tried to flip over, yet powerful hands held her down, pushing her shoulders to the floor. A knee dug into her back, and the man's weight crushed her rib cage, forcing a groan from her throat.

"Get rope!" a Torkin ordered.

Elia's arms were yanked behind her, and her legs bent back at the knees to meet them. She winced as her captors lashed a thin rope around her wrists and ankles, cutting into her skin like wire. Elia struggled to lift her face, but one of the men pressed a calloused palm against her cheek, forcing her head down until the knots were secure.

"Is that enough to hold her?" asked a disembodied voice in the gloom.

"She can't break free," reassured the Torkin who had pinned her. "The more she pulls, the tighter it gets."

A small flame flickered to life in the shadows and was passed forward to the man now towering above her. He was tall and menacing, though he appeared younger than the others. Like his companions, he had a bald scalp and bare chest painted with black designs. Leather straps were tied around his arms and leggings. A sickle with a sharp, curved blade hung from his waist, and a similar but much smaller crescent-shaped slice of metal had been stabbed through his eyebrow as a piercing. Both pieces flashed from a streak of lightning outside.

"Roahm, we can't keep her," someone cautioned. "It will endanger our mission."

Roahm studied Elia for a moment. "I'm sure she won't jeopardize anything. We just can't let her escape. And we have to be ready if more like her show up."

He crouched and rolled Elia from her stomach onto her side. She flinched as he swept tangled strands of hair away from her face. "Were you sent to find us?" he asked.

She glared at him. "No," she croaked, sounding weaker than she wanted.

"Will anyone from the city be looking for you?"

"No, I can assure you," Elia replied with as much confidence as possible.

"Then why are you here?"

"I'm running away."

"From what?"

"The city."

The Torkin dabbed a drop of blood from her bleeding lip with an unexpectedly gentle touch, though he wiped his finger on her sleeve, leaving a red smudge. He leaned in as if to have a private conversation. "You're not from this city, are you?"

"I'm from Above," Elia replied, blinking on purpose.

The Torkin saw the double eyelids close independently of each other, and he couldn't mask his startled look. "How did you get here?"

"I fell."

"And survived."

"Obviously."

He thought for a moment. "Anybody else?"

"No, I'm the only one."

Roahm turned to the other warriors. "Whether there are more like her or not, we stick to the plan," he said, "regardless of what the Agoans might know or expect."

"And the girl?"

Roahm looked down at Elia. "For now, the girl will stay as she is."

"She could be a spy."

"Yes, she could be, but a spy would not jump through our window if she knew this was our hideout."

"She'll hear things about our plan."

"If she's supposed to report to someone, she will not be able to deliver her message," said Roahm.

The pain from the ropes was becoming too much for Elia to bear. "Please, let me go," she pleaded. "I don't care what your plans are. I just want to escape this wretched city."

For a moment, it appeared Roahm was considering her request.

"Gag her," he ordered.

Another Torkin forced a long scrap of leather between her teeth. He tied it roughly behind her head, catching her hair in the knot. The leather was dry on her tongue, tasting like soil and salt.

"Now move her out of the way," commanded Roahm with a wave of his hand, "and everyone continue to stay back from the windows. Our orders haven't changed. We've waited this long, and we must continue to be patient. Tonight's the night when the last of us arrive, when all the units will finally be in position."

• • •

A nervous energy hung in the room like static about to crackle. Already edgy, the Torkins were clearly uneasy with Elia's presence as they stared at her, hog-tied on the floor.

The only person not watching her was the man Roahm had stationed at a window. The lookout pressed himself against the wall, peeking cautiously around the edge of the windowsill. Near the man's feet, Hokk's bag sat hidden in the shadows, and Elia hoped it would remain unnoticed. Her arrival had caused such a commotion, no one seemed to remember it was the first thing through the window.

Elia had given up fighting her restraints. Lying weak and exhausted, she felt pain in her neck and throughout her limbs. Her mouth drooled around the leather gag.

Though as a group their eyes never left her, the Torkins were busy with preparations, working in the dim light only briefly enhanced by bright flashes of lightning. She watched them meticulously inspecting small, wooden spears about the length of their hands. The spears had pointy tips and white, feathered fins at the opposite end. Those not straight enough were discarded, but the ones they kept were dipped into a gourd passed carefully between the men as if its contents were either too dangerous or too precious to spill.

"Careful what you throw away," said one of the Torkins, rescuing a dart that had not passed another man's inspection. "We're not going to have enough left."

The first man took the dart back and looked along its length. "It won't fly straight," he replied in a hushed voice.

"Test it," the other whispered.

Reaching behind, the Torkin grabbed a long, hollow pole and dropped the dart inside. "What should I aim for?"

"The girl," said someone farther back.

"She's too close," replied another.

The Torkin who had rejected the dart shook his head. "It won't matter. Like I said, it won't fly straight. I'll prove it."

The man stuck the blowpipe to his lips and pointed the tube in Elia's direction. All the others in the room stopped to watch, including the man at the window.

With a quick gulp of air and a burst from his cheeks, he shot the projectile from its narrow cannon.

Elia recoiled, her eyes closed. A split second later, she heard a thunk and a man's sharp breath. Looking up, she saw the dart embedded in the window frame, its feathers still quivering.

"Idiot," growled the man at the window. "That could have hit me!"

"Don't worry, it wasn't dipped."

Having jumped back to avoid the dart, the lookout now noticed Hokk's bag underfoot. He bent to pick it up. "Hey, it's her sack!" he announced.

"Give that to me," said Roahm, grabbing it. He squatted beside Elia and started to remove items, beginning with the lady-in-waiting's crumpled dress and stopping when he pulled out the wooden box. He held it up in the air like an offering, and a timely bolt of lightning flared to illuminate the intricate carvings. Noticing the latch, he gently placed the box on the floor and flipped the lid. As he lifted out an object, Elia strained to see at last what had been so important to smuggle out of the palace. She was unable, however, to identify the flawlessly polished silver cylinder resting in his hands. Roahm seemed equally mystified.

"What is it?" someone asked.

"I have no idea," Roahm replied as he tapped on the glass covering both ends. He held one end up to his eye and frowned. Then he looked through the other side and his body jerked with surprise. "But I like it."

He lowered the gag from Elia's mouth. "What is this thing?"

"I don't know," she murmured.

"It's yours, isn't it?"

"No. It's something I've just stolen, so I haven't had a chance to look inside."

Was that the right response? Elia didn't want them to think this was an object worth keeping, but they might destroy the thing if they considered it worthless.

"Is this why you were trying to escape the city?" asked Roahm.

"Yes," she replied. "Can I see?"

The Torkin held the cylinder to her eye and she looked through. The view of the room instantly shrank away as if at the end of a long tunnel. Roahm flipped it around, and when she looked again, Elia saw an image of the men opposite unexpectedly leap toward her. It was a dramatic effect for such a simple-looking apparatus. Though she had never seen one before, she had heard it described once by her grandfather. "It's a telescope."

"A telescope," Roahm repeated, sounding intrigued. He stood by the window and used it to gaze out over the ruins and up to the clouds. So full of amazement, he seemed to forget he was in full view.

"I might be wrong," Elia added, "but I think pulling it open makes it work better."

Perplexed, Roahm tugged on one end of the cylinder until the pieces extended and the instrument tripled in length. "I'm stunned," he said as he peered through it again, piquing the interest of the other Torkins. "It's a miracle!"

Interesting, yes, and useful too, but Elia could not agree it was a miracle, nor particularly amazing. After all her efforts to retrieve and protect the box, she was disappointed it contained nothing more.

Why would the lady-in-waiting sacrifice her life for a telescope?

Chapter 41

HOKK'S AFTERNOON WITH PREE DRAGGED on endlessly. The rain was merciless. Hunkered down inside the boxcar, neither of them grunted more than a few words while Pree gnawed raw corn and tossed the stripped cobs onto the wet ground outside. Nym sat obediently beside Hokk, resisting his usual instinct to explore.

They spotted horses flying overhead several times as they watched the bursts of lightning. At first, Pree choked with surprise, spraying chewed kernels from her mouth. She rubbed her eyes as if seeing an illusion and worried aloud about trusting her poor vision.

Though Hokk was stiff and uncomfortable, he kept thinking of Elia in the tunnel. Being stuck down there would definitely be more unpleasant than what he was enduring. He hoped he had made the right decision for her safety. He was impatient for nighttime to arrive so he could go find her.

Hours passed. No sign of Kalus. The man still had plenty of time, but Hokk wondered if he was having problems finding Twister. Successful or not, Kalus would demand something for his efforts, so if Hokk couldn't repay him with the box or gem, then returning here to face the man's anger would be foolish. It would be wiser to simply rescue Elia and escape the city without looking back. Yet finding that donkey was a promise he had to keep.

Hokk left Pree and the Junction as soon as it was dark. He stole two torches along the way, but lit just one. The second he tucked into his back waistband, where it was covered by his cloak. He would light it only when the first one fizzled, depending on how long it took to find Elia.

He hurried through the streets with Nym as fast as his sore knee would allow. Although the flaming torch made him more noticeable in the night, all was quiet. The storm had thankfully stopped, and now, with a strong wind, things would dry quickly.

Arriving at the hole, Hokk stuck the burning torch into the ground and dug out the lid, all the while counting on Nym to stay alert for the sound or smell of approaching danger. He flipped the cover and climbed down the ladder with his fox under one arm, shuddering as the gloom enveloped him. He scrambled up to retrieve the torch, then closed the lid over his head before descending again. The fox had already started sniffing along the tunnel floor and Hokk hurried to catch up, running in the direction where Elia had pointed. At the first split, he went left. Twice more, and then he only turned right.

Being inside the tunnels was worse than he remembered. When they were much younger, Davim had brought him down under various areas of the city, but it was always exciting back then. They never explored very far and the daylight shining through the hole in the street above was enough reassurance of an easy escape.

Now, however, the space was too low for him to stand straight, and after the openness of the prairies, such a tight enclosure was distressing. Hanging roots tangled in his ponytail and pulled his hair as if someone were trying to catch him from behind. His feet splashed in murky puddles through which Nym reluctantly followed, and the skeletal remains of rodents were scattered along the sides.

Panting and wiping sweat from his forehead, he wondered again how Elia had fared down here for so many hours. And how far had she gotten? He continued deeper, further confusing his sense of direction with each new curve or fork in the path.

The torch's flame had lost most of its strength when Hokk came upon the exposed hole overhead. He stopped and stared up at the night sky. Had Elia opened it? Or worse, had someone else lifted it to get in?

Nym whimpered at Hokk's feet, unhappy to be left standing in the puddle beneath the ladder. He gingerly lifted his paws, trying to keep them out of the water.

"Give me a second, Nym," Hokk said as he stepped up the ladder.

He poked his head above ground and was stunned to see the surrounding ruins. As he climbed farther, the strong wind blew out his torch and he cursed as he flung it away. Now he had nothing to light the replacement.

This far from the city center, Elia must have felt safe enough to leave the tunnels for better shelter. Hokk noticed a faint light shining from one of the dilapidated buildings. Perhaps she'd started a small fire with the remains of her torch. Smart decision.

Descending into the tunnel, he lifted Nym out of the puddle. Water dripped from the fur on his legs. They emerged outside and Hokk lowered the fox to the ground.

He stopped dead to listen above the wind.

Muffled voices?

With Nym following, Hokk hurried across the street and hid himself behind the remains of a wall. He held his breath.

There, more voices! It sounded like a group of men inside. Could Elia be in there too?

As he silently inched closer to a window to peer in, he heard a rustling on the opposite side of the road. A silhouette broke free from the blackness of a damaged building. A man crossed toward him, followed by a second, third, and fourth.

They were coming straight for him!

Creeping carefully, the men turned their bald heads from side to side, scanning in all directions. As they passed by just a few feet away, flashes of lightning deep within the cloud cover provided enough of a glow to see their painted skin.

Torkins!

Hokk's chest tightened.

Torkins within the city's boundaries? It couldn't be!

The voices inside immediately fell silent upon hearing a soft knock on the door. After an exchange of whispered words, the men were allowed to enter and the door was closed.

Moments later, another group of men crossed over. This time, the door opened quickly and they disappeared behind it.

How many were there?

Clearly outnumbered and stuck in a deserted area of the city, Hokk did not want to find out. He didn't dare to imagine what they might do if they discovered him. And he could do nothing for Elia if she was inside—or was she already dead?

Keeping as low to the ground as possible, Hokk darted to the hole and hurried down the ladder. Absolute blackness surrounded him. He could barely distinguish the area directly in front of him, even after his eyes adjusted. Stretching his arms wide until his fingertips felt the rounded walls on both sides, he scurried back through the tunnels, trusting only his sense of touch.

Chapter 42

ROAHM'S PREDICTION WAS RIGHT. Torkins had been arriving since nightfall, and their ranks had already doubled.

Hours ago, it had grown too dark to bother posting a lookout. Everyone stayed hidden from view of the windows, and voices were kept as low as possible. Red embers from an earlier fire were the only clue that might give them away, but it was a necessary risk. The glow was a beacon drawing in other Torkins wandering the ruins.

Though the extra men were expected, the initial knock on the door made everyone jump.

Roahm silently approached the entrance. "*The wind knows not which way to blow,*" he whispered through a crack.

"*Then patience be for those who sow,*" came the muted response from the other side. Roahm quickly unlocked the door and swung it open. The procedure was repeated many times during the night as more and more men found them.

"All quiet out there?" Roahm asked when the first group arrived.

"It's only us," one of them answered. "There's no way we were spotted."

"We can never be too sure," Roahm replied, pointing to Elia.

Still tied up, but no longer gagged, Elia was an unexpected sight for the men, and each new batch asked the same question: "Where did she come from?"

"A runaway from the city. She stumbled upon us by mistake."

One Torkin was so fascinated he knelt in front of Elia for a closer inspection. "She looks so unusual, but vaguely familiar," he said, speaking low. "I've seen her kind before."

Roahm nodded. "I suspect you have, but they were probably dead already. She's from Above."

"Yes, that's it," said the first man. "And what a surprise to find another one still alive."

"Another one?" asked Elia, unable to stop herself. Her words were ignored.

"This girl is quite young," the man said to Roahm before his gaze returned to Elia. "But I guess the other woman was young too when she first fell. Do you know who I mean?"

"I do. I have visited her a couple of times with my father," replied Roahm. "But I rarely trek through that area."

"Yet this one doesn't appear to be injured."

"No, surprisingly, she's not."

Another knock at the door made the men turn their backs. "Is there someone else like me?" Elia blurted out after them, but again, they paid no attention.

Had she misunderstood? No, he had said very clearly—a woman, older than Elia, had previously survived a fall from Above!

Like all the others, the men who appeared now through the door were filthy, looking more like displaced beggars than a band of menacing warriors. They seemed exhausted, as if they had been traveling for days, and their leggings were muddy up to the knees after crossing the city's dirt barrier. Though no longer wet, they had obviously been caught earlier in the storm's rain—the designs on their bare chests were smudged and had run down their skin like drops of black blood.

Their comrades didn't waste any time attending to the newest arrivals. Sticks of wood were pulled from the smoldering embers, and the flames were waved over the scalps of the newcomers, almost touching their skin, burning away any remaining hair. Once their heads were perfectly smooth, the flames were blown out and the charred ends of the sticks used to refresh the designs on their bodies. Elia expected to see the men flinch to have their skin touched by the searing heat, but they sat motionless during their transformations.

As the room filled, Elia struggled to piece together the stories shared quietly between the men. The Torkins had been out on the prairies for weeks, slowly moving toward the city, staying in small groups as they advanced undetected. Roahm and his men were the first to arrive, hiding and waiting in this shelter for many days until the others could join them. It seemed they had some idea about forcing trade between the neighboring populations and removing the extreme territorial restrictions that meant death to whoever breached them. The leader of the Torkins had decided the only way they could eliminate the archaic rules, as well as end their isolation in the mountains, was to overthrow the governing body of Ago.

Elia remembered how Hokk responded to their chance encounter with Torkins on the grasslands. How would he react if he knew they were surrounding his city? If all Agoans felt the same way, war would be inevitable.

She wondered how Hokk was faring since they had separated. Trapped now with the Torkins, she gave up hope he would find her, let alone save her. And, even if he was still alive, his injuries would make it very difficult to locate Twister in the streets.

Elia needed a new plan.

An abrupt knock on the door was loud and urgent. Every Torkin froze. Roahm hesitated before whispering his line of the rhyme.

The correct response was spoken.

Through the door came two middle-aged men. They were not bare-chested, but wore sleeveless tunics made of the same leather as their leggings. Black patterns were drawn only on their forearms and they had scruffy hair on their heads.

"We're glad we found you," they said.

"I was wondering if we could expect anyone else tonight," replied Roahm.

"We have already visited six groups in these ruins and the men are prepared."

"Looks like you've come straight from the villages," said Roahm, inspecting them top to bottom.

"We have. We've traveled nonstop to get here in time."

"And what news do you bring from home? Most of us have been out on the prairies or holed up here for much too long, waiting for all this to begin."

"The news is not good," one of them replied with a grim face. "And as we have told the others tonight, we come with an urgent message."

"What's that?"

"The orders have changed."

"Says who?" challenged Roahm.

"The Chieftain."

"Oh." Roahm paused. "What has my father ordered?"

"The strike must happen as soon as possible . . ."

"Which it will. We've been waiting for this last wave of men to arrive."

"But as soon as it's over, all have been ordered to return immediately to the villages."

"What? That's senseless!" Roahm objected with a laugh.

"We can't overtake their leaders and hope for change if we just turn around and leave."

"The Chieftain says it cannot be any other way."

"Then why are we even bothering?"

"Our villages have been attacked."

"Attacked!" Roahm repeated above a collective gasp in the room.

"They came from the air, on horseback. Demons from the clouds with faces of metal. They were looking for something and they demanded we turn it over to them."

Elia's heart pounded to hear the description. The Imperial Guards must have split into two search parties—one that traced her to Ago and another that invaded the Torkin villages in case she sought refuge there.

"When we fled into the fields to hide, the demons set them on fire to flush us out. Almost everything has been destroyed, including the crops, which were close to harvest. People will soon be starving."

Roahm and his men looked dumbfounded. No one said a word.

"They're Imperial Guards from Above," Elia said quietly. "They were looking for me."

Shocked faces turned to her.

"And they have already arrived in the city," she continued. The truth was a daring gamble, but perhaps she'd be released by the Torkins if they feared the Imperial Guards could trace her to this hideout.

"They're in the city now?" asked Roahm.

"Yes, I've seen them. Flying on horses, just as you described," said Elia.

"How many?"

"I don't know. But that's why I am trying to escape."

A wave of fear rippled through the crowd of men.

"Get rid of her!" someone cried out.

"Kill her!" others demanded.

"Silence!" ordered Roahm. He turned back to his father's messengers. "So what does the Chieftain command?"

"All able-bodied men must return. Though the raid of the city should still be carried out as planned, it is not to overthrow the governing powers, but to pillage. Take only what is required to ensure our survival. We need supplies, but more importantly, food. Lots of food."

"How much can we realistically expect to bring back with us?" Roahm wondered aloud. "And how long will it last before we're in the same situation? That's why establishing trade is so important. We need a different solution if we hope to—"

"What other option do we have?" interrupted one of the messengers.

"You have to replant your crops," Elia ventured to say, once again drawing all eyes to her.

"Yes, of course," said a messenger, dismissively. "But it can't be done. There's nothing left."

"I know a building in the city where they store a huge collection of seeds," said Elia. "Seeds will be much easier to carry back with you to replant your fields." A new strategy was forming in her mind. "I could take you there."

"Don't trust her," cautioned a Torkin in the group.

Roahm appeared to be considering her suggestion. He turned to the messengers. "And you have shared this same message with the other units?"

"Yes, we have. Though based on the numbers, we suspect there's one more out here that we haven't found yet."

"Well, we are certainly ready to strike tonight," said Roahm. "Now go, find that other group so they can be informed immediately about the Chieftain's orders."

"Right away," the messengers replied. They opened the door and disappeared into the blackness beyond.

The energy level in the room grew rapidly. The time for waiting was over. "Are we going to raid tonight?" someone asked.

"The plan remains the same. Strike at first light," Roahm answered. He crouched beside Elia and spoke in a hushed voice. "Where exactly is this building you speak of?"

"It's in the very center of the city. I can take you there safely under complete cover."

"Can we trust you?"

"Yes, but can I trust you in return?"

Roahm paused for a moment, then removed the sickle hanging from his waistband. Rolling Elia onto her stomach, he sliced through the cords around her ankles and wrists. She could barely straighten her stiff limbs as he helped her stand.

"What are you doing?" asked a man who charged at Roahm. "Are you insane?"

Roahm held him away while protecting Elia with his other arm. "This girl can help us," he said firmly.

"You heard her yourself. Our villages were attacked because they were looking for her!" the man protested. "And now these demons are in this city. If they find her with us, we're done for." When the men in the room murmured agreement, the Torkin continued. "You may be the Chieftain's son, but you are not experienced enough to understand the true danger we may face."

"And you are too dim-witted to recognize an opportunity," Roahm spat back. "We have to consider what will truly help our people, now and in the long run! Our other groups of men can storm the city, but we will follow a different plan of action. While they're looting the outskirts to make a fast getaway, we'll access its very heart!"

"Based on the lies of this girl?"

"I can lead you through underground tunnels," said Elia. "That's how I was able to escape."

"But why would you go back?" came the suspicious reply. "What's in it for you?"

"Your protection." Elia turned to look squarely at Roahm. "And after it's all done, I want you to take me with you. Take me to the woman who also survived a fall from Above."

Outraged, the other Torkin spoke before Roahm could respond. "These Imperial Guards, as she calls them, will recognize her immediately, and then we'll pay with our lives."

"They will not recognize me," said Elia, leaping forward and grabbing the sickle from Roahm's waist.

"Watch her!" someone shouted as those standing nearby braced to spring.

But the attack never came.

The Torkins stood entranced as they watched Elia begin to hack off handfuls of her hair with the curved blade, ravaging it until only a few stray wisps remained.

She handed the sickle back to Roahm. "Get rid of it all."

Roahm appeared pleased with her dramatic display. She could be trusted. And though shocked, the rest of the Torkins seemed just as impressed.

"Pass me a flame," Roahm ordered, and he was handed a blazing stick of wood.

Elia steeled herself as the flame came close to her head. The stink of burning hair was nauseating.

I must be crazy!

She held her breath while Roahm quickly caressed her scalp with the fire, followed by a hand to wipe off the singed hairs. When Roahm stepped away, she touched her head, finding it bizarre to feel nothing.

"Now draw on my face," she said, then pointed to the purple tattoo on her forehead. "And cover that up as well."

Roahm snuffed out the flame and waved the stick in the air before pressing the scorched end onto her cheek. Elia flinched from the heat, and struggled not to squirm as the rough tip was dragged over her face. After drawing the designs, Roahm held up his sickle to show Elia her reflection on its polished blade.

She gasped to see the Torkin staring back at her.

Roahm smiled wide. "You're one of us now."

Chapter 43

"WE'LL HAVE ENOUGH TORCHES IF we use the floorboards," Elia suggested.

"Then tear up the floorboards," ordered Roahm, and his men got busy.

The planks cracked and snapped as they were pried off, yet nobody was concerned with the tremendous noise. They wouldn't be here for much longer. Dawn was approaching. Nothing could stop them now.

Roahm scanned the room to ensure each man had a plank. "Make sure you all get a good flame going before we leave."

"No, not everyone," warned Elia. "Only some of you. The boards won't last long enough underground if we light them all at once."

"Fine," said Roahm. "Make sure to keep an eye on your flames so they don't go out. Light someone else's before they do." He lit one now for himself. "As soon as we emerge on the other side, the torches won't be necessary. We will not be using the tunnels to evacuate once we have taken what we need. And remember—silence and stealth are essential for our success."

The room quickly grew brighter as wooden planks were set ablaze, casting eerie shadows on the walls. The light seemed to energize the men, and their excitement reminded Elia of Hokk. She had noticed how captivated he became whenever he built a fire. Of course, fire was essential for surviving on the prairies, but his attraction to it seemed intense, as if it had a hold on him.

Roahm handed Elia his crude torch and she could feel the searing heat on her bare scalp. The dry floorboards were burning rapidly, so there was no time to waste. "Let's move out!" Roahm commanded.

With the blue dress, box, and telescope once again safely stowed inside Hokk's sack, Elia slung the bag over her shoulder. She was the first to slip noiselessly out the door, followed by Roahm and then everyone else. Enveloped by the silence of the night, Elia's eyes focused on the gaping hole in the ground, a black abyss against the ruins bathed in flickering light. It was a very short distance to cover.

A blur suddenly shot across their path.

"What was that?" whispered Roahm.

Adrenaline raced through Elia's system. It looked like a small animal darting for cover.

"Nym?" she called out, spotting the fox's eyes glowing in the nearby shadows. As Elia carefully approached, she saw more of the fox's face.

"Nym?" Elia repeated softly, reaching out her hand. The fox took a hesitant step forward, his nose twitching as if trying to match Elia's familiar scent with her unrecognizable appearance. Picking him up in her arms, Elia felt shivers in his small, fuzzy body. Nym nervously licked her fingers and the trembling subsided.

The Torkins had stopped, clearly troubled by this interruption. Elia ignored them as she scanned her surroundings.

If Nym was here, then Hokk must be too. She felt distressed to think she had given up on him, only to realize now he had tracked her down. Was he using the fox as a sign to let her know he had returned and was watching?

Elia spun around, her eyes searching for Hokk, but she could not make out anything beyond the small area of the ruins lit by the flaming floorboards. The anxious Torkins turned too, fearing they had been lured into a trap and were being surrounded by an invisible enemy.

"What's the matter?" Roahm hissed under his breath.

"Nothing," Elia said vaguely, lost in thought.

Hokk was here. Or was he? Had something happened to him that forced Nym to find her all on his own? Could Hokk actually make a rescue attempt with so many Torkins present? Would he even recognize her now? Or would he stay hidden, thinking she had switched sides?

"Everything is fine," said Elia, trying to look composed. The plans she had made with Roahm could not be changed now. "This is my fox," she added, "and we've spooked him. I can't leave him behind."

"All right, but let's get on with this!" Roahm urged, the strain in his voice obvious.

Roahm held Elia's torch as she descended into the hole with Nym under one arm, and then he followed her down the ladder. The two of them waited side by side as the men entered the tunnel. Elia struggled to remain calm. Hokk or no Hokk, she had a Torkin army to lead into the City of Ago.

Chapter 44

HOKK COULDN'T FOOL HIMSELF ANYMORE—he was lost. In the blackness, he had become disoriented. He could be anywhere beneath the city. Panic was setting in and his entire body was slick with sweat. He knew he wouldn't be able to last much longer in the tunnels. He needed space, fresh air, light.

Suddenly, a mass of dangling roots wrapped around his head like living tentacles, causing claustrophobic terrors to overwhelm him. Hokk bolted. He heard yelling reverberate off the rounded walls, so he ran faster, then realized it was his own voice. But he couldn't stop. He was losing his mind—maybe this time for good.

He tripped over something large blocking his path and crashed hard to the ground, knocking the air from his lungs. He struggled for breath as the sound of his shouting faded in the depths of the tunnels, replaced by the maddening echo of dripping water on all sides. Trying to compose himself, Hokk reached behind to touch the obstacle that had taken him down. He felt fabric. Strips of cloth. Running his hand along its surface, he realized it was a body.

Elia's grandfather!

Hokk immediately pulled back his arm and jumped up. A shiver of horror rippled through him. He had never had a reaction like this to a dead body, yet somehow, down here, it was the last thing he wanted to discover.

At least now he knew his location in the city. He also knew that overhead was an opening through which to escape. Locating the rungs on the wall, Hokk scrambled up the ladder and slammed his shoulders against the metal cover. He burst through, and the lid, with all the dirt on top, flipped onto the grass.

Hokk filled his lungs with satisfying gulps of cool air and then he climbed back down the ladder. "Okay, Nym. Let's get out of here."

He reached for his fox in the surrounding gloom, but Nym did not come to him. Confused, he called out again. "Nym?"

Hokk's mind struggled to trace back his last memory of the fox. He crouched in the tunnel, his desperate fingers clutching empty air. Then, realizing the awful truth, he grabbed the lowest rung of the ladder to stop himself from toppling into the puddle at his feet.

He had forgotten Nym in the ruins.

How could he have been so careless? Nym had no chance now of following his scent. And the very idea of going back through these horrible tunnels to retrieve him was unimaginable.

Hokk's legs had little energy to carry him back up to the surface. Once through the opening, he collapsed on the ground, his feet dangling in the hole. He was such a failure. And he felt so alone.

He didn't move for a long time. In his mind, only one course of action started to shine through as his best option—leave the city. Immediately. He cared for nothing here anymore. Elia must have been captured and was surely dead—the Torkins were such ruthless barbarians—so Hokk had no one to rescue, no donkey to find. Instead, he would head out and search for Nym along the way before crossing the dirt barrier. With Torkins hidden in the ruins, it would be a huge risk, but one that Hokk had to take. A solitary life on the prairies without his fox would be unbearable.

● ● ●

Hokk was breathing hard as he stepped onto the eleventh floor of the burnt tower. Focused on retrieving his abandoned supplies before dawn, he failed to notice the man reclining against a pillar in the darkness.

"So you're back," said an unfamiliar voice.

Hokk almost lost his balance as he whirled around. He could barely make out any of the person's features until the man lit a match. Hokk recognized him as one of Kalus's sidekicks.

"You look like you're empty-handed though," observed the weasel.

Hokk glanced at his one remaining bag on the floor beside his tent.

The man shook his head. "Don't try to explain. I know you got nothing." His match went out.

"So you've already rummaged through my stuff," Hokk said in the dark.

"Kalus ain't going to be happy you tried to take off without bringing him those treasures."

"That wasn't my intention. Things just didn't work out like I expected."

"Save your excuses for Kalus. I'm here to take you back."

Hokk snorted. "You think I'm going to follow you to the Junction?"

"And if you don't, do you really think he won't hunt you down?" the man replied. "He knew you'd return to this spot. Besides, you got too many people looking for you. Why make him angry if he's the one person who can help?"

The man struck another match.

"What's your name?" asked Hokk.

"Gwelth."

"Kalus has quite a hold on you, it seems."

Gwelth shrugged. "We have our arrangement."

Hokk needed an arrangement of his own. Perhaps Kalus would find it valuable to learn the city was about to be invaded by Torkins. Hokk had no other alternative but to find out. Escaping from this wretch, Gwelth, wouldn't be hard, but Hokk had to assume it was true that others were keeping watch over his movements. If Kalus had been able to infiltrate the Board's courtroom with a spy, then no place in this city was safe from the eyes and ears of the many people who had their own special arrangement with the man.

Chapter 45

THREE DARTS TOOK DOWN THE Imperial Guard. His knees gave out and he crumpled to the ground outside the only tower in the city with illuminated walls of glass. His winged stallion simply stepped out of the way. One dart would have been sufficient to make him collapse, but multiple hits meant enough poison was delivered to the guard's system to keep him unconscious for hours.

Locating the building so early in the morning had not been as easy as Elia had hoped. She wasn't sure which way to turn when they first emerged from the tunnels and had started second guessing her directions. Yet she couldn't let the Torkins see her uncertainty. As they crept along the edges of the streets, her anxiety continued to grow until, thankfully, the tower's lights were turned on, shining between the other buildings. She had not led them off course and Roahm seemed pleased Elia could deliver as promised.

Roahm split up his unit so waves of men could sneak into the building from different directions. He instructed four men to stay behind to provide cover. So far, the streets had been very quiet, and they'd had to shoot down only two Agoan farmers who were heading to work much earlier than the rest of the population. There wasn't any sign of the other Torkin detachments, but Elia had no doubt the silent ambush had begun full force on the outer limits of Ago.

Giving an all-clear signal, Roahm was about to advance with his troops when Elia stopped him, pointing to an Agoan shepherd in a nearby building, standing by his fire a few levels above the street. The young man had seen the Imperial Guard topple over and was now peering over the edge.

A small, feathered spear zipped through the air, impaling itself in the shepherd's thigh. Shocked, he could not pull it out of his leg fast enough before he fell backward, out of sight, overcome with the dart's venom.

Roahm moved out with his first group. Elia followed, holding Nym close to her body. Hyper alert, she searched the surrounding scrapers for more watchful eyes and then looked up to the sky where an island of Above moved slowly over the city. It seemed to be floating much lower than any other islands she had seen. She didn't recognize it as Kamanman.

All of a sudden, she saw an Imperial horse and its rider leap off the roof of the Board's tower. Roahm saw them too and raised a blowpipe to his mouth, expecting the beast to nosedive toward the ground. Instead, it soared with powerful wings, disappearing over the rooftops.

Elia felt relieved to duck under the cover of the building's first floor. Roahm's initial assault team was soon joined by two more. No words were spoken, but intense eyes surveyed the main level. Elia led them to the middle of the structure and peered down the hallway where she and Hokk had been held captive. The solitary light shone at the far end, and an Agoan, wearing a red armband, kept watch over the four doors.

With a single dart, the guard was knocked cold. Elia searched him for the key to operate the small cells, but no luck. Instead, she found stairs off the same hallway. "We'll take these."

Nym squirmed in her arms, eager to be released. She lowered him to the floor. "Stay," she said. The fox cocked his head. "Stay here," she urged once more, hoping he understood. She would retrieve him on their way out.

Elia climbed the stairs, and Roahm motioned for the other Torkins to follow. At each landing, they opened the doors to find the floors empty. They continued higher until they came upon a locked door, and a Torkin got busy picking the lock with the tip of a dart. Elia felt nervous, wondering what, or who, might be behind the barrier. The door swung open to a spacious room stacked only with tools and crates. An undisturbed layer of dust covered everything, including the floor.

Elia and the men carried on. The next few levels also had locked doors and housed similar supplies, all of it untouched. One floor higher, they found a large room filled with nothing more than rows of books and paper records. It was just as dusty, though footprints were evidence of recent visitors. Elia took this as a sign they were getting closer.

The unmarked access to the Seed Keeper's floor looked like all the other secured doors in the stairwell. But as soon as she saw what lay beyond, Elia knew they had reached the right spot. "This is it," she said as she stepped into the hallway of the twentieth floor.

Hokk had described a sealed room, which was exactly what stood before them. Tinted glass, installed from floor to ceiling, blocked the entire end of the hallway past the elevators. It was cool to the touch and fogged up from their breath as they tried to peer in. The door to the room, made of the same thick glass, had no lock to pick, and its seams were too snug to pry open.

"Find something to get us in," ordered Roahm, and several Torkins left to check the supplies below. They soon returned with pickaxes, which they swung into the center of the glass door. Though the noise was deafening, nothing shattered. After numerous strikes, only a small web of cracks blemished the surface.

"Hit where it's weakest," ordered Roahm, pointing to a corner of the door.

With his full strength, a Torkin slammed the pickaxe as instructed, and a small shard broke away with an unexpected rush of pressurized air. Another blow, and the entire door exploded into a spray of transparent pebbles that rained to the floor.

Though the entrance was now gaping, no one moved. They were perplexed by an orange light that had started pulsating within the Seed Conservatory. Roahm looked at Elia for an explanation but she could only shrug as she picked her way across a floor now littered with glass.

Inside, she immediately sensed a change in the air. It was drier and had a scent similar to freshly harvested hay. With the help of the flashing orange light and the morning haze from outside, Elia could see rows of covered bins running all the way to the opposite windows. On one side sat massive cabinets with drawers of various sizes. Opening one, Elia dipped her hand into a pile of tiny brown grains that flowed like water through her fingers.

Walking down the aisles, the men lifted lids to examine the contents. "How will we get enough of it back with us?" someone asked.

"With these," answered another, who pulled drawstring bags from a wooden chest.

"Tie two together and hang them around your neck," suggested Roahm as he lowered a bag into a bin and scooped handfuls of seeds to fill it. The other men started doing the same.

A horn suddenly blared outside, followed by another and another, resonating across the city.

"They know they're being attacked!" Elia shouted, racing to the nearest window, which was now foggy from the fresh, humid air filling the room. She wiped away the moisture but saw no activity in the street below. In the distance, however, a thick column of smoke rose into the sky. "We've got to hurry if we want to get out of here!"

Before pulling herself away, Elia saw two stallions take flight from the rooftop, flying in the direction of the smoke. It gave her hope. Perhaps the skirmishes on the outskirts would distract the Imperial Guards from the activity here.

The Torkins worked feverishly, and Elia helped tie the heavy bags before slinging them around the men's shoulders. Suddenly, a breathless Agoan charged into the room.

"Whoa! Whoa! What's going on?" exclaimed the elderly Seed Keeper. His eyes widened in horror to see the many painted warriors looting his storeroom. Frantically turning to run away, he fell as his feet slipped on the small chunks of broken glass. It was the dart in his back, though, that kept him down.

Elia focused on the pulsing orange light. Was it an alarm? She wondered if they had set one off not just here, but elsewhere in the building. "He won't be the last," she warned, and moments later, shouting could be heard from the stairwell.

The Torkins ducked behind the bins of seed as half a dozen red-banded security men swarmed the outside hallway. Darts whizzed through the door and the unprepared Agoans dropped unconscious to the floor.

"Take what you can carry, then get out!" Roahm yelled as he rushed to fill more bags. "Split up and head to the meeting point!"

Men burdened with full loads around their necks raced out of the storeroom, taking down several more Agoans arriving at the scene. The room emptied quickly, leaving Elia and Roahm with just a few others. When they could carry no more, they hurried from the room as well, crunching on glass and stepping over fallen bodies.

Two bags hung from Elia's neck. As she entered the stairwell, she stopped. "I forgot something!"

Just steps ahead, Roahm turned around, looking irritated. "We can't wait for you!"

Dashing into the hallway again, Elia could not believe she was so stupid to forget Hokk's sack. Behind her, the elevator dinged with a single chime as she rushed into the storeroom and took in the damage with one glance—bins tipped over, piles of seeds spilled on the floor, cabinet drawers emptied and flung everywhere. She found the precious sack abandoned near a window. Looking out, she could see growing chaos on the street. If she hurried, she could catch up to Roahm before he and his men left the building.

As she swiveled around, Elia heard a strange whirring sound through the air, then felt a sudden thunk against her chest. She froze. A knife stuck out from one of the bags dangling from her neck, and a stream of seeds poured onto the floor. Elia looked up in a daze.

At the shattered door, Commander Wrasse, with his faceplate pulled up, stood beside the Imperial Guard who had thrown the knife.

"They send children to storm a city?" Wrasse sneered as the other guard hurried forward. The man grabbed Elia before she could collapse, and tossed Hokk's sack to his commander.

"Little boys hardly make the best warriors," Wrasse mocked, catching the sack in midair.

Chapter 46

GWELTH LED THE WAY THROUGH the Junction, and as they got closer to Pree's dwelling, they heard her snoring long before they saw her. Hokk didn't think it could possibly be a sound made by a human until they came around the side of the overturned boxcar. The hefty woman was sprawled inside, passed out in the corner with her double chin resting on her fleshy bosom. After each deep breath, her chest deflated, forcing out through her nose a cacophony of snorts and whistles.

Her legs twitched, one foot moving dangerously close to the smoldering remnants of a fire. Gwelth added branches from the nearby pile and the dry leaves quickly blazed.

"Who's there?" mumbled Pree, still half asleep, but pulling up her legs to keep her toes away from the heat. "What's goin' on?"

"We're waiting for Kalus," answered Gwelth.

"Oh, it's you two," she said, glaring at them with only one eye open. "He ain't back yet."

"I'm just trying to get this fire going till he is."

She grunted. "Don't waste nothin'. I don't got much wood to spare."

Pree rolled over to face the wall and fell back to sleep. Sitting opposite, Gwelth closed his eyes to snooze as well, but Hokk remained standing in the dirt outside. Dozing off would be impossible with Pree's snoring, especially since the metal boxcar amplified every note of her nasal symphony.

Hokk lowered his tent and supplies to the ground and added another piece of wood to the fire. He was tempted to build it larger, but resisted, not wanting to run out of wood too soon. This fire was something to prolong and savor. The flames and heat made him feel invigorated. Less anxious. The crackle and hiss of escaping gases seemed to speak to him.

Dawn spread its pitiable glow across the sky and the darkness lifted over the Junction. Pree and Gwelth continued to sleep. An island of Above was suspended over the city. The leaves of one tenacious tree, growing in the skimpiest patch of soil on top of Pree's boxcar, rustled in the breeze, and a few long, trailing roots swung overhead, hanging down to seek fresh dirt. Still mesmerized by the flames, Hokk ignored it all. He did not even hear the approaching footsteps or see Kalus until he was right beside him.

"Got the stuff?" Kalus asked coldly.

Hokk jumped, snapped from his hypnotic state. "You're back!"

"Got the stuff?"

Glancing over Kalus's shoulder, Hokk was impressed, yet not surprised, to see the donkey on the end of a rope, straining to pull away. "So you were able to find him."

Kalus shifted to block Hokk's view. "I followed through with my end of the bargain. How about you?"

"No luck, unfortunately," Hokk replied, trying to control the nervousness in his voice. "I couldn't track down the box and the gem like I thought, though there's a very good reason."

Kalus frowned, suppressed anger boiling behind his eyes. He looked at Gwelth sleeping in the boxcar and then down at Hokk's provisions piled by the side. "But you went back to the tower," he said. "You were planning to disappear."

"No, I—"

"So you got nothing."

"No, but I've discovered information you'll find much more valuable if you take it to the Board."

"Oh, what's that?" Kalus asked skeptically.

"Torkins! I discovered them while trying to find the girl." Hokk could hear his voice choke up at the thought of Elia. "They've killed her and taken her stuff. And they're occupying the city limits."

Kalus grimaced but said nothing.

"There are lots of them," Hokk added. "I couldn't believe how many kept coming. I don't know exactly what they are planning, but I'm sure if you are the first to warn the Board, you'll be rewarded."

"I know about the Torkins," said Kalus.

"You do?" Hokk was stunned. "I don't believe you."

"Of course I know. I've already heard."

"From the lookouts in the towers?"

"Those fools notice nothing. They keep themselves stone drunk to help kill the time. No, it was one of my men who likes to get out and wander. He saw them, or at least their animals—a large herd of bison beyond the dirt barrier. It's been growing in size, but hasn't moved on to graze elsewhere. What could this mean besides Torkins?"

"So then you've told the Board?"

"Naturally, I have not," he replied with a wicked smirk. "Things will work out better for me if I just let them happen as they're meant to happen."

"But the Torkins are trespassing!"

"Who cares! I only care about the things I can control, and the things I can't, well . . . so long as I stay informed, I'm happy. Which makes me wonder, where is this girl of yours now?"

Hokk hesitated. "I told you." His voice tightened. "She was captured and killed."

"You're lying."

"I'm not."

Twister brayed and tugged to break free. Infuriated, Kalus kicked the donkey in the neck. The startled animal shrieked and leapt into the air with flapping wings, yet he could not fly farther than his short tether.

"Stay down, you stupid beast!" Kalus growled, violently yanking the cord. Pree and Gwelth stirred with the commotion. "This damn animal irritates me to no end. I should let it go. Or just kill it."

"No, let me take him," Hokk anxiously offered, reaching forward for the rope.

"He's all yours," Kalus replied loudly so his voice would carry. As he took a step away from Hokk's outstretched hand, Davim appeared around the corner of the boxcar.

Hokk staggered backward. "You've been followed!" he exclaimed as he tripped over the edge of the car's metal floor and fell hard on its surface. The unlit torch, still tucked into his waistband, pressed painfully into his back.

"I wasn't followed, you fool," Kalus laughed. "I brought him. He's an invited guest."

"Who's this now?" bellowed Pree.

"The brother."

"How many more you bringin' round?" she grunted.

Once again, Hokk was amazed how much his brother reminded him of their father—not just his features, but the way he walked and stuck out his chin. For a split second, Hokk wondered if maybe Davim had arrived to save him, as he had done in the Junction so many years ago, yet behind those eyes was that same deranged look he had seen earlier when his brother tried hauling him from his tent. The first spark of madness had appeared when Davim was a young teenager, but it was shocking to see how much it had overtaken him. Unfortunately, his drinking only made it worse.

Hokk scrambled to his feet as Davim stepped closer. "Stay away," Hokk warned and then glared at Kalus. "You betrayed me, you bastard."

"I knew I couldn't trust you," said Kalus.

"So whether I brought the stuff you wanted or not, I'd be turned over to him, is that it?"

Kalus shrugged, pretending to look sheepish. "I was hoping you'd have the girl with you too."

"Who cares about her," Davim seethed, his fists clenched.

"Stay away!" Hokk warned again, his voice faltering.

Davim advanced, forcing Hokk farther into the boxcar. Glancing quickly behind, Hokk saw Gwelth get to his feet, ready to grab him. Hokk moved his hand under his cloak until he felt the unused torch with his fingertips. In an instant, he pulled it out, jabbing it into the fire.

Davim charged, just as Hokk swung the flames around to stop him. His brother held back as Gwelth made his move, but Hokk waved the burning torch between the two men.

A smile spread across Pree's face. She was enjoying this unexpected entertainment.

Inching ahead, Hokk used his torch to force Davim backward, all the while keeping his eye on Kalus and Gwelth.

Davim grinned. "You just don't give up, do you?"

"Shut up!" Hokk growled. "Leave me alone. Forget about me!"

His brother laughed. "How can I do that when you're still in the city? You're like a parasite that can't be burned off."

"Trust me, I don't want to stay. I'm trying to get out of here."

"Shouldn't you be gone by now?"

"Shouldn't you be in quarantine?"

"I had a friend hide me," replied Davim with a sideways glance at Kalus.

Hokk should have known—they were a perfect pair. No wonder Kalus had been so well informed about Hokk and Elia's appearance before the Board.

Brushing aside the overhanging roots, Hokk moved into the open and scanned the area. With three men surrounding him, all ready to pounce, he could see no way to escape. It would be impossible to outrun them, especially here in the Junction where Kalus's cohorts were everywhere.

A lookout's horn trumpeted from a rooftop only blocks away. The smile on Pree's face vanished as the piercing sound was echoed by horns at other watchtowers across the city. "Things are happenin'!" she huffed, struggling to stand. "This ain't gonna be good!"

With his captors staring skyward as the alarms blared, Hokk recognized his chance.

He lunged at Kalus, catching his sleeve with the torch. The man shouted, releasing Twister's rope as he beat the flames on his arm. Hokk snatched the rope in midair and twisted it around his hand. Before the donkey could step away, he waved his torch in the animal's face with a simultaneous kick to its rump. Wings flapping frantically, the frightened donkey rose off the ground, and Hokk sprung with all the strength in his legs, still hanging onto the rope as he was yanked into the air. The donkey lifted them above the boxcar, but Hokk's weight pulled them both down onto its top. From up here, Hokk saw ahead of him a long, twisting line of similar boxcars like some ancient train wreck that had slid haphazardly off its tracks centuries ago.

Below, the men's shock quickly turned to fury.

"Get up there and stop him!" Kalus screamed as Davim and Gwelth started climbing the sides.

Hokk had to slow the men down. Standing beside the tree growing on top of the boxcar, he raised his torch into its lowest braches. The tufts of leaves burst into flames. This was a fire, however, that could not be enjoyed. Hokk sprinted along the length of the train carriage, and Twister followed, overtaking him. As they reached the far edge, the donkey once again beat his wings, lifting Hokk high above Gwelth, who clung to a ladder on the side of the hull, reaching up in vain to catch Hokk's leg.

Davim made it to the top of the first boxcar just as Twister and Hokk landed on the next one over. The man darted after them, ducking under and around the burning branches and leaping across the gap.

Hokk heard his brother crash onto the metal deck, but did not look back. As he reached the opposite end, he realized the distance to jump was much wider, with another tree in between. Hokk wasn't sure they could make it, yet there was no time to decide. Twister flew up, hauling Hokk across with the flame of his torch flaring in the air and his feet just barely clearing the tree's uppermost limbs before they both landed on the neighboring car. Pulling the donkey's rope to stop him, Hokk turned to watch Davim attempt the same jump, knowing it would be impossible for a man to do on his own.

His brother skidded to a halt at the edge.

"Do it!" Hokk taunted. "Jump! Come on."

"You better quit this!" Davim barked.

Back on the ground, Gwelth raced into view. As he began climbing after Hokk, Hokk leaned forward and dipped his flame into the tree he had just jumped. The tree immediately caught fire, burning like a torch itself. Gwelth was forced to drop down again, and Davim was blocked from attempting to leap over.

"I'm going to kill you!" Davim raged.

"Only if you can catch me!" yelled Hokk.

Hokk noticed several men from the Junction coming out of their hiding spots, their curiosity piqued by the shouting, the fire, and the horns that continued to wail.

Kalus appeared below and called out to the men, pointing to Hokk. "Don't let him escape!"

Hokk ran. And when there was no surface to run on, Twister lifted him into the air. Their pursuers could not keep up. Behind them, Hokk caught a glimpse of the two trees he had lit on fire, and could see the flames spreading through the weeds below. He threw his torch down onto the top of the boxcar and kept running.

He would leave the Junction and travel through the ruins until he reached the dirt barrier. Then the prairies and freedom beyond. He could not jeopardize this last chance to get out of the city. Ago would become a part of his past, not his future. Nothing could keep him here.

But he was leaving behind his tent and supplies. And what about the compass?

Forget it! Pree could keep everything. He had survived with nothing the first time. He could do it again.

Chapter **47**

COMMANDER WRASSE DIDN'T RECOGNIZE HER!

But how could he? With a shaved head, of course she looked like a boy.

Hauling Elia by the arm, the Imperial Guard followed Wrasse into the waiting elevator. The doors closed and the carriage started to rise.

"Search him," the commander ordered, pointing to the bulk around Elia's waist. "He may have concealed weapons."

The guard patted Elia's legs, then started pulling up her top, only to discover he was removing a dress from her pants, not a shirt. When Wrasse saw the dress tumble out, he grabbed Elia and threw her against the wall. With his hand pressing on her chest, she couldn't push him away. She knew he could feel her breasts under her uniform.

Commander Wrasse spit on her forehead, and with his thumb, rubbed the soot off the purple tattoo. "Such a stupid girl," he sneered. He let go and opened Hokk's sack, recognizing the contents immediately. "You came right back to me and brought exactly what I was looking for."

Elia dove for the bag and tried to wrench it from his

grasp. "You can't take that! What could you possibly want with a telescope?"

Again, Wrasse flung her against the wall, almost cracking her skull. His face fumed just inches away from hers. "Look inside and this telescope can reveal a truth that would topple the monarchy," he snorted, mucus spraying from his butchered nose. "And I won't let that happen!"

"Just by looking through it?" Elia shouted.

"Shut up!"

The upward motion of their carriage stopped. With a pleasant ding, the elevator doors opened and Wrasse mercilessly yanked her out onto the floor of the Board's courtroom. Another flashing orange light in the ceiling warned of the break-in several stories below. The space was a mess of overturned chairs and strewn papers, and Minister Crawlik was sorting through everything with the help of an aide. Out of his formal robes, Crawlik looked like a crazed old man, eyes bloodshot, spectacles teetering on the end of his nose. As Wrasse approached, he gave a startled jump, and wiped a pudgy hand over his perspiring forehead. His aide timidly stepped back, lowering his face.

The Imperial Commander ignored them both.

A secret door, normally flush with the wall, hung ajar and Wrasse charged through to another staircase, this one narrower and made of metal. He ascended the steps two at a time, and moved so fast Elia couldn't keep up. Stumbling, she fell painfully to her knees, and the other guard barely avoided tripping on her legs.

The commander plowed through a final door at the top, slamming it back with a crash. People already on the roof anxiously turned, all except a group of distracted Imperial Guards. Several Agoan men, wearing red armbands, stood in a huddle, nervously glancing back and forth between Wrasse and the young Minister Tollo, who was bound, gagged, and furious where he lay on the roof's floor. Nearby, free of any restraints, Minister Seeli stiffly rose to her feet, her face haggard, her normally intense eyes strained.

"We've found what we wanted," Wrasse snarled, storming past Seeli.

Staggering behind the commander, Elia made eye contact with the minister and saw the old woman's confusion replaced with a look of surprised recognition.

"Let's get ready to mount!" roared Commander Wrasse as a flying horse overhead, carrying a rider, prepared to land on the rooftop, its wings backpedaling the air for a graceful touchdown. "It's time to finally . . ." Wrasse began to say before his voice trailed off, his attention captured by something in the sky.

"It keeps dropping lower," said one of the guards.

Elia twisted around to see the amazing sight. A massive island of Above had moved directly over the city's center. Drifting slowly between the buildings, its jagged tip now hung dangerously low. At this altitude, it would inevitably smash into one of the taller scrapers.

"Can anyone identify this island?" asked Wrasse, though he was too impatient to wait for a response. "Never mind," he said, as he grabbed Elia's arm. "Any island is better than remaining down here any longer. Bring me my steed."

His pure white stallion, a regal specimen, was brought forward. Its mane and tail were braided with shiny rings of silver that jingled as it walked. Haughty and temperamental, the animal's eyes flared an instant before it reared up, pawing the air with its front legs. The commander moved quickly to avoid being hit, releasing his grip on Elia as he reached automatically to steady his horse.

Elia bolted.

The guards grabbed nothing as Elia dodged their outstretched arms. Staying low, she was almost clear of them when a man caught her ankles. She toppled like a falling tree.

Before she could get to her feet, Wrasse seized her around the waist in a vice-like embrace.

"No! No!" she screamed, kicking and squirming to break free. His grip tightened.

Commander Wrasse carried her to his stallion and tossed her stomach-down across its back, pinning her with his hand as he climbed up. An Imperial Guard hurried to tie Hokk's sack to the saddle, and as soon as it was secure, Wrasse climbed on and barked, "We're done here!"

Hanging over the side of the horse in front of Wrasse, with the saddle digging into her ribs, Elia saw the rooftop drop away as the horse became airborne. As they rose higher, there was sudden shouting and commotion on the roof, accompanied by zipping sounds in the air. Elia heard Wrasse grunt as he tried to turn in his saddle. At the same moment, she recognized the unmistakable markings of Torkin warriors swarming the rooftop below.

Roahm had returned, but too late to save her.

Wrasse's stallion faltered in midflight, tilting to the side as if a wing had stiffened. The crushing pressure of the commander's hand was gone. Horrified to feel herself slipping off, Elia struggled to hang on to the horse's mane. Twisting her neck, she saw a glazed expression on Wrasse's face. His arms hung limp. With what seemed like a last breath, his body deflated and he slouched forward until he was lying on top of her.

Trapped beneath his bulk, Elia desperately tried to push him off. Only when he teetered over precariously to one side did she notice the feathered darts sticking out of his back.

Chapter 48

ELIA FOUGHT TO STAY ON the horse, and managed to turn so she was facing Wrasse. The commander had slipped so far over in his saddle he was dangerously close to falling, but as Elia attempted to push him off, the man stirred, and his head bobbed back up. With his blurry eyes losing focus, he tried swiping at the side of her head like a sleepy bear, though after only one attempt, his heavy arm tumbled down. Wrasse was unconscious again.

Omi and Opi are dead because of this man, Elia reminded herself. Probably her mother and brother too.

She gave a tremendous shove, but the commander was saved by his feet braced firmly in the stirrups. Elia kicked furiously at the straps to loosen them.

"Stop!" yelled an Imperial Guard who had caught up on his own flying horse.

"I'll get her!" shouted a second.

It was impossible for either guard to bring their stallions alongside Elia's without the wings colliding, but one had a spear in his hand that he stabbed at Elia. She barely avoided the sharp tip as she continued to frantically kick at the stirrups.

One of Wrasse's feet finally came free. With all her might, Elia pushed against the commander and felt his weight shift.

"No!" screamed a guard as Wrasse slid from his saddle.

The commander plunged headfirst, his limbs lifeless as he plummeted toward the ground, landing in a crumpled heap. They were flying too high to hear the commander's bones break, but Elia could imagine the satisfying *crunch* they must have made. Surviving the fall would be impossible. As his body lay in the street, she noticed an Agoan man snatch the winged helmet from Wrasse's head and wondered what would be left of him after scavengers picked him clean.

The spear came at her again, dangerously close to piercing her rib cage. Elia's only chance was to somehow take control of her stallion. But as she carefully swung her leg around to face forward, the horse suddenly lurched, pitching her off. She grabbed the saddle just in time and dangled against the animal's side. Frightened the guard's spear would easily skewer her in the back, she looked up, but was bewildered to see both men now far overhead.

Her horse was dropping!

The wing above her continued to flap, but its rhythm was off and the horse's legs kicked with an awkward gait as if its joints were beginning to seize. Elia could see a dart had stung the animal's back leg, embedded in the flesh like a large, ravenous mosquito.

The stallion's mass was sufficient to prevent it from becoming overwhelmed by the toxin; however, the animal was losing altitude. They descended rapidly between the buildings, cutting through layers of drifting smoke. Elia felt her grip weakening. The ground raced closer. She let go of the horse an instant before its hooves touched down, but she rolled helplessly out of control along the grass-covered street. The stallion skidded to a jarring stop a short distance away. Its flesh was quivering and it flapped its wings as though trying to shake off the effects of the poison.

Dazed, with her head throbbing, Elia raised herself to take in the surrounding pandemonium. She was now close to the outskirts of the city, where Torkin invaders had ransacked buildings before setting them on fire. And it seemed as if the entire population had emerged from underground in response. As flames licked the sides of the buildings, confused Agoans raced everywhere, shouting as the flames spread at street level.

This frenzied commotion further agitated the already anxious stallion, and it reared up on its hind legs, beating its wings as it started to move away from her. But Elia couldn't let it take flight—getting back on was crucial. She could fly this horse to Above!

Elia sprinted until she was running alongside the stallion, yet realized she could do nothing to pull herself up onto the saddle. She only had the chance, at the last possible moment, to snag Hokk's bag before the animal broke into a crazed gallop.

The stallion rose high into the smoky air, but by the time it climbed to the height of the closest building, its wings gave out once more. Circling down like a leaf caught in the wind, the ill-fated creature dropped behind a wall of fire on the roof, and Elia lost sight of it.

She was suddenly pushed aside by a panicked woman trying to herd a flock of distressed sheep. Scorched wool still smoldered on their backs. The woman's eyes were filled with hate. "Here's one! Here's one of them now," she shrieked, pointing at Elia.

Elia didn't wait for the response, darting instead in the opposite direction. The air was thick with choking smoke that irritated her eyes and throat. She ran blindly, dodging people until a man grabbed her. A Torkin man.

"You're going the wrong way. It's too dangerous back there," he explained quickly, pointing toward the city center.

Elia looked up and gasped. The tip of the floating island was about to hit a tower just a few blocks away!

"Where's Roahm?" she shouted.

The man was already steps ahead of her. "He's out here somewhere," he called back, waving toward the other Torkins caught among the frightened civilians. The warriors were all fleeing in the same direction, some of them carrying torches, which they had no doubt used to start the many fires.

A horrendous rumble thundered between the buildings. Everyone, both Torkin and Agoan, stopped to watch the mass of rock smash into the tower, sending wreckage raining onto the streets. People directly below screamed and dove for cover, while others raced to keep ahead of its path. Elia ran too, glancing over her shoulder every few steps.

The island pulverized the top floors of the first tower and moved on to its much taller neighbor, shearing it completely in half. Clouds of dust billowed up. Huge chunks of falling concrete and metal battered the streets. As a third building was hit, this one already burning, debris showered down like a cloudburst of fiery hail.

But the Torkins did not look back. On and on they ran toward the prairies. The number of people in the streets diminished. The few they encountered were quickly silenced by a dart.

By the time the warriors reached the decomposed buildings of the city's outer ruins, Elia had fallen behind. She struggled to push on, but was wheezing so deeply she started to choke. A few more steps and she stopped, bending over to relieve the cramps in her gut while gasping for air.

"Don't quit now," encouraged one last straggling Torkin as he overtook her.

Elia was relieved to see it was Roahm. "I'm not," she called out after him as she forced herself to continue walking. "And thank you for coming back for me!"

Roahm slowed his pace. "We were too late though."

"Just in time, I'd say," replied Elia before coughing again.

"Can you keep up?" he asked.

"I'm trying, but I don't know what's wrong with me."

"You've inhaled too much dust and smoke," replied Roahm, jogging backward. Besides his blowpipe and the bags around his neck, he carried something in his arms.

"You've got Nym!" Elia declared, stunned to see the fox.

"Of course."

"I would have never . . ."

"How could I leave him behind?"

"Thank you," Elia said. "Can I carry him for you?"

Roahm shook his head. "You've already got that sack to worry about," he said, breaking into a run again that left Elia no choice but to follow.

Along their route, remnants of abandoned buildings gave way to indistinguishable grass-covered mounds. Beyond these, the dirt barrier. Elia could see Torkins struggling to make their way across. She stepped in the muck, which threatened to hold her fast. Footprints stretched far ahead. It seemed too risky to leave such obvious tracks, and she glanced nervously behind. Except for a few remaining Torkins trailing the pack, no one was in pursuit.

The view of Ago was astounding. From this distance, the city seemed eerily silent as it burned. There was no sense of the bedlam in the streets. Columns of thick smoke rose into the sky as if to nourish the blanket of gray clouds that were growing darker and heavier. The island overhead, having plowed through the city's core, was now floating over areas where the buildings were too low to be damaged. Following the air currents, it would soon be drifting over the vast prairies.

Elia scanned the expanse of dirt and the endless grasslands beyond. How could she possibly survive another trip over that barren landscape? It had been one thing to travel on the back of a gazelk, but by foot seemed to be almost an impossible challenge.

"Are you taking me with you?" she asked.

"Yes," replied Roahm.

"Back to your village?"

"Yes."

"And I'll be safe there?"

"You will. And you'll meet the woman we've protected all these years who also fell from the sky. Back then, they searched for her too."

Elia shot a startled look at Roahm. "They did?"

"But we concealed her well. They never found her. Perhaps she'll share with you why it was so important she stay hidden."

Yes, Elia had to meet this woman. If there was no way to return to Above, then living in Below might be tolerable if she had someone with whom to share the same memories—the blue sky, the warmth, the sun.

As if to taunt her, Elia felt the first kisses of rain on her cheek. "Please no," she groaned.

The clouds opened up with a downpour that instantly soaked her. Water ran over her naked scalp and trickled down her face, streaking the designs on her skin. She tasted soot on her wet lips. By the time they stepped onto the grasses on the other side of the dirt barrier, Elia's pants and the bottom of her dress were completely coated with mud. Roahm's leggings were filthy too. His face was wet and smudged. He appeared younger than Elia had originally guessed—just a few years older than Hokk.

Hokk.

She stopped walking as though the thought of Hokk had paralyzed her body with sadness. He was surely dead. And how strange that she should survive so much. Hokk had brought her to the city in equally wretched weather just days before, but that seemed so long ago. She had been filled with hope, but now she was leaving and nothing had changed except her travel companion.

No, that wasn't true. She had the telescope. And she had learned that somehow, by looking through it, it would expose a lie that the Twin Emperors would do anything to hide.

"We'll travel much faster once we reach the bison," said Roahm, noticing she had fallen behind.

"Bison?" Elia said with surprise, trying to ignore the heavy lump she felt in her chest as she started walking again. "We don't have to travel on foot?"

"Of course not. It would take us far too long."

Encouraged, Elia kept her head up, alert for any sign of the colossal beasts. Led by the scattered procession of Torkins ahead of them, they trekked for quite a distance until they came to a depression in the prairies where at least a hundred animals were waiting, an ever-shifting sea of brown, woolly fur. The Torkins who had conducted the raid on the city's outskirts were already assembled and busy loading their plunder. Besides the many bags of seeds, she saw bulging sacks of stolen vegetables, clutches of squawking chickens, and even a few piglets and lambs being tied to the bison.

Men mounted the animals and soon a convoy snaked away from the herd. Roahm selected a bison and then counted how many were left unclaimed. "We've lost men," he murmured in dismay.

He corralled a second beast for Elia. "You can ride this one." With his help and a fistful of soggy fur, Elia pulled herself onto its back. Roahm passed up Nym and the sack, then climbed onto his own steed. He whistled to catch the attention of two men, and waved at the remaining bison. "Round them all up. Don't leave any behind."

The low-lying island of Above floated ahead of them as they joined the tail end of the procession. Rain roared down from the sky, and the dark clouds threatened more to come. The wind blew as if to snatch Elia's soul.

Stroking Nym's head, she gazed back in the direction of Ago. There was nothing to see in the swirling mist. No city. No Hokk.

Elia rocked with the lumbering gait of the bison between her legs. She was exhausted. Her stomach was empty. Her wet dress and muddy pants clung to her freezing body. Her heart ached.

This was misery. But she would not let this be her life.

Chapter **49**

HOKK KNEW HE SHOULD FOLLOW. He had waited long enough and hadn't seen anyone pass by for quite a while.

He was hidden in one of the derelict buildings, surrounded by four walls but no roof, with Twister tied inside to a post so he couldn't fly away. Hokk had watched the Torkins escape, weaving their way through the ruins to get to the dirt barrier. They were overloaded with stolen loot, yet he didn't care what they took. He was finished with this city—and he needed a new plan, especially given what he had just seen.

Elia. Alive!

She wasn't a hallucination. It was definitely her. The gray dress, with the pants underneath, gave her away. Had she quickly raced by, he might have missed her, but she had stopped, choking and bent over in pain, clearly struggling as a hostage of the Torkins.

It was barbaric the way they had burned off all her hair and painted her skin to look like theirs. She appeared too exhausted to keep up, and Hokk saw Elia exchange words with one of the Torkins, who forced her to continue. He shuddered to think of the man's threats and what else they might have already done to her. Whatever reason they had for keeping Elia alive could soon be meaningless, so he had to rescue her before that happened. And Nym too! Hokk had to look twice to confirm it was his fox in the Torkin's arms.

Imagine how thrilled Elia would be to see him arrive with Twister. Here was a chance to fulfill his promise before returning to the prairies.

Yes, leave now and follow.

Untying the donkey, Hokk stepped out into the open. Earlier, he had heard distant crashing sounds, then had seen through the missing roof a suspended island drift into view. Curious to see whether the rock was floating any lower, he turned around to look.

His legs almost gave out beneath him.

The city was on fire!

How could this be? So many flames. Such beautiful flames.

Hokk was captivated by their flickering allure, just like that fateful day six years ago when he dared to play with fire and lost control. That was the last time he had surrendered so completely to his obsession.

Fire was so natural, so powerful, so wonderfully tantalizing. And at this very moment, right in front of him, was a spectacular display to admire. A wave of euphoria swept through his body.

Yet at the same time, Hokk was appalled to feel such exhilaration. Fire was his frightening addiction. His fascination from an early age had turned into an almost uncontrollable fixation, made worse by the death of his parents. Creating fire seemed the only way to distract himself from the stress and fears that threatened to unhinge his mind.

Hokk now forced his eyes away from his city in flames. He looked down at the scars on his arms and hands and remembered again the chickens burning alive. Compelled by a crazy impulse, he had ignored his uncle's warning that day and had struck his flint against a heaping pile of wood as the birds began to molt. He started to play with their feathers—at first lighting just a few of them on fire, but quickly progressing to handfuls that he'd hold like a bouquet until the tips flared to life, then throwing them high up into the air to float around the eleventh floor like drowsy fireflies. Where they settled, the dry grasses immediately caught fire. The spreading flames sent the chickens into a frenzy, and they shook off plumes of loosened feathers. These ignited, as did the birds themselves that hadn't begun to molt, and in their panic, many of the burning chickens flew to other levels of the tower and set them ablaze too. Mesmerized by this awful scene, Hokk didn't break free of his trance until it was too late, when the flames had already taken over the entire floor. Horrified by what he had started, he desperately attempted to put out the fires with his bare hands, only to be forced by the smoke to climb to the roof.

This was the true story he couldn't share with Elia. But both versions ended the same way. Eight people died because of his obsessive play. Fire had destroyed their future as well as his own. He might never stop paying the price.

Finding it irresistible even now, Hokk's gaze returned to the towers engulfed by the inferno. It could have only been caused by the trees he had set ablaze in the Junction, the flames spreading faster than he could ever have imagined. And it was all his fault. He was to blame again.

Drops of rain hit his face. Looking up to the clouds, he felt like weeping with relief. He prayed for a downpour.

But then, out of the corner of his eye, he spotted a body high above, falling from the island overhead. Similar to the others he had seen before, it was white, though one side glowed like an orange ember, leaving a trail of smoke as it spiraled down. Seconds later, it came into clearer view and he realized his mistake.

It was a stallion on fire!

Flames, fanned by every frantic beat, were consuming one of its wings. Though it had risen to a great height as it flew out of the city, the animal was now dropping quickly. With a dreadful thump, it collided with the ground.

Hokk charged forward, pulling Twister along as the donkey rose into the air.

The terrified stallion shrieked and twisted in agony, rolling on its side to extinguish the flames. Its nostrils flared; its eyes bulged. Silver ornaments braided into its mane and tail jingled as the animal struggled.

Hokk let go of the rope and Twister hovered beside him. Removing his cloak, Hokk tried to smother the flames without getting kicked by the horse's flailing hooves.

Burning feathers drifted down in the air, and fizzled with a *hiss* as the rain fell harder. The clouds released their blessed deluge, and steam and smoke rose from the wing as the flames were finally doused. The stallion labored to get up. Once standing, it faced Hokk with its head down, its wings spread as if to rinse them in the downpour. One soggy wing was still intact, yet the other was blackened and limp. Only a few feathers remained. Would the rest ever grow back?

Hokk placed a soothing hand on the horse's forehead. The stallion relaxed enough to fold its wings against its body. Twister landed gently on the ground beside Hokk and nudged his other hand.

Behind them, the City of Ago was enveloped by the storm's torrents, and Hokk knew the rain would be its savior.

Endless drops of water from the sky, always falling down, never to return to Above. It was the fate of everything claimed by Below, his home beneath the clouds.

And what was above those clouds? A ball of fire traveling across a sky of blue? It seemed impossible, but there was only one way to know for sure. And one person to show him.

Hokk headed into the grasslands, leading the donkey and the wounded stallion. They had a long journey ahead and he could afford no further delay.

He already had so much to make up for.

End of Book One

Acknowledgments

My evolution from number cruncher to published author has been a challenging yet exciting transition, and I succeeded because of the following people to whom I wish to express my immense gratitude.

Thank you many times over to my dedicated agent, Daniel Lazar, from Writers House in New York City. Dan, you were the first person to recognize the uniqueness of my vision, and I am so fortunate to have you as a champion of this novel.

I am especially grateful to the award-winning team at Turner Publishing Company for their enthusiasm and ongoing commitment. I owe this amazing opportunity to Todd Bottorff, President, and Stephanie Beard, Executive Editor of Acquisitions, who both immediately appreciated my inspiration and my passion for the written word. Working alongside my editor, Jon O'Neal, has been an absolute pleasure as well, and I couldn't be more pleased to see the culmination of our efforts. Special recognition must also go to my publicist, Jolene Barto, who is delightfully creative with promotional ideas for a book launch, and to designer Maddie Cothren who conceived such a breathtaking design for the cover.

ACKNOWLEDGMENTS

From my own writing community closer to home, I most certainly have to acknowledge three individuals who I greatly admire: Hadley Dyer, Maria Golikova, and Catherine Dorton. The wise advice offered by each of you has made all the difference as I pursued my dream of entering the publishing world.

I am who I am because of my wonderful family. Love always to my incredibly supportive parents, Jo-Ann and André, as well as my brother, Jeff, and his wife and children: Jennifer, Jack, and Kate. I'm inspired by each of you and hope to always make you proud.

Thank you to Jazz Rai for being a dear friend and confidante all these years. You've had to wait the longest to read this book, but I wanted it to be perfect before you did.

And for the many happy times I've shared with Shawn Shirazi, I realize just how lucky we've been to live them. My most heartfelt thanks and appreciation to you, Shawn, for the forest therapy, the nights out on the town that left our feet sore, and for the peaceful moments spent admiring the beauty within a saltwater aquarium.

THE BROKEN SKY CHRONICLES

WILL CONTINUE IN . . .

ABOVE

FEBRUARY 2017

FROM

TURNER
PUBLISHING COMPANY